LIGHT AND SHADOW

Book Eleven of the Hayle Coven Novels

PATTI LARSEN

PURELY PRESS PARANORMAL

Find out more about Patti Larsen at **pattilarsen.com** or **purelyparanormalpress.com**

Also by

PATTI LARSEN

The Hunted Series
The Hayle Coven Novels
Blood and Gold Trilogy
The Clone Chronicles
The Diamond City Trilogy
The First Plane Trilogy
The Lychos Cycle
The Hayle Coven Destinies
and much, much more.

Find your new favorite author at
pattilarsen.com or
purelyparanormalpress.com

Sign up for new releases
bit.ly/pattilarsenemail

I grinned at the enthusiastic, if off-key, rendition of "Happy Birthday" and added my own pathetically energetic voice. Twenty or so young witches, all about the same age as the birthday girl, sat around her as she gazed with wide, happy eyes at the candles on her impressive cake.

Mom may have been distant and a little cold the last six months, but she went all out for Meira's eleventh birthday. Guilt driven? Maybe. Still, I found it hard to stay mad at her no matter how little time she seemed to have for either Meira or me these days.

My heart ached every time I thought of Dad.

No room for sadness today, though. Even Mom smiled and clapped her hands when the singing was over and Meira finally blew out her candles. The giant cake was covered in them, a model of our house back in Wilding Springs complete with a big, black dog in the back yard for Galleytrot, a furry silver Persian in her window for Sassafras and the whole family in the front driveway. Well, not the whole family. We lived in a coven, after all. Mom, me—I refused to look too closely at my candy sculpture after the first glimpse I had made me think "prostitute"— Gram and Meira. No Dad.

Ouch.

Despite his obvious absence, Meira squealed in delight over the monstrosity and its many glowing candles, happily spinning tiny whirling balls of air to help her put them all out as she made her wish.

It would have been nice to host her birthday back home, in the real thing instead of standing next to its facsimile, but Meira was still in school. I'd been home over a month now, the spring semester over. Amazing how quickly I grew accustomed to my own bed again and how weird it felt to be back at Harvard, even if only for a few hours.

Mom's sitting room was as gloomy and dark as ever, but the giggling witches, balloons and animals shaped out of magic cavorting in the air above our heads made it feel much more festive. I swatted at a herd of unicorns galloping past my right ear, but couldn't help smiling.

Meira's friends piled in around her, handing her presents, holding out plates for their chunk of her cake. I hung back, not wanting to interfere, saving my gift for when she returned home tomorrow. Maybe it was silly of me to make the trip to Harvard for her birthday, but I hadn't missed one yet and didn't plan to start any time soon.

I was a little ashamed of the wave of jealousy I felt, seeing my little sister the center of what seemed like genuine affection and attention. I hadn't had access to other witches my age when I was growing up, partly because the age gap in births just happened to spread to older and younger than me, for some odd reason, but also because I spent sixteen years rejecting my magic.

Yeah, my own fault. Still.

Lucky kid.

Mom met my eyes briefly over the heads of the pack of laughing eleven-year-olds, though her gaze dropped just as quickly. Erica Plower, once Mom's second and now the Hayle representative on the Council, hurried forward, taking over as Mom eased away. Good old Erica. No matter how much responsibility she had now, she still looked out for Mom. My mother had run out of steam, I could only guess, and was getting ready to retreat.

I slid around the crowd, heading for Mom, just wanting a word, a moment, something to tell me the woman I loved still lived inside her. No matter what she said, I still blamed myself for the fact Dad was gone, his mating to Mom broken, now ascended to the Second Seat of Demonicon, one of its two Rulers. If I'd just listened to Mom and Gram, Dad wouldn't have to be Prince, take a demon wife, have demon children.

And Mom wouldn't avoid me like she was doing right now.

Did she hate me? The question crossed my mind many times in the dark of night over the last six months. I wouldn't blame her. I kind of hated myself, though I refused to let it show. The coven needed me to be strong for them. Even though Mom wasn't leader anymore, had no connection to our family magic-wise, they still felt the grief of Dad's loss, if only because he'd been a part of their lives as long as Mom and Dad had been mated.

I reached her and placed one hand on her arm just before she disappeared behind her office door. She turned to me, the barest of smiles remaining, the lines around her eyes and mouth deeper than I remembered. Losing Dad seemed to be aging her even more.

When did my mother start getting old?

"Syd," she whispered, kissing my cheek though her lips were dry and cold, her hands icy as they touched the sides of my face. "Take care of your sister."

I tried to pull her back, but she was gone already, in heart if not in body, then both as the door slid shut behind her. It was hard not to sigh and lean my forehead against her door, or to pound on it with both fists and tell her to wake up.

I did neither. Wouldn't do any good. Instead, I turned back and faced the party, smiling at Meira whose amber gaze must have followed us as we retreated, sadness in her eyes.

Love you, Meems, I sent. *Happy birthday.*

I didn't last much longer than Mom. Once the cake was devoured and the presents torn open and admired, most of the kids left, picked up by their witch parents who treated me with a mix of deferential awe and fear due a coven leader. Well, I guess I was okay with that. Better than hate and revulsion.

Yup, I'd take it.

Erica hugged me as I stood, Meira huddled with three friends, giggling over something.

"How are you, Syd?" She stroked my cheek. Erica had been Mom's second since I was little, and had always treated me like she was my mother. She had new wrinkles too, though not as pronounced as Mom's. The old me would have brushed her off, anger rising. But my arms reacted without my consent and hugged her close.

"I'm great, Erica," I whispered in her ear. "How are you?"

She pulled away after a moment, teary eyed, but smiling,

a real, happy smile. I think I surprised her. Surprised myself, actually. But ever since I'd come home from Demonicon I felt hyper aware of the people around me, the ones I loved, cared about. How fragile they were.

Part of me wished my demon grandmother, Ahbi, had never told me I was immortal. But at least it made me more empathetic. And appreciative.

"I'm wonderful," she said, blonde hair back to its old bob, the one I missed. It swung around her face in shining gold strands and I found myself grinning at her.

She didn't get to say anything more. Meira burrowed her way between us and hugged me, her forehead pressed into my shoulder. She was getting so tall and had matured so much in the last year, it was hard for me to remember she was only ten.

Wait. Eleven. Wow.

"Thanks for coming." Meira grinned up at me, cute black horns shining in the low light of the room, amber eyes lit from within. "I'll see you tomorrow?"

I nodded, hugged her again, pulling her tight before releasing her to go back to her friends. I waved at Erica, not prepared to go into any kind of deep conversation with her and headed for the elevator.

Charlotte stepped out of the shadows, my bodywere

practically attached at my hip as I waited for the doors to open. She seemed to suffer no ill effects from my prolonged stay on Demonicon, despite the powerful reaction she'd had to my absence. I was happy to know she didn't suffer any permanent damage thanks to Ahbi's arrogance. Still, Charlotte insisted she remain in close contact these days.

I found I didn't really mind, though there were times it would have been nice to open the bathroom door and not find her waiting for me on the other side.

Guess I could get used to anything.

At least things had been quiet since we returned from Dad's plane. As Charlotte and I stepped out into the Yard and I reached for the veil, I felt a tiny shudder go through me at the memory of being trapped. Yes, the fear stayed with me that somehow when I rode the veil one day, Ahbi would be waiting to pull me over and keep me prisoner there forever.

Silly, maybe. And yet, I wouldn't put it past the old bat.

Powerful Ruler or not, the grandmother I'd met was a conniving politician without morals who used her family on a regular basis to get whatever she wanted. I'd take my witch grandmother over her anytime.

As Charlotte and I stepped into the veil, the rubbery membrane holding the two planes apart, sliding through toward home, I thought of Gram with a twinge of worry. She'd been absent more and more lately, wandering off on her own. Not that I worried about her, not in the least. Of anyone in our family, Gram had proven to me without a shadow of a doubt she was more than capable of taking care of herself.

No, I missed her. It was that simple. The air felt warm on the other side of the veil as Charlotte and I stepped out into a secluded area of the park near the house, outside the reach of the family wards, neither of us missing a stride as we began the short walk home. Gram was my constant, even when she was still lost to us, spiraling in and out of madness. Now, back to her abnormal self and about as stable as she was ever going to get, her constant presence and her support in our co-leadership of the coven was something I counted on without question.

When she disappeared on me, I finally felt alone.

The sun was just setting as I walked through the back door. One quick sweep around the house told me Gram still wasn't home. A bit bummed and missing my family, I said an early good night to Charlotte and retreated to my bedroom, closing myself off a little.

No more poor me. I'd made that vow and I intended to keep it. But still, there were times I just needed to be alone.

Good book in one hand and a half-bag of chips dug out from under my bed in the other and I was gone for a while.

One touch was all it took. I didn't hesitate, didn't think, just ran for the stairs, the back door.

The yard.

And him.

The screen door slammed behind me, bare feet instantly chilled by the damp patio stones.

Didn't matter. Could have been the dead of winter and I wouldn't have cared.

"Quaid." I forced myself to a halt, refrained from throwing myself into his arms, covering his shadowed face in kisses, letting his power wrap around me like a blanket and stir things inside me. He still had that effect on me? Damn it. I thought I'd gotten better at cutting off my feelings for him.

Had lots of practice at school where we did our best to ignore each other and go on with our lives as if we didn't feel anything.

"Syd." He held himself rigid, body tall and still inside his black Enforcer's robe, a thin band of blue at the cuffs marking him as a trainee. *Did* he feel what I felt?

Did I care?

"Nice to see you." I'd seen him, of course I had. We attended the same school, after all. But we both avoided each other, for the most part. He had his life, I had mine. There were moments over the course of the year I'd wanted to reach out to him, when I thought he'd been ready to do so himself, but either we had the worst timing on the planet or I imagined his need to reconnect.

I pulled my heart and my demon, who begged me to grab him and kiss him until he begged for more, under control. He'd made his choice back in the fall, abandoned me when I thought we would always be together, and I wasn't about to be an idiot and fall into that old trap again.

Wasn't.

"You too." He paused, one hand reaching out a little before it fell to his side. "You look great."

"So do you." What I could see of him. Maybe it was a good thing he wore the robe. That way I didn't have to watch his wide shoulders pull against his t-shirt, the way his thighs filled out his jeans. For all I knew he'd gotten fat and was hiding it.

Sigh. Yeah right.

As long as he kept his distance, I could handle it.

"I wanted to bring you this." He did hold out his hand this time, a small box with a silver bow on top shining in the outside light. "And for Meira." His other hand held a bag. "Happy birthday."

A month late. Still.

"Thanks," I said. I couldn't bring myself to move. Tried to convince myself I was aloof, cool, collected. Held very stiff as he approached, offering the gifts to me. By the time he stopped, it was worse case scenario. I smelled him, felt the heat of his body and found myself shivering, hugging my arms around the thin tank top I'd worn to bed, aware at last of my cold feet as the struggle inside me intensified.

Even after he'd broken my heart, I still loved him. Needed him. Wanted him around. The magic tied to our supposed destiny was a sneaky little bastard.

Yeah, blame fate. I was such a sucker.

"Sorry," he said softly. "You must be freezing. Here." He swept off his robe, slid it around me. Took a step closer to drape it across my shoulders.

So close. Too close.

Oh, Syd.

It was my fault. Or was it his? I'm not sure who moved first or if we did it together, but the moment his robe touched me his hands were in my hair and my fingers clutched the front of his shirt and we were pulling each other in desperate need.

One touch of his lips and I was lost.

His brown eyes were black in the dim light of the moon shining through my bedroom window. I curled on my side, forehead almost pressed to his, the sheets pulled up to my chin, wanting to stroke the warm skin of his arm and shoulder, to trace the pattern of the pentagram tattoo he wore. But I held still, just breathing, my body relaxed and happy while my heart hurt.

"I'm sorry," he whispered, fingers stroking hair out of my face. "This was a bad idea. I never should have come to see you."

Even as he spoke, the pain inside me eased. I could feel it, the grief trapped in him, the agony of our separation. He did feel it, too. I wasn't the only one.

It was enough.

"You have to know I still love you, Syd." Quaid's face crumpled, as sad as I'd ever seen him. "It breaks my heart every time I see you, knowing we're not together."

I nodded, swallowed. "You have to follow your dreams, Quaid," I said, finally letting go of my need to make him do what I wanted. Maybe it was the fact I knew I could never have him now, not really, not knowing what I did about myself. Or maybe the fact he was so young and yet had so little time compared to me it broke the terrible hold blame, guilt and anger held over me. I reached for him, kissed his forehead, sighed against his skin, loving the hot scent of him, the way his power held onto me. "I'm glad you did."

He shook his head. "I'll quit right now." Quaid grasped my hands, kissed them, kissed my mouth. So much desperation, confusion. He was still conflicted. How could I let him choose me when I knew he'd regret it?

"There's something you need to know." We'd been in touch over Christmas, but my offer for him to spend the holidays with us had been rejected. Now I knew why. Every time Quaid saw me he doubted his choice. It wasn't fair to either of us. But now I had a way to ease his conscience.

And, maybe, mine.

I told him everything, about the trip to Demonicon, fighting for status, Dad's ascension. And about my immortality. Quaid didn't say anything as I spoke, but he did pull me into his arms, bare chest against my naked skin, arms holding me close as he breathed softly over my cheek, fingers sliding through my hair over and over again.

When I finished, I cried, not for me, not really, but because I needed to cry. For us. For what it meant, no matter the choice he'd made.

Not wracking sobs, though. Just soft tears wept into the arms of the man I loved while he held me and loved me with all his heart.

I pulled away a little at last and smiled up at him while one of his wide thumbs wiped moisture from my cheek. "Good thing we're not together," I said, "I'd hate to have to dump you."

Quaid didn't laugh. It was a terrible joke anyway.

"I'm just happy to have you in my life," I said, meaning it, knowing this was enough. "I can't promise you anything and you can't either." He nodded. "So maybe we have this and that's all. Are you okay with that?"

Quaid sighed, deep and long, his chest collapsing as he exhaled. When he finally took a breath, he nodded, though there were tears in his eyes. "I'll take it," he said.

"Now," I snuggled closer, "tell me about your training."

His body relaxed. Was that all it took, for me to accept him and the choice he made for this mess to heal between us? Maybe, maybe not. But for the moment, I was happy to think so.

Quaid's voice rumbled softly in the dark of my room as he told me with growing enthusiasm just how much he loved being an Enforcer trainee. From learning offensive magics and counter-intelligence spells to the camaraderie of the corps, by the time he wound down, voice sleepy, my own eyes falling slowly shut, he actually sounded happy.

Maybe I shouldn't have brought it up, but I needed to know. "And your friend?" Funny, no twinge of jealousy at the thought or mention of the blonde with the rack. Wow, I really was growing up. Either that or being in his arms diffused it enough I didn't feel it.

Quaid didn't tense, didn't react, really. Just sighed. "It's been over for a long time," he said. Was that regret? "I kept comparing her to you. Drove Payten crazy."

I choked on a laugh, but held it in even as jealousy—yes, I was jealous of her even though they weren't together anymore, go figure—popped up and said hello. "Poor her."

Oh, Syd. Bad girl.

Snort.

"I just want to love you," he said.

"Me too." Made sense to me.

"I'm sorry about your dad," he whispered.

Not going there. So I dragged the subject back.

"Besides," I said, "we're young, right? Well, I'll be young for a long time." He laughed at last. "No rush. Just the two of us when we can manage it."

Quaid's arms hugged me. "I really do love you, Syd."

When I woke a few hours later and he was gone, I smiled into the darkness, hugging the pillow he'd laid his head on.

Not with some silly girl dreams of my prince charming and riding off with him on his white horse. But at the thought of just enjoying Quaid when we were together.

What a novelty. No pressure, no requirements. Just fun. And he was very, very fun to be around. My demon chuckled wickedly while Shaylee flushed and giggled. Only my vampire core remained quiet. As usual.

Stick in the mud.

I rolled over onto my back and stretched, settling into a comfy position, hand brushing over the small box with the silver bow. There was no hurry. And no future. Just the understanding that not everything in my life had to weigh a ton and a half or make me feel like I'd done something wrong.

Twinge. Liam's handsome face prodded me with some guilt. He still insisted he loved me, immortal or not. But I'd never once made him any promises. In fact, I told him we couldn't be together now that I knew I'd outlive him by quite probably millennia.

No more guilt. I pulled free the shining ribbon, lifted the lid and peered inside at the pair of pentagram earrings nestled in black velvet. Smiled. Slid them into my ears, fingers rubbing them into place flat against my skin. They were perfect. Or about as perfect as any gift was going to get.

With that, sleep won again.

I'm in the veil, but it's different somehow. Incomplete. No, I'm not in it. I'm creating it.

What the...

You must be careful. *I turn toward the voice, see a shape floating next to me in the dark, glowing softly iridescent, all the colors of the rainbow and others for which I have no names.*

Of what?

The sound and feel of the shape is feminine. She lifts her arm and points. I see them then, below and before me, two vast armies stretching out over an empty gray plane, facing each other. But they've not yet begun to fight. I recognize witches and vampires, Sidhe and demons, other creatures I've never laid eyes on, crowding one side. On the other side are humans, feeling empty and cold, though their power crackles around them like electric fire.

You must be ready. *My companion's voice is very sad, makes tears rise in my eyes.* The war is coming and you only have a little time left to prepare.

I reach for her, wanting to ask her more questions. War? What war? And who is she, who are they, why are we fighting. But she flickers, waves her hand, and I'm falling, faster and faster, my heart pounding, a shriek of terror escaping me as

I flip slowly over and see I'm on Demonicon, plummeting from the side of the Seat mountain, and the ground is right there—

Charlotte was beside me when I jerked awake, eyes gushing tears, my chest on fire from my screams. She rarely touched me, but this time she held me close, rocking me gently as I got a freaking grip already.

"Nightmare?" Her wolf flashed in her eyes.

I shook my head. It was too real. "Something's coming," I said, trying not to sound too melodramatic.

Fail.

The light of day helped me gain some perspective, wiping away my fear and making me doubt what I'd dreamed.

"You've dreamed before," Charlotte said over a steaming cup of the thickest coffee I'd ever choked on. She insisted on making her own, our American brew just too weak for her Old World tastes. "And those dreams have been warnings, foreshadowings."

It was kind of nice to have someone in my life who actually believed me when I said something was happening. And yet, I found myself shaking my head as I slid into the seat at the head of the table, my back to the basement door, and toyed with my glass of orange juice. "I dreamed about falling on Demonicon," I said. "If this was some kind of warning, why did I have the same nightmare at the end of it?"

Yes, nightmare. I'd been having the falling dream pretty regularly since we came home from the other plane. My near-death experience left a stamp of terror on my psyche, the absolute fear I'd felt as I slid over the side of the disabled elevator, protective wards shut down by my murderous cousins always making me shudder, awake or asleep.

"Perhaps." Charlotte was a were of few words, though her Eastern European accent was strongest when she mulled something over, as if thinking too hard made her revert to her native language.

"At any rate," I said, the golden juice tart and sweet at the same time as I took a sip, "I hardly have enough information to go on." Without knowing who the opposing army was, or even what kind of a threat they posed if this warning was the real deal, raising a red flag would likely give me a "cry wolf" complex. No pun intended.

A rush of power outside sent me running, though I knew it wasn't Quaid in my back yard this time. I stepped through the door in time to hug Meira as she ran from the three Enforcers who escorted her home. She only had one small bag with her. The sight made me a little sad, though I knew it was logical she'd likely go back to Harvard and Mom regularly rather than spending the whole summer with me.

I glanced up at the three black-robed witches and was startled to find Pender Tremere in the lead. He bowed slightly to me, the others following suit as I crossed to shake his hand.

"Nice to see you." The tall, thin leader of the Enforcer sect's hand felt cool and dry in mine.

"And you, coven leader," he said with real warmth. There had been a time he'd tried to help our family against the threat of Batsheva and her evil husband, Dominic, and another when he'd been too weak and bound by the rules of his order to act. But I had to agree with Mom, he was a great choice for leader, sunk into honor and duty as if it was all he had.

I just hoped Quaid wouldn't turn out like him. There was more to life than being an Enforcer and following the rules.

My eyes flickered to the others and I received another surprise. The honey blonde who hid behind the cowl on the end was none other than Quaid's old flame.

Interesting. I felt a shot of smugness rush through me at the memory of what he and I had been doing last night and couldn't resist baiting her.

"Hi, Payten," I said. "How's Quaid?"

Her eyes widened, I guessed because I'd addressed her directly. She hesitated before speaking. "He's wonderful," she said softly. "I'm very lucky to have him."

Um. What?

Pender spoke again, distracting me from pinning the

hussy to the ground and demanding to know just what she was talking about.

"When would you like me to send Enforcers for Meira?" I turned to him, almost gaping myself, pulling my heart and my wits together.

"I'll run her back when she's ready," I said, grateful for the lightness of my tone. "Thank you for bringing her personally."

He bowed again. "My pleasure," he said. "Good day."

The three left without another word, power surging around them as they shuddered as though holographic and vanished with a soft pop of magic.

I stood there a long moment, listening to the sound of Meira talking to Charlotte, unable to draw deep breaths or find the will to move.

He'd lied to me. Quaid lied openly, with his power touching mine, at a time I didn't think he should have been able to lie and get away with it. And yet, I couldn't muster anger, or even sadness. Just a dull numb spreading from my middle outward until I felt disconnected from everything.

Um. Hang on a second. I was trusting some random girl with an obvious like-on for the guy I loved and I was trusting her word over his? From someone who had never lied to me before?

Really? Really. Sheesh. And though the doubt remained, it was diminished enough I could shake my head and poke fun at my own instant jealous breakdown into drama.

I'd be asking him next time I saw him, he could bet on that. But until I did, could see the reaction on his face, feel his magic flinch—or not—I'd give him and our love the benefit of the doubt.

"Syd?" Meira's hand on my arm snapped me out of it. I turned to her with a smile, hugged her, already feeling better.

"Hey, Meems," I said. "Want some breakfast?" Whatever hold the news of Quaid's possible betrayal had over me was broken. Just like that. I guess I'd really meant what I said last night.

Just the two of us when we could manage it. Love and no promises.

Either I could live with it or I couldn't, and I found I could.

The old me would have fallen into a fit of rage and spent the day in her room sulking and sobbing and beating herself up over being such an idiot. The new me, knowing how little and yet how very much each moment meant, chose to run, laughing, up to Meira's room and collapse on her bed, to enjoy my sister's company for the time I had her and not look back.

But I'd be reevaluating my relationship with Quaid the next time he came around.

You betcha.

The only person who seemed unhappy with our choice of hangouts grumbled and spit, his silver tail thrashing against the comforter, ears flat to the sides as demon fire flashed in his eyes. Sassafras had come home from school with me, for the peace and quiet, he said. Tired of Meira's endless parade of little friends, he said.

I was sure it was because he wanted to keep an eye on me, but I let him have his subterfuge.

Meira squealed with appropriate excitement as she opened my gift to her, sticking her fingers into pots of color, trying out her new eyeliners on the back of her hand. She'd fallen in love with makeup all over again in the last half a year, thanks to our visit on Demonicon. Better she liked it for the right reasons, than because of some evil witches making her feel like she couldn't be herself. I still owed the Dumont family for their particular brand of torture when Meira had been helpless at camp and brainwashed into hating herself and the rest of the family.

Her hug told me I'd done well. "These colors are perfect for my skin tone," Meira said like she knew what she was talking about—because I surely didn't—the palette spread out in front of her. "Both of them." I had Sashenka, my roommate and bestie, to thank for the choice. She'd taken one look at the handful of makeup I'd been about to buy with a desperate look on my face and firmly removed them from my grip, choosing with care and an amazing eye for detail everything my sister would need for her personas—both human and demon.

Quaid's gift was a cute t-shirt with a band's logo on it. The Witch Doctors were a popular rock group made up entirely of coven members from the Courtney family. Meira hugged it to her, the dark blue fabric also perfect for her.

"I'll kiss him when I see him," she said, winking slowly.

Um, yeah. Okay. What? Ack.

"So what do you want to do while you're home?" I rested my head on my hand as Meira reclined back into her pillows, spreading on some lip gloss and smacking her mouth to smooth it around. "Maybe a movie, go to Johnny's, shopping?"

Her face fell a little. "I don't have much time," she said, apology in her words and her voice. "I'm sorry, Syd, but I have to get back."

Odd how that bothered me more than Quaid's lies. "Okay," I said. "What's up?"

Her eyes sparkled as she leaned forward and hugged me. "I'm taking some advanced training," she said. "I can't wait!"

Sassy perched nearby, nap disturbed, cleaning one of his spotless front paws with his very pink tongue. "I'm certain that's why you're so excited to go back," he said in his droll and cutting way.

Meira's blush made her already red-tinted cheeks turn crimson. I looked back and forth between them as Meira squealed his name and threw a small pillow at him. Sassy dodged easily and went back to his cleaning.

"Okay," I said, grinning myself, "'fess up. What's so interesting back at Harvard you won't take time out for your sister?"

Meira stuck her tongue out at me before falling back onto her pillows again with a happy sigh.

"Emery," she said.

"And what or who exactly is an Emery?" I poked her side, making her squeal and twitch from the tickle.

"Emery Chate," she said, that dreamy look in her eyes I, myself, knew so well. "He's a witch."

Of course he was. I vaguely recalled the three young witches she'd hung out with at the party yesterday. Was one of them a boy?

"Dish," I demanded. "What's he like and why is he worthy of my sister?"

"Oh, *Syd*," she gushed. "He's *awesome*."

Sure he was. And if he touched her in any way I didn't like, I'd rip his arms off.

"Go on," I said.

"He's a year older," she said, like that was a big deal, "but they put me up two semesters, so we're in the same classes." Glitter sparkled in her eyes. "He likes my horns," she said.

Oh. My. Swearword. Was Mom not keeping an eye on her? Tell me my little sister wasn't dating. I was barely ready for me to be dating, damn it.

Breathe, Syd. Just breathe.

Meira went on, oblivious, thankfully. "He's from a small family," she said, sliding over so we were face-to-face, playing with the chain of my pentagram necklace. I'd found the gift from Mom before leaving for Demonicon and hadn't taken it off since, the only real connection I had left to her magic now that she'd withdrawn from me. "I had no idea, did you?"

"What?" At least we weren't talking about dating anymore.

"There are witches who don't live in covens." She seemed appalled at the notion. "Emery's family is one, though. But he has friends who are on their own, just the immediate mom and dad and kids for support." We'd both grown up children of the most powerful coven in North America. I had to admit, the idea of not being surrounded by so much magic would have been a bit of a shocker. I'd been powerless once and could only imagine it felt kind of the same.

"There are ten in his coven," she said. "His mom? She and her sister had a fight and she broke away and made her own family." Meira looked sad at that. "At least he's the younger brother of the heir to his, so he understands me."

"What do you mean?" I didn't mean to frown at her. Her sadness turned defensive as she let my chain go and shrugged.

"Being second has a stigma," she said like she knew what that word meant. "Not so bad if you're a boy, worse if you're a girl. Knowing you'll never be leader and all that. Being in your older sibling's shadow."

Sassy had fallen very still next to us, staring at her, but I ignored him as I nodded.

"We had this talk, kind of," I said, "on Demonicon. But Meems, I told you. You're not second in my eyes. Not ever."

She actually looked at me like I was a child who needed to be straightened out of my thinking, patting my hand.

"Syd," she said very slowly, as if I didn't get it and never would, "I'll never lead our coven. Even if something happens to you," she winced a little, "the coven will never accept me. Not looking like this." She held out her black-fingernailed, red-tinted hands.

Sassy told me as much years ago, back when I just wanted out of the family life, but I'd never believed him. But Meira understood. How did she grow up faster than I did?

And yet, she didn't seem upset or angry. Just so matter of fact I wanted to hug her.

"Meems..." I didn't know what to say.

"Doesn't matter," she said. "You're immortal anyway, so it's not like the coven will be forced to let me down gently. But..."

"What?" I stroked hair back from her cheek, suddenly sad with the way our conversation was going.

"What would you do if I left?" She seemed tense all of a sudden. Was she expecting me to give her a hard time? "If I wanted to start my own coven?"

I leaned forward and gathered her against me, hugging her and kissing her cheek. "I'd miss you like absolute crazy," I said, eyes tingling with unshed tears, a little hoarse as I went on. "But I'd support you in any way I could. And

Meems," I pulled away a little as Sassy started to purr, "I'd be so proud of you I wouldn't be able to stand it."

Meira beamed at me, hugged me back. She'd been through so much in the last few years, I was amazed how mature she'd become.

I wanted to talk about it more, but her computer dinged and she squealed in excitement.

"Emery," she said before answering the Skype call that basically dismissed me.

I left her to talk to the boy who was certainly the first of many conquests Meira would make and softly closed the door on her, Sassafras weaving out between my legs as we left her to her giggling.

Why was it my default location when I felt sad had Liam in it? Not that I was deep in the doldrums or anything, but thinking about Meira leaving me was enough to set me off in search of comfort.

Didn't help Gram was still nowhere to be found. The rest of the house felt so quiet. Maybe that was why I couldn't stand to stay around while the sound of Meira's laughter and chatter echoed from upstairs like she was in another world.

I sealed the wards on the house as I left, sending her a soft touch of magic to let her know where I was going. She hugged me quickly back, a flash of a very cute guy passing between us before she blocked me out, giggling. I was a little surprised to find Sassafras at my feet, tail twitching, as I locked the kitchen door.

Who was I to question why he needed out of the house? Maybe Meira's growing up bothered him, too.

Not feeling super talkative, but in the need for exercise,

I led our small procession, Charlotte at my side, toward town hall and my Sidhe friend.

It was a beautiful day, the leaves fresh on the trees, the beginning of summer just around the corner. A few deep breaths helped raise my spirits as did the memory of Quaid's visit the night before. Sure, he may have lied to me about the blonde, but no way was I letting it ruin the fact I had a great time.

How grown up of you, Syd.

Galleytrot lay in the entry, big head on his paws as we entered through the green glow of the Sidhe wards. He looked up as we did, nose lifting, sniffing. I reached out to him, gave his ear a scratch on the way by, only to hear him grumbling to himself.

"Quaid," he said.

Oh no he *didn't*. I withdrew my hand, suddenly cold despite my rising temper.

I already told you to mind your own business. My mind snapped against the black dog. *And I meant it.*

Galleytrot shut me out, rising to pad toward the archive, ignoring me. We'd had this argument already. About Liam. Galleytrot's concern was touching, but irritating at the same time. Liam was a big boy and knew perfectly well I was in no position to be his girlfriend.

I'd told him enough times. I just wished he'd listen.

Happy mood now tainted with anger and a bit of guilt, I stomped my way through the door, Sassafras scampering ahead of me to take his favorite chair. I had a brief after-image of him in human form, draped sideways over the arm, one foot up on Liam's desk, a book in his hands and had to shake my head as the silver Persian curled up into a ball, tail tucked around him and stared at me with glowing amber eyes.

"Syd!" Liam rushed toward me, hugging me, a book pressed uncomfortably between us. "You must be psychic."

"Sorry?" I rubbed at my breastbone where the spine of the thick, brown leather book had made an impression.

Liam grinned. "I was just about to call you. You have to read this." He pulled me into his office toward a cluttered old desk of heavy, carved wood in Sidhe motif. Piles of parchment and books lay everywhere, his only nod to the present his silver laptop open to one side, a spinning vortex screensaver making me dizzy.

He pressed me down into the chair I usually took, the velvet seat shaping almost perfectly to my butt as he laid the book in my lap with something like reverence. One scan of the scrolling handwriting and I shook my head, looking up into his excited hazel eyes, green flecks winking at me.

"You know I don't share your ability for languages." I let my fingers trace over the writing, feeling something familiar about it, but not able to make a connection just yet. "What is it?"

Liam set one hand on it, not taking it from me, the pressure of his touch weighing the book more heavily on my legs. "It's maji," he said.

Maji? We knew so little about the magical sect, long since extinct, or so it was believed. I knew almost nothing of their history, until the chamber under the vampire's mansion was discovered. I did know they used to be the big boys, until their power started to fade, but came up empty when I tried to remember why.

Liam finally took back the book, stroking the side of the page as he smiled down at it. "This was written by one of their scientists, a powerful and brilliant woman named Iepa."

Okay, why did that name make me shudder? Not in a bad way, but as if I should know what it meant?

Freaky. And yes, I was used to freaky, but then again, did anyone really get used to freaky?

It did prompt me to recall my dream from last night, though. Which struck me as odd. "Why are you researching the maji?"

Liam sank against the desk, open book cradled against his chest as he frowned a little. "I'm not sure. I was looking into Sidhe court rituals when I stumbled on this by accident." He tapped the cover with one hand.

Sassafras perked immediately while Charlotte twitched where she leaned against the wall behind me.

"There are no such things as accidents in a place like this," Sass said. Hmm, true. The archive almost had a mind of its own, showing the seeker exactly what was sought from the endless stacks going back into who knew where.

"Sass is right," I said. "This is too much of a coincidence." The misty form I'd seen, the ancient feel of her, the way the veil seemed new, not old. The woman in my dream. Was she somehow tied to the maji? Or was she really some random nightmare I remembered because I woke up from falling? Just in case, I told them all what I'd dreamed about, Charlotte silent though she'd heard it before, the others tensed as I wrapped up.

"My falling dream," I said, eyes on Sass. "The Demonicon one." He'd comforted me a few times since, so he knew what I was talking about and I didn't have any secrets from Liam.

Well, I did have one. But I wasn't going there right now.

"I thought you said it was nothing?" Charlotte's soft tone cut nonetheless.

"I guess I was wrong." I turned to see her lips twitch. Yeah, she could have her private little laugh fest.

"Why the falling dream in conjunction?" Sassafras stood up, ears flickering back and forth, his gaze lost in the distance. "Or is there a correlation between the two?"

I didn't want to think about my falling dream though he mirrored my thoughts. "I think the more important question is how valid is the warning?"

Liam frowned over the book. "You said it was like the veil was new, like you were making it. Could this woman have been controlling it, not you?"

"What are you suggesting?" Sassy's ears flickered, whiskers twitching.

"I don't know," he smiled, embarrassed, cheeks flushing from it. "Just a stupid theory."

"Spit it out," Galleytrot said.

Liam cleared his throat. "What if she was maji?"

That was a stretch, wasn't it? Or was it?

Sassafras nodded, nose wriggling as he thought it over. "From what little we demons know, it might make sense. Worth exploring, anyway."

Galleytrot chuffed softly. "The Sidhe respected the maji," he said in his rumbling voice, the echo of thunder from a rainstorm rolling through me when he spoke. "Considered them beyond nobility. Almost as gods."

Well that was interesting. "Why's that?"

He shrugged his great shoulders, red fire dancing in his eyes. "I don't know," he said. "Only that my handlers were almost afraid of them."

The arrogant Sidhe? Afraid? Even more interesting.

"You met them?" Liam closed the book and set it aside, though one hand never left it, fingers steepled on the cover.

"One," the hound said. "A woman. And her very presence made my blood go cold."

Liam was nodding, flipping the book open. "They were beyond Spirit," he said. "Iepa knew she made others uncomfortable."

I shook my head, frowning. "There's nothing beyond Spirit." Or so I'd been taught.

Sassafras grunted softly, tail twitching. "And in all your nineteen years of accumulated wisdom, you've learned everything there is to know, have you?"

I hated it when he did that. "Okay then, smarty pants," I said. "What's beyond Spirit?"

Liam saved Sassafras the trouble of answering. "They are outside Spirit," he said. "Pure Universal energy. According to Iepa, they were literally the hands of creation."

"Were?" I felt my hands clenching together as the wavering image of the woman I'd seen in my dream hovered in my mind's eye. "Where did they go?"

Liam looked suddenly sad, the book thudding shut. "They fell when the sorcerers attacked." I felt my stomach ripple with something unpleasant. "The maji were pure creation power, without offense. The sorcerer's sect was offense only, drawing power from the world around them, destroying what they used to fuel their magic. The maji didn't stand a chance against them."

The compulsion to get up, get up, GET UP was so strong I found myself on my feet and heading for the door before Liam was through speaking. I forced myself to stop at the threshold and turn to the others.

"I'm going to the mansion," I said while the pull of it grew stronger. "Coming?"

As I turned once again, giving in to the need of whatever led me, I heard Quaid's voice in my head, telling me not to go looking for trouble.

If trouble would leave me be, I'd be happy to take his advice.

I wasn't surprised to find out I was far from alone, either.

We were a quiet bunch heading back to the house. Liam was lost in thought and his own inner geeky excitement, grinning at me from time to time, a kid on his way to a toy store. Galleytrot padded beside him, tongue lolling out, Sassafras perched on his wide back. I almost told him to get down, but just rolled my eyes.

This town was weird on its own. A silver Persian riding a giant black dog wasn't going to be news.

And Charlotte? Well, she was Charlotte. Chatty Cathy, that one.

Naturally, when we piled into the van waiting in my driveway, I was stuck driving. Not that I minded. I liked to drive. But there were too many of us to fit in a normal-sized car, so I was forced to take the family minivan.

Yup, really cool, Syd.

I still missed Minnie, my turquoise and white Mini Cooper, cursing the Dumont brothers, Jean Marc and Kristophe, under my breath yet again at the memory of my exploding car. Jerktards. While their attempt to kill me had failed, thanks to Charlotte's timely arrival, I secretly wished she'd shown up before they'd gotten their greasy little hands on it.

And while riding the veil was more fun and I probably should have just pulled my companions all along behind me to speed the trip, to be totally honest, there were times a girl just wanted to drive a car.

Galleytrot leaned through the gap between the front seats, Charlotte firmly belted into the passenger's side, and breathed his earthy smelling breath on me. Not that I normally minded, but his head was the size of three dogs and was very fluffy, black fur brushing against my cheek.

"You said there was writing on the walls of the maji chamber?" His tongue swept out to lick his chops, making me shudder and cringe sideways. I loved the big mutt, but he was creeping me out.

Guess I just wasn't used to having him so close anymore.

"Yeah," I said. "Gram said it was maji, so I took her word for it." My attempts to reach her and tell her where we were going fell on empty air. Wherever Gram was, she didn't want me interfering.

Fine, leave me out of important stuff yet again and see what kind of trouble it brings.

Bitter? Who, me?

Galleytrot retreated, much to my relief, Liam taking his place.

"I can't wait," he said, magic so tightly wound it made me nervous. Didn't they realize I had to concentrate to drive? "I can't believe I didn't think of exploring the cavern under the mansion before."

More coincidence?

"You're certain the vampire's human servants won't mind our intrusion?" Sassafras sat in Charlotte's lap, every once in a while standing up and putting his paws on the dash so he could look outside, chattering at a bird or some other interesting thing moving past. He hated it, but he was still a slave to his cat nature at times.

"I'm sure." Well, mostly sure. I'd only been to the mansion once when the sun was up and the Council not occupying the property, shortly after Mom's trial. I'd shown up a few minutes too early to say goodbye to Uncle Frank and Sunny. The clan butler, for lack of a better term, had been very gracious and didn't hesitate to let me inside.

Mind you, now that I thought about it, then it had only been minutes to dark and I was alone. Maybe carting a vanload of paranormals, one of them a werewolf, into Sebastian's house while he was still asleep wasn't a good idea.

Too late. I pulled into the driveway and checked the clock on the dash. Just after 2pm. We had hours yet before vampire wakey-wakey, eggs and bakey. I shrugged to myself as I parked in front of the big main door. If we weren't allowed in, we'd come back later. A pain in the rear, but we'd survive.

The moment I knocked, the door swung open and my worries were extinguished as the tall, slender man in the black suit on the other side smiled at me and held out his hand to take mine with real warmth.

"Coven leader," he said. "Welcome."

I gestured behind me as the gang trooped their way up the stairs. "I hope it's okay," I said. "We want to have a look at the chamber under the house."

He bowed to us, still smiling. "Of course," he said. "At your service." He pulled the door open wider, wavy black hair streaked with liberal gray glinting in the sunlight shining over the marble floor. More confident, I entered, Sassafras darting around my legs and into the house while the rest followed more slowly.

The big door thudded shut behind us as I turned to face the butler. He gestured with slow grace toward the wide hallway I remembered. "My lord has instructed me to allow you entry at any time," the butler said, striding along beside me as we moved deeper into the house, past carved wooden doors along a carpet so red and plush it felt like walking through clouds.

"Thank you." I struggled with his name. I knew it, didn't I? Been introduced before. Shaun? Stanley?

I sucked at people.

"Stewart, coven leader." His smile was soft, kind. How did he know I couldn't remember? "Here we are." He paused by the door as memory gripped me. The last time I'd stood here, Gram waited for me on the other side, Mom's trial in full swing. I half expected the crazy old lady to be there again, disappointed to find the room empty.

"If there is anything I can do," Stewart said as he bowed again. "Please, do not hesitate to ask. And if you are still here when my Lord awakes, I'll inform him of your studies."

"Thank you, Stewart." I found myself smiling back as he turned and walked away in his same long, slow stride, eating the distance, until he was gone around the corner.

Charlotte was already at the wall, hands reaching for the stones when I joined my posse inside the large room. I ignored the fancy furniture, the walls lined with bookshelves and what were probably priceless paintings and tried to follow Charlotte's hands as she pressed the right combination. Good thing one of us remembered. I'd been watching, but Gram had been too quick for me. Charlotte selected each slotted piece with precise confidence. Within a tense moment where Liam practically quivered in anticipation, the floor beneath us groaned and dropped away, revealing a set of stairs.

"After you." Liam tried the gallant thing, but I just laughed.

"You're kidding, right?" I gave him a gentle shove and watched as, grinning like a little kid at Christmas, he trotted fearlessly down the steps and into the darkness below. Galleytrot went after him, Sassafras waiting for me at the top, tail wrapped around his paws. I bent and lifted him into my arms without thinking and was a little surprised he didn't protest.

"What's wrong, Sass?" I stroked his fur while he shivered slightly.

"I don't know," he said. "There's something..."

He was right again. I felt it too, now he'd made me aware. It could have been the mix of my magicks kept me from noticing it at first. And my initial visit was wrapped up in fear for Mom and anxiety over Gram's plan. But now, standing there with myself in balance and with Sass's attention to focus mine, I became acutely aware of the pressure of something, as though walking down the stairs would be the equivalent of going under water.

"Did you want to wait up here?" I half-bent to put him down only to have him swat me.

"Don't be ridiculous." He growled softly, though made no attempt to leave my arms. "Well? Are we going or not?"

I laughed under my breath as I descended, the underwater feeling dissipating as I passed the third stair. Was there some kind of protection on the staircase? Likely. Though there didn't seem to be one on the mechanism controlling it. Odd. But at least Sassy wasn't shivering any longer, so he must have noticed the release as well.

By the time I joined Liam at the bottom, his green Sidhe magic lighting the way, I was a little creeped out. Not by where we were, but by the memory of why I'd been here last time. I knew Gram was a good enough Necromancer there was no way even a smidge of the echoes of the people she'd raised would be hanging around. But, on the other hand, she'd pulled a large number of ghosts out of the gray place where they lived. Even someone as talented as her could have made a mistake.

But no, I was lying to myself. It wasn't the ghosts she raised making the hair stand up on my arms or driving me to form a large ball of witch light I shoved before me like a beacon. It was the ghost who latched onto me when the doorway first opened, the one I was responsible for, the one I blamed myself for.

Alison. Part of me feared there might be part of her still here. But worse, that the monster she'd become might use this place as a hideout. Meeting up with blood-sucking Alison's echo, now a twisted and black creature influenced by Ameline Benoit, in a dark and creepy underchamber hidden below a vampire lair was the stuff of horror movies.

The ones where the heroine dies in the end.

I almost yelled at Liam not to go into the side chamber. Wasn't the handsome guy always the first one to bite it? Instead, I shook myself internally and got a freaking grip. Sometimes I had to remind myself I didn't have to worry about horror movies.

I was way scarier than any Hollywood creature, thanks.

A breath of air passed over me as I walked into the circular room, but it was welcoming, almost a blessing, as though someone bent to kiss my cheek. I relaxed instantly, my witch light floating up into the darkness, lighting the room like a sparkling chandelier. I was proud of my control, considering a few short years ago I could barely shield a lit candle for more than ten seconds before distraction killed the flame. But no one paid attention to how awesome my skills had become and, with a little shrug for vanity, I let it go.

Hard not to. Especially when I could barely keep the grin of affection off my face. Liam dashed around the room as if he didn't know where to start, hands running over the carvings, entire body quivering in excitement. When he turned to me, his eyes glowed with Sidhe magic and his smile so wide his white teeth caught the light from above.

"This is amazing!" He went back to his studies, whispering to himself while Galleytrot stayed close. I almost told the big dog to back off and let Liam have his space only to bite my tongue. Liam was important, very, very important, to a lot of people. Um, to the whole world, actually. As Keeper of the Gate in Wilding Springs, only he was able to answer the knock when the Sidhe came calling. Which made Galleytrot, a hound of the same Sidhe, uber protective.

Fair enough. And Liam had to be used to him by now, not even tripping over the massive black galoot as my friend wound his way around and around the room, starting first in the middle of the wall only to swear at himself and crouch-walk his way again only this time focused on the bottom, near the floor.

I sighed and set Sassafras on the altar pedestal in

the center of the room, looking around, now a little bummed since I couldn't read any of the words myself. The apprehension of meeting up with Gram's ghosts was banished in favor of boredom.

Charlotte prowled endlessly, as though restless. But when I asked her what was wrong, she just shook her head and growled before beginning her pacing again. I felt calm, more calm than I had in a long time, and even Sassafras acted like this was no big deal so I let the weregirl have her nervous explorations and hopped up to join my demon cat on the stone.

"This is definitely maji," Liam said, spinning toward me. "Do you feel the energy?"

I shrugged, picking at a hangnail on my thumb. "So?" I looked around a moment before sighing. "There's nothing here." The pull forcing me to pile my friends into the van was now gone as if it never existed. Curious, yes. But unless the source of that pull made herself—I was now positive this Iepa was manipulating us in some way—known, we'd wasted our trip.

Liam laughed, shook his head. "Oh, ye of little faith," he said. "Give me a few minutes and I'll show you something that will blow your beautiful mind."

I flushed at the compliment, but he was already at it

again, moving faster this time, whispers turning to mutters as he circled and circled. By the time he stopped again, he was straining, hand above him, touching the stones, unable to reach any further.

"Amazing." Liam's awe-struck tone took my attention from where I played catch-a-paw with Sassafras. "Do you have any idea what this is?"

I drew a breath, a sarcastic snark on my lips, only to let it out in a puff of irritation. "Do tell."

Liam hugged himself. "This is the history of everything," he said.

The what? "What do you mean, everything?" I turned where I sat, eyes roving over the stones he'd been studying the better part of three hours.

"I mean, everything." He pointed at the floor, to a stone with an irregular shape, right by the entry door. "The birth of the Universe," he said, hand traveling along as he spun, "the creation of suns, planets, nebulae." His arm raised, finger still showing us the way. "The fabric of all life, all planes, the creation of the divides between them. At the hands of the maji."

I didn't want to be a wet blanket, but most religions had their creation theories. Why wouldn't the maji be any different? The idea they actually created everything sounded pretty ludicrous. But Liam was on a roll so I didn't shoot him down. Not directly.

"Cool," I said. "Now what?"

He frowned at me before rushing to my side, lifting me from the pedestal and setting me on my feet in front of him. I was a little breathless from the contact, how his power buzzed with energy, but he didn't give me a chance to stop him as he pulled me toward the wall opposite the doorway. He stopped and pointed.

"I have an idea," he said. "But you have to trust me."

Galleytrot growled softly while Charlotte rumbled her own distress.

"Will it put us in danger?" I met Liam's eyes, only to see his desperate need for me to believe in him shining from the depths.

"No," he said. Paused. "I don't think so."

Before the two overly protective canines could put a kibosh on the idea, Sassafras wormed his way between Liam and me.

"Not like we haven't faced a little danger before," he said. "This feels important, Syd."

Weird. "Did you just say I should purposely do something that might be stupid?" Who stole my cat and put this imposter in his place?

Sassafras shuddered, licking one paw a few strokes before settling again. "I'm just... I feel like there's something more here we need to know."

I opened my power, all of it, from demon to witch to Sidhe to vampire and drew a breath, closing my eyes. Felt around. Let the combined magicks I controlled wander around the room. Only to be led back here, to this wall. Something pulsed inside it, beckoning to me. The pull I'd first felt earlier, in Liam's cavern, bringing us all here, was focused in these stones. Anything able to penetrate the wards of the Sidhe to reach me had to be powerful. The cavern itself was protected by the most earth magic I'd ever come across, not to mention its own little shift in planes, making it close to impossible for normal magic to penetrate. I'd only ever felt anything reach through when something catastrophic was happening. And yet this embedded magic was so soft now, so subtle, it took searching to find it.

I let my eyes drift open, six stones glowing softly in my vision as I did, the illumination fading from them as I blinked and let the light in. I squinted and was able to see again, just barely. Without thinking, I did as Charlotte had done, pressing each of the stones. Only the ones I touched didn't depress, but began to glow, the same iridescent light

I'd seen in my dream shining from them, until all six shone with happy power.

The intensity of the light grew as Liam took my hand and led me back, away from the wall, toward the center of the chamber. Charlotte clung close, snuffling the air, quivering while Galleytrot chuffed and licked his chops over and over again. Sassafras was the only calm one of the three, though his tail wrapped around my ankle, one front paw resting on the toe of my shoe.

"Here." Liam pointed to the altar and the words etched there. "This one. It means enter."

I didn't need him to tell me what word to touch, or its meaning. Now that the light glowed from the stones across the room I could feel it to my bones, what I was meant to do, supposed to do. This was my fate, my destiny and it called me from deep inside the earth as surely as if it had a voice, a heart, a soul.

But Liam was wrong. The word didn't mean enter. Not quite.

It meant *Come.*

The moment I touched it, it began its own glow, the energy rippling upward from my finger tips and through my arm, all the way to my heart and the vampire core hiding there.

She cried out as the light reached her, but not in pain. In joy.

"I knew it," Liam said as the floor began to sink, silent this time, flickers of the same multi-colored magic flowing as a spiral staircase was revealed. "You have the power of the maji."

Like I needed another kind of magic to worry about.

Liam was gone like a shot down the stairs, yet again leaving us to follow. But this time he was slowed by the writing on the walls of the narrow flight, twisting back and forth from one side to another, cries of joy and exclamation bursting from him, kind of like this:

"Mesopotamia! Holy, can't be, how cool is—Egypt! The pyramids are what? Now I have to go to—Greece. Yes, of course. Of course! Why didn't I guess that might be the—Rome? No, really? All of Rome? How did they control the flow of—"

He stopped below me, hand hovering over the wall, and when he turned to face me there was so much sadness in his eyes I descended to share his step and hug him while he shook.

"So sad," he whispered. "The Dark Ages."

Ouch. Not a great time for those with magic. "The Inquisition?" All witches knew about the Spanish Inquisition, their unholy need to eradicate all of us from the face of the earth, only to ultimately fail because we were simply too smart for them.

"It wasn't what we thought," Liam said, fingers stroking the etchings as the others crowded in to listen. "The Inquisition was run by sorcerers who claimed to serve the Church, but who had their own agenda."

"They missed us, at least," I said, squeezing his arm. "Though innocent women were killed in our place."

Liam's head hung a moment before he shook it. "Witches weren't the real target," he said, voice breaking. "They were hunting maji."

Um. What?

"Not pure maji," he said, "but their descendants. Look, it's all here." I wished I could read what he translated for myself. "The innocent women and men who died were the sons and daughters of powerful maji creators, gone while their blood lines carried on." He paused. "The sorcerers were too late, though, to catch everyone. The pureblood maji's children had already spread far and wide."

Liam turned and continued his descent, my witch light floating ahead of him and lighting his reading. I was a little startled to reach the bottom, stepping down onto ground level before passing under a curved entry and into another round stone chamber.

The iridescent glow I'd noticed in the writings above us was stronger here, flooding the place as we crossed the threshold, shining from everywhere and from nowhere. The very rocks glittered with it, making it as bright as day, if daylight was equivalent to stepping into a complex rainbow.

I let my witch light fade, looking around with awe, noting the threads of white, green, blue, brown, amber and red magic weaving themselves through the room. Liam was already studying and, for the first time, I worried he might hurt himself someday, rushing into a situation he couldn't handle out of the desire for knowledge. It took me this long to see it, but I no longer doubted Galleytrot's need to protect the absent-minded and driven O'Dane and, in fact, I was grateful to have him watch over my friend.

"This is different," Liam said, excited again. "The history is done. These are names." He looked over his shoulder at me with a little frown. "Lists of names?"

I joined him, touched the walls, though nothing glowed beneath my fingers. "What kind of names?"

He ignored me another moment before letting out a heavy breath of air. "Families," he whispered, reverential in his tone as he stepped back toward the middle of the room and the long, bed-like slab of stone resting there on a raised pedestal. I'd noted it when I'd first entered, along with the alcove-like seats placed at regular intervals around the chamber.

"Chapter markers?" I raised one eyebrow at the thought, pointing at the alcoves and, though Liam couldn't possibly have known where my mind went after that cryptic comment, he suddenly laughed.

"Yes, of course, Syd. Brilliant." He turned to the door again, began his sideways motion around the room. "These are family trees, the lineages of the maji. The ones they left behind." I backed out of his way as he hurried past me. "With these, we can find every line of maji blood still here on this plane."

"To raise an army?" Galleytrot sank to his haunches. "For the war?"

Liam paused, shoulders sagging. "I hope that's not its purpose," he said.

I shook my head, crossing my arms over my chest. "This feels like a record," I said, "not some battle manifest."

Liam opened his mouth to say something only to freeze and gasp. When he looked up at me, he was grinning again.

"The Hayle family," he said. "Your blood line is here."

Sassy scampered to his side. "Who begins it?"

"I couldn't even start to tell you," Liam said, looking up

the wall. "The story reaches way back here," he pointed to a line of text above his head, "mixed with this one," another line, this time on the other side of an alcove, "and has many, many branches."

Liam's hand fell to Sassy's head, stroking his fur as the Persian stood up and placed his paws against the wall.

"But it ends early," Liam said. "With someone named Auburdeen?"

"Auburdeen Thaddea Hayle," Sassy said, voice cracking for a moment before he cleared his throat and returned to all fours. "Why does it end with her? She had children, obviously."

"I don't know," Liam said, fingers tracing the bare stone below my ancestor's name. "It just stops."

"The record keeper must have passed on before he or she could find a replacement." Galleytrot's tongue lolled out, though his dark eyes were sad.

"Makes sense," I said, feeling a little sad myself, almost as if I knew my ancestor Auburdeen now that I stood here in the presence of her name etched in stone. Who was she and what was she like? I'd have to ask Sassafras. If he'd be willing to talk about it. I'd never been able to convince him to share any of his past with me before.

Maybe this would change his mind.

I turned from the wall, to look down at Sassafras, only to see a thin snake of red power coil around him and let go again. It drifted toward me even as a similar strand of blue flittered across Liam's shoulder, a fluttering piece of green teasing the ends of Charlotte's hair.

"All the magicks," Liam said. "The power of the creators."

I reached for the red strand, let it slide over my palm. "This is blood magic." Usually just thinking about the forbidden power made my stomach crawl. But standing there in the maji chamber, I had to wonder what all the fuss was about.

"Were you right, Liam?" Sassafras's voice was low, vibrating with wonder. "Did the sorcerers really find a way to prevent witches from using their magic?"

I'd known my Sidhe friend was correct all along, had told me ages ago how witches, working for the church, cast power over all of our kind to prevent the use of blood magic. The geas was still in place and even just the thought of using what we now referred to as negative magic made my stomach churn. And yet, knowing what I did, that the lie created to stunt our power still existed, I hadn't done anything about it, aside from tell Mom when she was in no position to act, still a prisoner of the Council. I had to talk to her about it.

It suddenly felt very important.

As I turned toward the door, the compulsion to speak to Mom growing more powerful as I considered what had been done to witches by the very sorcerers I now knew were the other side of this war I'd been warned about, my eyes settled on the slab and I paused.

Approached without thought. Heard a whisper of a voice I recognized, the same one from my dream, pulling me closer, asking me to reach out and touch the stone as power flared—

—I'm in the dream again, watching the two armies face off, the ghostly specter of the maji woman hovering next to me. Only now the battle has engaged, power slashing between combatants, death and life coming together in a mix of screams and the discharge of opposing magicks.

I want to help, reaching for them, but the maji holds me back.

Iepa. *I turn to her, see her face more clearly with contact, and know I'm right, it is she, the author of Liam's book, who has brought us together, to this place, with purpose.* I have to stop it.

You will have your chance. *Her voice is liquid in my mind, gentle and soft.* I hope. But not in this moment, Sydlynn. This is but an image of what could be, a possible future. If we were to go elsewhere in this place, you would see far different outcomes than this one. And yet, the possibility of its coming to pass is enough to bring us worry.

Us. *I turn back to the battle, heart pounding.* The maji.

She doesn't answer, just watches with me for a moment.

This future is terrible, *she sends*. One which could mean the end to magic on your plane, spreading outward to others until it consumes the Universe.

Then what do I have to do to stop it? *My hands have clenched into angry fists at my sides, beating against my thighs over and over. I feel the impact, though barely, as though my body is far away.*

Be open, *Iepa sends*. And say yes to them when they come to you. Their safety is paramount.

I'm about to ask her who she's talking about when the image changes, a large, jagged cut appearing through the battle scene as though I've only been watching on a big-screen television. The two edges jerk aside, the stuff of the veil parting to show me what I need to see.

Two kids run toward me, a girl, tall with dark hair, glasses, her hand clutching the boy beside her, shorter, younger, with the clearest, most intense blue eyes I've ever seen. They are in darkness, fleeing through trees, heading toward me, but never reaching the veil.

The light and her shadow, *Iepa sends*. Remember.

I lunge for them, the compulsion the maji has placed on me pushing me forward, the need to protect them so powerful I can barely catch my breath. My fingers brush the edge of the veil, almost, almost—

"Syd."

I leaped back, away from Liam as he touched me, my hand lifting from the slab, the vision over, though my need to reach the kids hadn't gone anywhere. I stared at the empty air above the pedestal, searching for a glimpse of the kids, some way to reach them, but they were gone.

"Damn it." I pulled free of Liam as he tried again, rubbing my hands together while they tingled, the iridescent magic of the maji still clinging to me. "I have to find them again." I touched the slab with my fingertips, but nothing happened. It wasn't until I pressed both palms to the plate I realized I'd lost whatever connection I'd had.

Hard not to be angry at Liam for breaking it.

"Syd, what's wrong?" Sassafras hopped up on the slab and came to my side. I resisted the urge to lift him free of the stone, feeling as if his presence there was some kind of sacrilege. I really had to get my crap together. At least, from the way my friends were looking at me, I did.

"I saw something." I told them in a halting voice, about the battle, the conversation and the two kids. I shook myself a little as I spoke. The girl had to be near my age and I was calling her a kid? Something about going through all the life-changing events I'd been through made me feel like anyone else my age was still just a child.

Not fair of me, though. For all I knew, those two had seen as much trouble as I had.

"None of you saw any of it?" I wasn't really surprised, though I hoped I'd have some backup in case I was accused of looking for trouble. Funny how Quaid's reaction from months ago still clung to me and made me feel guilty.

"I'm sorry," Liam said. "I shouldn't have touched you. But you were shaking and looked like you were in pain."

Charlotte hung back, her breath coming in soft pants. I turned and went to her, taking her hands in mine. "What is it?"

"You were gone so long," she said softly. "If Liam hadn't broken the spell, I would have."

I spun back on the others. "How long?"

"At least a few hours," Liam said. "We were going to let it run its course, but then you became so agitated."

Wow. It felt like minutes to me.

"Okay," I said, trying to pull my thoughts together through a burning need to find the two kids in my vision. "So here's what we know. It seems the sorcerer's sect is prepping for some kind of war against all other magic races. But they aren't ready yet. Unless we find a way to stop them, magic as we know it could be destroyed."

Sassafras shook, his fur standing on end. "And the children you mentioned?"

"According to Iepa, they have something to do with the light and the shadow, whatever that means. I do know they are both important in the war." I ground my teeth together and crossed my arms over my chest. "You know what? I'm getting mighty tired of all this crap. Just for once, couldn't something be easy?"

Galleytrot snorted. "I'm sure the powers controlling this are most contrite about their methods," he said. "I'm sure if you ask the maji to just come out with it, they'll be happy to oblige."

I scowled at him, but couldn't hold it, a grin winning. "And here I thought Sassafras was the smartass."

The big dog bowed his head, tongue hanging out as his tail wagged a few times in answer.

"There's not much more we can do here," Liam said, looking around. "I did as much study of the family lines as I could without equipment to log the information."

"Unless you think you can reconnect with the maji?" Sassafras finally hopped down on his own and I found myself breathing a sigh of relief he'd done so.

I shook my head. "For whatever reason, our time was up." Yeah, Syd, like you'd over-used your broadband or something. Right. Still, it felt like I had what I needed.

I just had to find the kids and... what? Protect them? Help them? Lock them up?

Okay, so I didn't have everything. But maybe once I had them in my grasp they would be able to tell me more.

Shadows flickered, the room taking on a cold edge just as the air seemed to part and Sebastian appeared beside me. I turned toward him, the pull of his nature calling to my vampire core. The moment I did, he moved as well, all tall, dark and deliciously undead of him hovering over me, eyes full of something reminding me I hadn't had dinner yet.

"Sydlynn." His cold hand touched mine, skin temperature telling me he hadn't stopped to eat either before coming to see what we'd uncovered.

"Sebastian." Grrrowl. I'd always had a crush on the devastatingly handsome blood clan leader, even before my brilliant idea to rescue him from the essence threatening his life and now residing inside of me. Even more so now I knew what his broad, strong body looked like mostly unclothed. But the feeling of wanting to be with him was much stronger than I remembered. While I blamed my vampire core, I couldn't help the grin lifting the corner of my mouth or the naughty urge to stroke his hand with my thumb while I imagined stroking other parts of him—

Yeesh. Okay, down, girl.

I think Sebastian must have had the same reaction to me. And the exact understanding of why in the moment I did because it seemed like we pulled apart in the very same instant, his body, once curved toward me in sensual offering now rigid as he took a step away and clasped his hands behind his back.

There was just enough of my awareness left to register the flash of jealousy on Liam's face.

Like the poor guy needed another rival to worry about.

"Incredible." It was probably a good thing Sebastian was instantly fascinated with the chamber. Otherwise, I wasn't sure I'd be able to show as much restraint as he did. Part of me was sad when he walked away, eyes locked on the carvings on the walls, to think we'd used to be as close to friends as we could get, and now this thing between us could only end in disaster. I knew he'd been avoiding me since the fall, the only time I'd seen him since then an awkward and uncomfortable moment of him standing across the room muttering platitudes. He'd felt the vampire inside me when I'd asked for his help looking into the Star Club, so he was forewarned. But this was the first time we were actually in contact with each other and I fully understood why he held his distance.

Sucked. I'd have to talk to my vampire about it and see what we could do. Because now that I knew I was immortal, Sebastian and his blood clan were the few people in my life I could have a very long relationship with.

Liam lost whatever anger he'd been feeling, or at least found a way to hide it, because he eagerly joined the blood clan leader, the two muttering over the find before Sebastian turned and fixed me with his very blue eyes. I felt my cheeks heat, and not from embarrassment. Rather, the desire to run my hands over his face, to find out what he tasted like so strong I had to look away.

"This must be studied," he said, kindly not mentioning my moment of weakness. "I would be honored to assist you, Liam, in any way I can."

My Sidhe friend laughed a little, almost nervous. Was he afraid of the vampire? But no, not Sebastian, after all. "I'm not much of a scholar," Liam said. "But I'd really like to explore this further."

A few more flickers and three vampires joined us. I recognized Anastasia immediately, the cold, blonde vampire one of Sebastian's most trusted clan members. Her face twitched as she met my eyes, hunger burning in her gaze before she shuddered and crossed to Sebastian, staying away from me. The other two did the same, eyes looking everywhere but at me. My vampire core acted like a repulsion beam, though I knew part of the reason they avoided me was because they felt the opposite and struggled with the need to have access to her again.

All of a sudden I didn't feel so welcome anymore.

I turned without a word and retreated, climbing the stairs, letting my fingers run over the carvings as I did, feeling my bodywere close on my heels, the press and warmth of Sassy's furred shape against my leg as we emerged in the chamber above.

Time for me to be going. Now that the vampires were awake, it was probably a good idea for me to make myself scarce, though I was sure Liam and Galleytrot would be here for a while yet.

My mind returned to the two kids and Iepa's warning as I emerged into the main house level and walked the hall toward the front door, head down, eyes locked on the carpet, mind far away. I needed to figure out a way to find the pair, but I had no idea how.

Arms slid around me and since Charlotte didn't protest I assumed I knew the owner of those arms. I hugged Sunny back immediately, feeling the warmth of her, thankful she at least had eaten before I ran into her and wondered if hunger for blood made Sebastian's problem with me worse. It was much more likely his troubles stemmed from the fact he was host to the essence for so long.

Uncle Frank took Sunny's place, grinning like a kid, handsome face perfect, two blue eyes shining down at me. I couldn't help but remember how he used to look, the bubbling ruined orb, the melting scar. All thanks to Ameline and Odette Dumont.

And while my Sebastian troubles were thanks to the vampire essence, Uncle Frank's wholeness was too. And if having to hold my distance from the blood clan leader was the price for my uncle's healing, I'd pay it.

There was obviously something on their minds as they pulled free of me, holding hands, both smiling and exchanging glances. Sunny was gorgeous, the most beautiful woman I'd ever seen, but she glowed with a radiance now making her usual appearance pale in comparison, no pun intended.

"Spill it," I said, unable to resist the grin pulling at my lips or the stirring of excitement inside me. Yup, something was definitely up if my witchy senses were tingling.

Sunny reached for my hand with her free one, her vampire power pulling me close and tying me to the both of them. "Oh, Syd," she said with a low, throaty laugh, "we were planning to see you when we heard you were here."

Uncle Frank leaned in and kissed my cheek, hand cupping the back of my neck, the circuit of our physical touch complete. "We wanted you to be the first to know."

"I assume I'm welcome in this conversation? Or shall I wait in the van?" Sassafras's testy tone just made Sunny laugh and she released me to bend and scoop him into her arms, stroking his fur and rubbing his cheeks until he purred.

"Silly boy," she said. "You, my love, are always welcome." She kissed the top of his head.

"Naturally," he said, though there was now laughter in his voice. "Proceed."

"Thank you, oh wise and noble demon cat," Uncle Frank said. Again he and Sunny gazed at each other, but this time with so much love I thought they'd melt. Kind of gooey and all that, but I was just girly enough still it made me sigh and wish.

"We've decided to blend our blood," Sunny finally said. "And we want you to be there with us when we do."

Whoa. Blending blood was like getting married, only way more intense and totally for life. Which, to vampires, was eternity.

"We'll share our blood and be our own family, our own little clan," Uncle Frank said. "Will you stand with us?"

Um, hello? Dumbest question ever asked ever. I lunged for the two of them, hugging Uncle Frank and Sunny as a pair, Sassafras squashed between us until he squeaked a little in protest.

When I pulled back, I wasn't surprised they wavered before me in a mist of moisture, not when my throat was so tight from emotion I could barely swallow.

"I'm so happy for you," I wailed. What was wrong with me? Sunny set Sassy in Uncle Frank's arms and hugged me for real, one of her amazing hugs where she put her whole body into it. Uncle Frank did the same, from behind, making me the center of a nice vampire sandwich. Not that I minded even a little.

"Syd," Sunny whispered, "are you really?" She pulled back a little, concern on her lovely face. "We didn't want to upset you."

I swiped at my tears and latched onto her, my heart churning even as I sobbed into her blonde hair.

"I'm r-r-really, r-r-really h-h-happy for you," I pushed out around my tears. "I s-s-swear."

She laughed as Uncle Frank released me and returned to her side.

"Silly," she said. "Then why are you crying?"

I wished I knew. Except that looking at the pair of them, seeing them perfect and young and knowing now Sunny would always be a part of our family, made facing my immortality almost bearable.

"I won't be alone," I whispered, bending to scoop up Sassafras who licked at my tears with his sandpaper tongue and purred me into quiet. "I guess I've really been worried about it."

Sunny's face fell, hands reaching for me again while Uncle Frank's concern came at me in waves, but I laughed and shook my head and cuddled my demon cat.

"I'm fine, I promise," I said. "No more meltdowns. And I really am very happy for you both. This is so awesome, you have no idea." Okay, huge mood swing. I was beaming at them now, body vibrating with joy.

Much more of this and I was sure they'd have me committed for observation.

"So you'll do it?" Uncle Frank slid one arm around Sunny as she leaned into his side, the perfect couple. "Stand with us, I mean?"

Damn it, tears, freak the hell off. "Yes, of course," I babbled this time, fighting the need to wail all over again. But this time it was from a place of absolute joy. "Thank you so much for asking."

Syd. Seriously. Get a grip.

I left them in their mix of happiness and worry for me, sending a quick message to Liam the keys were in the van, riding the veil with Charlotte and Sass back home. Neither of them said much, Sassy devouring his meal with his usual cat-like grace while my bodywere served me dinner before joining Meira and me at the table. I spent the entire meal waffling between sobbing my heart out and giggling like a little kid every time I thought about Uncle Frank and Sunny, filling my little sister in on their important news while she squealed in excitement, which naturally set me off again. Those moments of joy and pain were punctuated by the faces of the two kids Iepa insisted were important.

I retreated from my family at last, leaving Meira chattering happily away to Charlotte about her little boy friend, suddenly tired, eyes so heavy I could barely keep them open, the day having worn me out completely. I collapsed on my bed, the memory of the kids rising just as I fell asleep.

—war, this time full out war, the battle going badly for us. I am in the middle of it, my shields crumbling, my power lashing outward, but doing little damage against the

sledgehammer destruction of the sorcerer's assault. Panic grips me. The cacophony of sound pushes me down as witches and Sidhe and demons die around me, faces I know, faces I love even as the sky itself seems to explode and rain down on us. Shattered shards of the veil holding us on this plane break apart and fly free.

I'm falling, we're all falling, good and bad alike, the sorcerer's final attack ending this plane in a rush of flaring light—

A breeze ruffled my ponytail, bits tickling my face. I opened my eyes, brushed at them, drew a breath.

No. Way.

I'd found myself in the park before, back in the days when my demon and I didn't exactly get along. She'd taken the opportunity to seize control of my sleeping body while my conscious mind was lost in dreamland, using the chance to run off and use my body all willy-nilly. It scared me then, terrified me, actually. But now?

Now I was just annoyed.

Okay, I sent the thought inside me as I looked down at the wet hems of my pajama pants, bare feet covered in newly cut grass. *Which one of you thought this was a good idea?*

My demon rumbled her anger and denial while I hugged myself, the breeze cold on my bare arms, tank top not designed for a late spring dead of night.

Shaylee protested in her Sidhe way, her earth magic pulsing, the very idea she was responsible an affront. And though my vampire was my most recent personality to join me, I was more inclined to believe she had nothing to do with it, even before she softly sent me her denial with a bemused feeling to her touch.

Grumph. Well then. If not them... ? I looked around, reached out with all of my magic, feeling for the someone or something who'd managed to get me out in the middle of the night. But we were alone, so my fear of outside manipulation faded. Okay, so I wasn't possessed. At least, not any more than usual.

Maybe I'd taken up sleepwalking? Lovely.

As I turned to go back, my power returning home where it belonged, the touch of maji magic spun me around. I barely had time to draw a breath of surprise when the air before me split in half and tried to part.

A portal, a veil portal. But weak and unable to fully form. I reached for it without thinking, my demon surging out to grab the edges and rip them apart, the rubbery membrane of the veil doing her bidding so easily I almost staggered, prepared as I was for a fight. But this parting felt different, shallow, as though we weren't severing the wall between planes at all.

More like someone was riding the veil in this plane and couldn't find the exit.

A crushing weight hit me, driving me backward to land on my butt in the dew-wet grass, pressing all of the air from my lungs as the portal began to collapse. My demon roared her fury, diving for it again, snarling her rage as she sliced open the resealing edges and wrenched it wide.

The pressure increased. My body slid away under the intensity of its push as I reinforced my shielding to hold off whoever wanted this portal closed. I recognized the feel of it, though I was at a loss what to do to stop the sorcerer on the other end of the attack from getting what he wanted.

Namely, to shut the portal down.

I had no idea what would happen if whoever rode the veil became trapped inside, unable to escape, but I wasn't about to let it happen on my watch. Anchoring myself to the ground with every ounce of earth magic Shaylee possessed, I forced myself to my feet and, with the vampire's power tied to my spirit magic, I conjured a battering ram of my own, driving it into the gap and slamming it into the power of my opponent on the other side.

The magic attack collapsed, opposition vanishing in a flash. I staggered, falling to my knees from the loss of pressure, just as my demon's roar of triumph told me she'd managed to hold the portal open.

Two bodies tumbled out, landing on me, sending me back into the grass with an *oof* of released air. I caught a glimpse of trees on the other side of the veil, a scene I recognized from the vision in the maji chamber, just before my demon let it go and the portal snapped shut.

Protect them, Iepa's voice whispered in my mind. *The light and her shadow must survive.*

Now I knew who managed to get me out of bed in the middle of the night.

It was a short trip across the park and to the back yard, but I worried the entire time. Despite being careful, I didn't want to be caught by a normal while levitating the two kids now in my charge. I could have used the veil, but I hesitated in taking them into it so soon after the attack. Besides, the wards on the house and surrounding property wouldn't let me ride the veil all the way to the back door anyway, so I figured a little quasi-illegal magic use was worth the risk.

As luck would have it, not too many people were out an about in the middle of the night in Wilding Springs. None, actually. Only me. Surprise, surprise. Oh, and my very anxious bodywere and demon cat who both came bounding across the grass toward me as I crossed the wards and entered the family property.

Charlotte looked very unhappy. And when the weregirl showed her emotions, it was all kinds of bad. Sassafras stopped in his tracks at the sight of the boy and girl, wrapped in glowing blue magic, floating beside me. I eased them gently to the ground, releasing the air element I'd used to keep them moving, settling them, still unconscious, onto the ground.

"I see you've made some friends." Sassafras's sarcasm was exactly what I needed. I laughed and sagged a little while Charlotte slid close to me, snuffling and tense.

"You know me," I said. "Always dragging stuff home." I sighed as the weregirl touched my arm as though doubting I was there at all.

"I didn't feel you leave," she said, forehead creased, tone vibrating.

"Yeah, well, I didn't choose to." I squeezed her hand. "Blame the maji. I do."

Sassafras sniffed the kids, the girl's glasses catching the light of the motion-sensitive lamp over the back door. "I take it these two are connected to what's going on?"

"Yes," I said, crouching next to them, remembering the moment of shock I'd felt when I pushed their limp bodies off me and realized who I'd rescued through the veil. "These are the two I saw in the maji chamber."

"The light and the shadow," he said. "Interesting. She is familiar. Her power, at least."

I agreed, letting my magic slide over her. "She's maji," I said.

"But he feels empty." His silver tail twitched. "Syd..."

I shrugged and sighed. "Let's just get them inside, okay? The back yard probably isn't the best place to hold this conversation."

Sass grunted something under his breath, but when I tapped my power to lift them again, his joined me. Together, Charlotte looking around like we were about to be attacked, her energy that of a wary guard dog, we floated the passed-out pair to the door and into the house.

Not even thinking, I headed up to my room, settling the two of them side-by-side on my rumpled covers, watching as Sass jumped up beside them and sniffed them over again.

"Mind telling me what happened?" His amber eyes met mine. "And where you went?"

Charlotte's gaze bored deathly holes through me as she waited for the answer.

I rolled my eyes. "Sure. Like I had a say in the matter." I filled him in, heard him grunt again though he kept silent as I relayed the battle over the two of them.

"Syd?" Meira poked her head in my door, rubbing sleepily at her eyes, those same eyes widening as she realized we weren't alone. "Who are they?"

Again with the story. I was getting good at telling it,

though to be fair Meira missed the entire thing earlier. My sister perched on the end of the bed while she listened, eyes locked on the boy. When I finally wrapped it up, I noticed the sky wasn't quite as dark as it had been.

Morning already? I shoved down a yawn though it still made my eyes water. I really needed to find a way to catch naps during these times of crisis.

The girl groaned, a soft, deep sound, louder than it should have been in the suddenly quiet room. Sassafras's tail twitched as he watched her wake, one of her sneakered feet bobbing over the edge of the bed. Her long, dark hair tangled around her neck and face, glasses slightly askew. She was pretty, very pretty, skin darker than the boy beside her, hair almost black, rims of her glasses a match. The dark denim jacket she wore hung from her thin frame, tank top under it showing her ribs. He wasn't much better. The pair of them were skinny and almost wild looking, his hair overgrown, a smudge of dirt on his cheek and a tear in the knee of his jeans. But they both had an innocence about them I trusted immediately, the feel of them telling me I'd done the right thing listening to Iepa.

Speaking of the maji, if she was so worried, where the hell was she? A little help would have been nice.

Dark brown eyes bordering on black flashed open

behind smudged glass. The girl sat up abruptly, grabbing for the boy, pulling him to her as she shoved herself backward into the wall, scrunching my comforter and sheets under her dirty sneakers as she tried to escape.

"Whoa," I held out both hands, Meira standing and backing away as Sassafras started to purr, the soothing sound augmented with his magic. "It's okay. You're safe."

Her eyes flickered from me to the cat at the end of the bed, to Charlotte and over Meira before returning to me again.

"I'm just supposed to believe you, is that it?" Her voice snapped like a whip, aggression pouring off her as she slid sideways, the boy firmly in her grasp, finding her feet only to crumple under his weight, face paling.

"Fair enough," I said, a little more sharply than I intended. I'd just saved her miserable hide and that of her companion. What more did she want? Still.

Deep breaths, Syd. Try tact.

Because, yeah, tact was my strong suit.

"Who are you and why did you kidnap us?" She jerked on the boy, managing to make it to her feet though her attempt to pull him upright and support him despite his unconscious state ended with her falling sideways onto the bed again.

Um, what? "Excuse me," I snapped back, "but you were

about to be trapped inside the veil by someone and I just happened to save your sorry ass. So a little gratitude and less attitude, if you don't mind."

No. I did not just sound like my mother. Did *not*.

The girl's scowl told me my tone was dead on bossy parent. "Who asked you?"

Okay then. Throwing her to the wolves felt like the ideal thing to me. Perfect.

A wall of maji magic flashed into being, cutting off her and the boy beside her from the rest of us. It shimmered and eddied like the veil, and when I touched it with my magic it felt like the same rubbery substance.

The family magic oozed and eddied around them, rising through the floor in reaction to my anger and the presence of foreign magic. I soothed it, though it didn't seem aggressive, instead curious, winding its way around the shield as if tasting it.

"Trill." The boy was awake at last, voice tired and weak. But when he looked up at me, those incredibly blue eyes met mine and I knew the maji was right.

I had to help them, no matter what.

"Owen." She forgot me, about all of us it seemed, turning to the boy and touching his face, rubbing at the dirty spot on his cheek. "Are you okay?"

He smiled, swiped at her hand. "I'm fine." Owen sat up, a grin on his face as he met my eyes again. "Thanks for the ride, by the way."

"You're welcome." I glared at the girl, Trill he'd called her, while Owen groaned and rubbed his head.

"I was sure we were goners." He poked Trill. "Told you to trust whoever was on the other end."

Trill glared at me, cleaning her glasses on the hem of her tank top as Owen swung his feet over the edge of the bed and stood. A moment of wobbling and he seemed okay.

"I was right, wasn't I?" He held out one hand to me and, despite her continuing glare, I took it. "You're witches."

"More than witches," Sassafras said at his most dry. Trill jumped while Owen turned and stared before laughing.

"Wicked," he said, one of his blue eyes winking at me.

"Demons." Trill let out a deep breath. "And a werewolf."

Owen nodded to Meira and then to Charlotte before focusing on me again. Funny, he was the younger, but seemed to be their leader. "I'm Owen, in case you hadn't figured that out." His smile was a sunny day, a refreshing walk in a warm rain. I adored him immediately. "And that is my sister, Trillia."

"Trill," she grumbled.

Owen flashed his very white teeth. "Trill. Zornov."

Sassy hissed softly at the name, but didn't comment and Owen must have missed it because he went on. "It seems we're in your debt."

He had a way of speaking that seemed beyond his normal age, maybe eleven or twelve.

"I didn't have much of a choice in the matter," I said. "You have a powerful guardian angel watching over the two of you."

They both looked confused. "What are you talking about?" Trill seemed nervous again, standing to join her brother, pulling him against her, one arm in a protective hold around his shoulders.

I waved it off. "That can wait," I said. "But I'm assuming I'm right to say you are the light," I pointed at Trill whose eyes flared wide, "and you are the shadow?" Owen's frown was more sad than angry.

"Yes," he said, before his sister could shush him. "Where did you hear about us?"

"Guardian angel, remember?" I looked back and forth between them. "Mind telling me what your cryptic titles mean?"

Trill stiffened, but Owen shrugged.

"Simple," he said. "My sister is maji. That's why she's the light. Creation magic, you get me?"

I nodded, already knowing what was coming. The empty feeling of him, I knew it, had felt it before.

"And you?" Sassafras had no compunction speaking up.

"And I am a sorcerer," Owen said with so much sadness I wanted to hug him. "And I'm going to be her downfall."

10

Even though I felt bad for the boy, a twinge of nerves put my back up. After all, according to Iepa, weren't we going to war with sorcerers? How smart was it to have one in my house?

And yet, there was no way the sweet-faced kid standing in front of me, his crushed expression telling me how much he worried about his own abilities, could possibly be a threat. At least, not on purpose.

I'd take it.

His sister, on the other hand, had this way with my last nerve that was about to get her a serious smackdown. She grabbed her brother and shoved past me, heading for the door, a harsh, determined look on her face. I naturally reached for her to pull her back. No way was she storming out, not after I'd saved their butts from whoever was trying to hurt them.

My fingers slipped over the denim of her jacket, caught her hand. The moment our skin touched, power rippled between us. Trill came to an immediate halt, turning to face me, her eyes at my height, slim body quivering.

"Why haven't you finished it?" She held onto my fingers, a stab of anger passing between us through the connection. "You're so close to balance."

I jerked my hand free of hers and glared at her. "Maybe if I knew what you were talking about, I could answer you."

Owen looked up at his sister. "What's wrong?"

Trill held her hand against her body, as if touching me had hurt her in some way. "Never mind," she snapped. "If you're too stupid to figure out what you are, I'm not going to fill you in."

Violence wasn't in my nature. Much. But if this chick didn't stop being such a bitch, she'd be out on her behind and I wouldn't think twice about it.

Sigh.

I didn't get to wring her neck. Just as I was considering my coven leader options, the door slammed wide and Gram strode in, a huge smile plastered on her face, thin, lined hands rubbing together like finding two strange kids in the house was par for the course.

"Who wants pancakes?" Her faded blue eyes sparkled as she reached out and rumpled Owen's hair. He shook his head to resettle his do, but he was smiling so I liked him even more. Trill just scowled at the crazy old lady, one arm going around her brother, pulling him back and away.

"Gram." Relief flooded through me, the tension I'd been carrying since this fiasco began releasing in a rush. I was careful to stay calm on the outside, not wanting to give the nasty girl anything to criticize, but happily reached for my grandmother and let her feel how much I needed her.

Gram's gaze flickered to me, smile disappearing. "We have a lot to talk about," she said, voice low and vibrating with something making my anxiety return. Where had she been and now what? But when she finished, she grinned again and poked a finger into Owen's tummy. "I put chocolate chips in my flapjacks," she sing-songed in a little girl voice before giggling and covering her mouth with one hand. "Yummers."

I had to laugh. Had to. "This is Ethpeal," I said, "and I'm Syd. That's Meira," she bobbed her head, smiling shyly at Owen, "Sassafras," the silver Persian flicked his tail when I said his name, "and the weregirl is Charlotte." No response. Yeah, hardly a shocker. "Now, if we could all just get along for five minutes, I'm starving."

Trill opened her mouth, protest all over her face, but I held up one hand, the very idea of arguing with her making me tired. "Gram might be a little light in the load," I said, "but she makes amazing pancakes."

The maji girl caved, though I could hear her softly grumbling to her brother as they preceded us out the door. I sent Meira after them, her with a nod of understanding to keep the two occupied while I grabbed Gram's arm and held her back.

"Mind sharing where you've been?" I pulled her into a hug, felt her arms squeeze me back.

"After breakfast." She tweaked my nose with two fingers, a little smile on her lips though her eyes seemed troubled. "You had to bring them here, didn't you?"

"You're assuming I had a choice."

She moved off, dancing a little dance in her familiar fuzzy socks, humming to herself as she left the room. Sassafras leaped down from the bed and followed her, his tail high and quivering behind him. That left only Charlotte and me and I knew exactly what she was going to say before she said it. Partly because she waited to say anything until we were alone.

"You left without me." Ah, the guilt trip of the wereguard unable to protect her charge. I'd grown accustomed to Charlotte's poking me with shame ever since her meltdown when I was trapped on Demonicon.

"I wasn't given a choice." I crossed my arms over my chest. "Besides, I thought you watched over me so things like this wouldn't happen?"

A slow flush of red colored her cheeks. "Forgive me," she choked, but not in her own guilt. Oh boy, was she pissed at me.

I sighed and hugged her, waiting until her rigid body softened. "The next time a maji takes over, you'll be the first to know."

Charlotte's lips finally quirked, her version of a giggle. "I suppose it will have to do."

I was surrounded by smartasses.

The kitchen was a bit of a bustle when I finally reached it, kids and Gram and Sass hustling to set the table, make pancakes, pour milk and juice.

Within a few minutes, we were all seated and eating. Even Trill seeming to appreciate the deliciousness of Gram's pancakes. Owen laughed over the magic the old lady used to continue to make breakfast, spatula wavering in the air over the hot frying pan while the glass bowl full of batter rattled impatiently for its turn to pour more goodness. Gram seemed to ignore what she'd set loose while she piled her own plate with butter and syrup, eating large chunks while drips of stickiness trickled down her chin.

I sat back after my first batch was devoured and took a sip of milk. "Can I ask how it is the two of you ended up in the territory of the Hayle coven?"

Trill kept her head down, now frowning at the remains of her food, stirring the pools of syrup with her fork while Owen answered.

"Nona sent us," he said, like that meant everything. "We've been on the run for so long, but we've always managed to stay ahead of the Brotherhood." Sassafras's snarl was louder than his hiss had been at the name Zornov. I really had to talk to him, it seemed. "But somehow they knew where we were last night, found a way to track us." He turned sadly to his sister, fork clattering to his plate. "It's my fault, Trill. I'm sorry."

"You don't know that," she snapped back. "Stop apologizing. They could just as easily have found a way to track me."

Owen nodded, glum. "Nona felt someone watching, said she'd been sensing another for a while. She said whoever it was felt different, not a threat. When she cast her cards, they told her the person she was feeling could be trusted."

Confused. "Nona?" I hated to pause the story, but without further information I'd have to have him repeat it.

"Our grandmother," Trill said, for the first time with a soft tone. And worry.

"She's maji too?" The girl's nod, joined with Owen's agreement, answered that question. "What's this casting cards?"

Gram snorted before either of them could say anything. "Tarot," she said, as though it were some insult. "Still, seems they did the job."

Witches didn't use Tarot, finding them unreliable at best. Our magic tended to influence them one way or the other, depending on how we were feeling. But since maji were creationists, I guessed it was possible they would work better in their hands.

"It was a close call last night," Owen said, hands now clenched on the table in front of him as he stared sightlessly into his empty plate. "We'd just crossed over into Tennessee when we were cornered. Nona made us stay with the RV while she left us to lay a false trail."

"We should never have let her go alone." Trill had the biggest chip on her shoulder I'd ever felt, bigger even than the one I'd carried around for years. I let my magic touch her, felt her mix of guilt, shame, blame and terror, all smothered in so much rage it was a wonder she could function.

"We heard her tell us to run." Trill looked up at last, as though she knew I was feeling her out, met my eyes, gaze cold, but angry. "So we did."

"From the Brotherhood." I glanced at Sassafras who nodded to me.

"Sorcerer sect," he said. "I had no idea they were still around."

Definitely needed to talk. "How did you manage the portal?"

"Nona," Owen said. "She tried, but the sorcerers blocked her, using up the air around us. That's how they—we—work." He shuddered softly before going on. "Maji create but sorcerers, we destroy for gain."

"So your Nona reached for me." I set my milk aside, thinking about Iepa. "She was right about one thing—I'm the perfect person to help. With my demon power, I'm able to open the veil and do it all the time."

Trill was staring at me like I was a little simple. "It's not your demon power the gives you that ability."

Gram cleared her throat and sat forward while my demon rumbled her confusion to match mine. "Why are the sorcerers chasing you, children?" All serious again, no hint of the fruity nutcake she tended toward.

How much of it was an act?

"I won't let them take my brother." Trill's angry response didn't really answer the question, but did at the same time.

"Why do they want Owen?" I hated secrets, half-truths, bits of information. So not helpful.

Owen shook his head, reached out and took his sister's hand. "It's not just me," he said. "Trill's as much at risk because of me as I am because of her." He let her go, sitting back again, tone matter-of-fact if tinged with regret. "They want me for their army," he said, "and they want Trill so they can strip her maji power and kill her."

Breakfast wrapped up pretty quickly after that, Meira and Owen volunteering to clean while Gram's magic interjected from time to time to speed the process. Trill and I left them to it, retiring to the back yard.

"You might not be able to reach your grandmother through the family wards," I told her as the cool grass crumpled under my bare feet, the touch of the Sidhe Wild Hunt, sleeping far below the earth whispering to me in its slumber. "But then again, I have no idea what maji power is capable of, so it's worth a try here before you expose yourself."

Trill's lips twisted, a hint of arrogance on her face. "All that power," she said, "and you still have no clue."

My fists clenched at my sides, good will fading rapidly. "Listen," I said, getting all up in her personal space, letting my demon out to snarl. Trill didn't back down. "I'm here to help, remember? You're freaking welcome."

Trill's nostrils flared, but she nodded. "You're right," she said. "I'm sorry. It's just... you really have no idea?" When she sighed, the loss of air seemed to crush her a little, tight shoulders sagging, face going from angry to sad. "There are so few of us."

"I have no idea what you're talking about," I said, not even trying to hide my confusion.

She nodded. "Let me try to reach Nona and then we'll talk."

I felt her power stir, drawn to the warmth of it, the sizzle and pop as it woke, the growing heat as she reached outward. It felt familiar, like Iepa's magic, creation energy rippling easily through the wards in search of Trill's grandmother.

She shook her head after a moment, tears in her eyes. "I can't reach that far," she whispered. "I'm just not strong enough yet."

I took her hand immediately, opened up to her. "Are any of my magicks useful?"

She looked so shocked at the offer, as my power spread wide like a welcoming flower, I had to laugh.

"I realize you may never have been able to trust anyone," I said, respect and sadness for her shoving aside my irritation at her attitude, "but you can trust me. And my family. Now, will any of my many personalities be able to help you or am I hanging it all out there for nothing?"

She tried. I felt her fishing around, winced a time or two as she attempted to shove past my vampire core and reach deeper still, but without success. With a final grunt of frustration, she pulled her hand free as my magic coiled back around me.

"It's no use," she said. "You've buried it."

Okay, what the freak? "Buried what?"

Trill's brown eyes were black with frustration. "Your maji gift, Sydlynn."

"Syd," I said absently while my brain churned. Oh boy.

Another one?

"You're saying I have maji blood?" Um, hello? Remember the whole family tree in the cavern thing? Knock, knock, Miss Brilliance. That train left ages ago.

Trill just shrugged. "Somewhere inside you," she said. "But your powers are so muddy, it's impossible to find it and isolate it enough to use it."

Muddy? My demon snarled while Shaylee sniffed in disdain. But the vampire essence twitched, sighed. Was she right? Did the combining of my magicks make things harder for me?

"No," I said, knowing she was absolutely wrong. "Integration has saved me more times than I can count.

I refuse to believe I'm doing it wrong, not when trying to keep the powers separate has only made me vulnerable."

"That's not what I meant," Trill said, perhaps more sharply than she intended because she paused before she went on. "Your powers are separate, whether you like it or not. I'm sure there are times you reach near perfection with them, when they combine and meld. But until you are able to do so on a permanent basis, your control of each will be limited."

Interesting. "And you know all this how?" Like she'd encountered someone like me before or could possibly know more than I did?

Snort.

"Nona," she said. "And the teachings of the maji. You're not unique in history, Sydlynn Hayle, but you are unique in this time and place."

Cryptic. "If you have it all figured out," I said, "tell me how to fix it."

Trill stuffed her hands in the back pockets of her jeans. "I don't know how." Ah, finally admitting while maybe she knew the concepts, the actual follow-through needed work.

So helpful.

"None of this matters," she said, turning away from me, heading for the back door. "Thank you for catching us," it seemed to hurt her to say thank you, "but we can't stay."

I grabbed her arm, pulled her back, purposely touching her skin. Our power connected for a moment. "You can't just leave," I said. "Your Nona sent you to me for a reason. And that guardian angel I mentioned? Yeah, I think she'd be a little miffed with me if I just let you go."

"What are you talking about?" Trill tried to pull free, but I held on.

"First things first," I said. "We need to hide you and Owen so the sorcerers can't find you. If they have some way of tracking you neither of you is aware of, smothering that ability is our first priority." I wanted to kick myself. They'd been here in Wilding Springs for what, four hours or so? Yes, the family wards would offer some protection, but without knowing if the sorcerers were, in fact, able to track the brother and sister, I could very well have left the door wide open for the Brotherhood to find my coven.

Still holding onto Trill, I let my power out, but this time weaving a net of protection around her and, through her, Owen. Sidhe, witch, demon and vampire magic swirled together, each as individual as a snowflake, with their own taste, scent, feeling. By the time I finished and let Trill's hand drop, tying off the net of energy, she stared at me wide-eyed like I'd done something she thought impossible.

I reached for her, now that she was contained, let my power ease around her. While there was still the barest hint of her magic bleeding through, I was fairly confident if she didn't try to use her power the barrier I'd built should keep her muffled enough until I found a more permanent solution.

"Well done," she said, totally grudgingly, but at least she said it. Not that I needed her approval, but if I was going to help protect her and Owen we had to at least try to get along.

"It will do for now," I said. "I think. I have no idea if sorcerers can see right through this or not. We need a better plan, somewhere they can't penetrate, no matter what." Shaylee prodded me, the whispering of the Wild Hunt a little louder as she offered the solution.

Brilliant. Sometimes having multiple personalities was a good thing.

"Come on," I said, marching to the back door and into the house. "I think I know what to do."

As we entered the kitchen, I saw Owen staring at his own hands, eyes wide. He met my gaze, his full of wonder.

"What did you do to me?" He flexed, his skin seeming

to shine as though the surface were coated in a soft layer of frost.

"Shielded you," I said, "at least for now. But I have a much better idea."

Gram's eyes narrowed as she chewed her thumb nail. "The cavern."

"Exactly." I motioned for Owen to rise and join us. "Since you don't know if the sorcerers can track you, we'll put you somewhere they'll never find you, even if they can feel you're around."

"Should work," Gram said while Trill scowled.

"Where?"

My turn to have a secret. "You'll see," I said. "Let's go."

Girl. Gram's mind touched mine. *We need to talk.*

Where have you been? Damn, I didn't mean to wail at her like a hurt child.

Hunting. She paused. *I've been feeling someone sniffing around Wilding Springs for some time now. Ever since the trial, when we opened the maji chamber.*

My stomach clenched as I fixed my eyes on her while the others gathered at the door.

Sorcerers?

It's been worse since yesterday.

When we found the underchamber.

Gram didn't comment, didn't have to. We were closely enough linked I knew she was already aware of what we'd found at the mansion.

It has to be the Brotherhood, she sent. *Tracking maji magic. So it's the girl you need to shield.*

Of course. Though I doubted telling Owen would make him feel better.

Just be careful, Gram sent as she shooed me out the door, Charlotte close beside me, Sassy scampering out between my legs to follow Trill and Owen into the driveway. *I'm going to have another look around.*

And if I tell you to be careful? I paused long enough to hug her, kiss her powder-soft cheek.

I'm always careful, she cackled suddenly in my mind. *They can just look the hell out.*

I opened the veil, taking the others with me, still worried no matter Gram's assertions.

And yet, I wouldn't want to piss her off.

I hadn't bothered to warn the two siblings about our mode of transportation, considering how they'd arrived in my life to begin with, though from the glaring anger on Trill's face when she stumbled forward out of the darkness I probably should have.

Yeah, not.

Shielding still firmly wrapped around the pair, I led our small group into the library and down the back stairs, to the entry to Liam's safe haven. Which I was counting on for Trill and Owen, too.

He was waiting for me when I crossed the green barrier, arms wide as he hugged me, kissing the top of my head. I absorbed his warmth, the scent of him so familiar and wonderful, all fresh turned earth and fabric softener mixed with his own subtle taste. His smile didn't waver as he released me to hug Meira, stroke Sassafras's fur and nod to Charlotte before turning his attention to the newcomers.

A quick introduction and I had him up to speed.

"Fascinating." He stared at Trill like he wanted to dissect her, or at least ask her a million questions. I found his attention irritating for some reason, but ignored it and plowed ahead.

"So the idea is, if the Brotherhood can track Trill, the cavern's out-of-plane shift might keep them from finding her." I'd had a hard enough time myself when Shaylee first warned me about the Gate, back before I'd met Liam or knew he was the Keeper. I'd discovered not only did the cavern have its own Sidhe protections, there was the subtlest of shifts in its plane location, not quite on our plane, but not quite anywhere else either, as though it hovered between my home and the Sidhe realm behind the massive portal.

"Yes, that makes total sense," Liam said. "Unless sorcery can penetrate the plane system like demon or Sidhe magic?" He addressed Owen and Trill rather than me. It felt weird to share his attention and I found myself unhappy with the little jealousy burning in my chest.

Like I had the answers he needed. Grow the hell up, Syd.

"That is one power sorcerers don't have," Trill said. "Sorcery is only able to function through the destruction of objects or the theft of power. Creation, pure creation, is beyond its ability." Was she smiling? Acting coy? No, my imagination. But she did seem softer around my tall, handsome friend. Mind you, the sweetness of his nature radiated out of him, a sure-fire way to put anyone at ease. Liam just had that effect on people. Still.

Grrr.

"What do we know of this Brotherhood?" Galleytrot's deep voice echoed softly in the hall of the cavern.

"Excellent question." Liam rubbed his hands together with a huge grin, like this wasn't life and death or anything, but a mystery he couldn't wait to unravel. "And I know exactly where to look for answers."

"So do I," I said, fixing my eyes on Sassafras while Liam turned toward the archive. The silver Persian ignored me, scampering after the Keeper, while Owen looked around in awe, one hand resting on the shoulder of the big black hound.

"Cool digs," he said.

"Thank you," Galleytrot said.

I let them go ahead, eyes locked on Trill who, instead of joining her brother and my sister with Liam, instead turned and walked ahead, into the Gate room. I grit my teeth together at her presumption. This was Liam's home after all. How dare she just wander around like she owned the place?

Okay, big fat reality check. I really needed to get a grip on my animosity. It wasn't like the Gate was under some kind of lock and key or anything. It stood there, a massive doorway of carved wood and iron bracers, humming softly with Sidhe magic. I held back as Trill examined it, felt Liam join me, the touch of his hand on the back of my neck making me shiver.

"It's a Gate," he said, speaking to Trill who turned and nodded.

"I know," she said. "Nona spoke of such portals between planes. How the Sidhe chose to retreat from this place and how the maji created their plane for them."

Whoa. What?

"The maji made the Sidhe plane?" How cool was that? So maybe their creation myth stuff wasn't all a crock of overcooked crap.

Liam left me to stand with Trill. "I've been reading up on your kind," he said. "I have so many questions about the creators."

Yikes. Jealous much? I had to hug myself to keep from jumping between them as Trill turned and smiled up at him, just a little.

"What would you like to know?"

I should have left. Walked away. I had absolutely no

reason to be jealous. Or at least no right. And yet, I couldn't bring myself to just leave them alone. So I stood on the outside, heart in knots as Liam and Trill spoke.

"You're correct," she said. "About the planes. And the Gates. My people," she paused a moment, "the original creators from who I'm descended, they made all of this." Her hands made sweeping gestures before her. "Though the art of it is lost to us. And maybe the power." She shook her head, backing away a step. "Our bloodlines are so weak now, too many generations gone."

"I'm sure that isn't true," Liam said. "And if so, maybe if you worked in a group, together—"

Trill shut down like he'd slapped her, face flat and cold. "I need to find my brother now."

I stopped her, blocking her path. "There's something you should know," I said, though part of me wanted to keep things from her, just to punish her. Seriously? No backsliding.

"Then tell me," she shot back, "or get out of my way."

Snap. I would have smacked her, I'm sure of it, if Liam hadn't appeared at my side and slid his arm around my shoulders.

"There's a maji stronghold not far from here," he said, saving me from snapping her damned head right off and spitting it out. "In a mansion controlled by vampires. Friendly vampires." He punctuated his caveat with a smile. "Syd's family, no less." His arm hugged me, Sidhe power stroking my magic in slow, soothing pets.

Yeah, it worked. Liam might have been gentle and mild and all that soppy mess, but he knew how to manipulate me.

Trill's closed expression opened a little. "What kind of stronghold?"

"A history," he said, excitement returning to his voice. "Of the maji, of everything."

Trill nodded slowly, sliding her glasses back as her black hair rippled around her shoulders. "I've heard of such places," she said. "Nona says there are buried chambers all over the world with family records, bloodlines tracked for centuries."

"Exactly!" Liam let me go, his happy energy enough to finish off the last of my irritation.

"I can take you to see it," I said. "If you want."

Again she closed off, but not completely. A crack of life still showed through her mask. "Just tell me where it is," she said. "Owen and I can go there ourselves."

What was her problem, really? Was this some kind of character flaw or did she get a kick out of pissing me off? She had no idea what a pissed-off Syd was like. And she didn't want to find out.

Liam's power reached for me for the second time, but this time I batted it away, even more annoyed.

"You're not going anywhere," I snapped. "Forget I even asked."

I turned away from her, needing to get out of her space, far enough so I could cool down before I did something I'd regret later. Maybe regret. Maybe not.

I was leaning very heavily toward not.

"You can't trap us here." Trill grabbed me, pulled me back, rage showing in her eyes, in the tension of her hand and the coiling of her magic. The shields I'd built around her flexed as she pushed against them, but they held.

"I'm not," I snarled back. "In case you forgot, I saved your life. And I'm still trying to. I'm trying to keep you safe. You know what? Just forget it." I jerked free of her grip. "Why don't you and Owen just wander off then and see how far you get before the Brotherhood finds you?"

She stared at me in impotent rage, her whole body trembling, hands fisted at her sides. She wanted to strike out at me—I could see it in her, feel the aggressive energy pouring out toward me.

"Better be sure," I said, ever so softly, leaning in. "You just better."

Liam's gentle magic slid between us, cutting the cord of

our mutual anger. Trill stepped back, turning away, though her hands didn't relax. I glared up at Liam who shook his head with sadness in his eyes.

"Please, Trill," he said, turning to her. "You're maji. We need to protect you. If what Syd's been told is coming is true, you're very precious to us."

Holy. Enough with the freaking jealousy already. I almost kicked him and made him look away from her with those begging hazel eyes, big hands held out to her. No way did he pick her side.

Syd. Breathe. Liam was right. If Iepa was correct, and I had no reason to doubt her, we did need Trill. And Owen.

On the other hand, here I was blindly trusting an entity who invaded my dreams and dragged me through a mental battle that hadn't even happened yet only to force me to rescue two kids I'd been informed were important.

I hated being manipulated, especially when the manipulator just assumed I'd fall in line.

Which I had.

Damn it.

I needed more information, to talk to Iepa again and this time she'd better be more forthcoming with me than sharing some vague warning about a war and showing me things I couldn't trust.

"I'm going to the mansion." I turned from Liam and Trill, not caring if either protested or not, though I did pause to glare at the maji girl. "If you want to leave, fine. But don't put your brother at risk because you're a stubborn idiot."

I left her to chew that over while the accusation rang in my own head.

13

I was already in the hall, heading for the stairs, when Liam burst through the barrier and caught my arm, turning me to face him. He didn't speak, just wrapped his arms around me, holding me with his whole body.

One thing about Liam? He gave the most amazing hugs ever.

He let me go then, with a farewell wave and a smile just for me. And while part of me was embarrassed and ashamed I needed such confirmation of his feelings, the truth was his love did wonders for my mood.

And what right did I have, really, to be jealous? Considering my own personal predicament.

Sigh.

Though I intended to ride the veil to the mansion, when I stepped out into the open air I made a different choice. I had a lot to think about and the drive would give me time alone to work things out. Mind you, with Charlotte attached to my hip, it wasn't like I'd be going alone. But

I was used to her by now, no longer feeling like I had to entertain her or anything. Liam dropped the van off at the house the day before, so I headed home, a heartbeat in the veil before I again touched down in my driveway, reaching for the kitchen door.

I felt someone watching me.

I spun, hair on the back of my neck rippling as goosebumps leaped into action all over my body. Charlotte snarled, low and deep, her body between mine and the end of the driveway. I pushed her gently aside, entire body tensed as I watched a black town car, the windows tinted too dark to see inside, cruise past my house.

My demon chuffed, sniffing around, but there was no sense of power, of magic of any kind about the vehicle. Still, a weight of dread pressed against me, shoving me backward toward the house and the safety of its walls.

I refused to retreat, Charlotte vibrating beside me, watching with a blank expression as the back window hissed down, a man's face visible for a moment on the other side as the car oozed past my driveway. He nodded once to me before the powered window closed again and the driver hit the gas. I walked down to the street, catching the ominous black car turning the corner at the end of the road and disappearing behind a neighbor's house.

No power. But emptiness. Unnatural emptiness. Like the way Demetrius Strong felt, the leader of the Chosen of the Light, the one sorcerer I'd had dealings with. So. I'd just met the Brotherhood.

Despite their creepy act, I was unimpressed.

"Feels like trouble." I jumped a little as Gram spoke, turning to find her standing next to me, a holey pink sweater wrapped tightly around her as she glared toward where the car vanished. She grinned at me suddenly, giggled. "I like trouble."

"Yeah," I said, "I've noticed." I met Charlotte's eyes. She looked anxious, confused.

"Nothing good will come of this," she said.

Great. Doom and gloom from my bodywere. Just what I needed.

Gram grasped her hand, pulling her close. "You have the sight?"

Foresight. Right. Sunny possessed the talent, though the beautiful vampire had only shared it with me once, when I was in danger. Yeah, being in danger for me was a regular occurrence, so it wasn't so much of a shocker. But Charlotte?

"Some," the weregirl said. "Enough." Her eyes flickered to me. "Barely enough."

Weird. So the sight wasn't just a vampire thing. How ironic, considering vampires and weres usually hated each other intensely, that they shared such a gift.

Or curse, depending on how it was used. Right now I had the sneaking feeling Charlotte had more control over hers than Sunny and was using it to keep track of me.

Not like I could stop her or anything.

"No matter." Gram let Charlotte go. "It seems your plan is working, though of course they know the Zornov children are here."

I felt myself relax a little, hoping she was right. If the Brotherhood could pinpoint the pair, they'd be at the library by now, not scoping out my house.

So, too close for comfort, but far enough away maybe things could work out after all.

One way to deal? I could make the Brotherhood leave.

Gram must have known where my thoughts were going because she jabbed me in the side with one if her sharp fingers. I clutched at the offended part of my person, scowling at her, but she just scowled right back.

"Don't be a fool," she said. "What will you do if you catch up with them?"

I felt my anger rise to her challenge. "Kick their sorcerer asses out of my territory." How dared they invade a coven town?

Mad was good. Really good. Raised all kinds of interesting thoughts and possibilities.

"Just when I think you're going to turn out all right," Gram said, "you revert into an idiot."

Ouch. "What do you propose we do?" If that car showed up again, I wasn't taking any chances. Engines used gas and demons used fire.

Easy math.

Brotherhood go boom.

Stupid Gram link. She grinned at me, sudden ferocity making me nervous. "You leave them to me," she said. "I'll track them, make sure they get themselves lost a time or two. But I won't act against them until I have all of my questions answered."

"Such as?" She turned and walked up the drive, leaving me to trail after her, Charlotte still humming with tension behind me as we entered the kitchen, Gram's power pulling the door shut behind me.

"Never you mind." She spun on me, one socked foot tapping the floor. "We have something else to talk about, miss."

Like I needed more problems. "One disaster at a time, yeah, Gram?"

She shrugged. "I'm getting tired of pulling your slacker weight," she said. "It's time you chose a second."

What, now? "But—"

Gram came to me, pinched my cheeks, kissed the end of my nose. "It's time, girl," she said. "I want a little freedom, you see?" Her hands dropped, squeezed my shoulders. "And you need to know what it's like to stand on your own."

I hugged her, heart constricting, fear taking me hostage. "You're not going anywhere, are you?" She couldn't leave me. Not ever.

Gram chuckled and shook me just a little. "Where would I drag this old carcass even if I wanted to?" She danced a little jig in the sunlight pouring into the kitchen, turning in a circle before coming to a halt, her eyes rimmed with extra moisture. "Just give an old lady a break and pick a damned second."

14

While I had intended to sort through my feelings about Trill and Liam and this whole mess, I instead spent the drive, silent Charlotte beside me, running through the entire family roster in my head and discarding each and every one of them in turn.

The twins? No freaking way. Not only were Estelle and Esther creepy, though I now adored the two old ladies, they were the same age as Gram. Yes, there were older witches I could choose, but none of them really seemed to fit the bill. And the younger ones, well... they were all parents with small children. I had absolutely nothing in common with them and, aside from being family, I'd never made a real connection, not enough to call on one of them to be my second.

It was a huge responsibility, taking on the job. I thought about Mom and Erica, how my mother chose her best friend so many years ago, when she herself was a new mother and sudden coven leader, Gram crippled by the Purities. Mom picked her not only because she adored her, but because she knew Erica served best as second, as a support system, someone who would never challenge her for leadership, too weak to lead herself, but as faithful as her own heart.

I briefly touched on Meira, but mentally shook my head. My sister was too young. And besides, after the conversations we'd had about her wanting more than to live in my shadow, as sad as that made me, there was no way I'd saddle her with the position.

She'd never forgive me.

Which meant I was out of luck. And while I knew Gram was right and I needed a second, my heart protested. She and I were a great team and, since she was never allowed to leave me, why should things change? Except, she'd given up her life, her own dreams and plans, to rule a coven she never wanted to lead, only to lose herself for seventeen years in madness so that same family would be safe.

She deserved a happy retirement.

I was in the mansion driveway, pulling up to the front of the house just as I realized the truth. There wasn't one witch in the Hayle coven I wanted as my second.

Which meant I had to look outside the coven.

It certainly opened up a great number of possibilities. I mused over the witches I'd met as I climbed the stairs to the front door, Charlotte at my side, my mind going right to my roommate and new bestie, Sashenka Hensley. Who I immediately struck from the list. Not because I didn't want her or trust her. In fact, the more I allowed my mind to linger on the options, the more I realized she'd be a perfect fit.

But she was already a second, to her sister, Tallah. They at least didn't have the same issues as Meira and me, happy to support each other.

Jeeze, Syd. So not fair.

Meira had the right to her own life, just like Gram did.

Stewart let me in with a smile and a murmured, "Coven leader," before leaving me to my task. Which, it turned out, evolved into several hours of swearing, kicking the stone pedestal deep underground while I used my magic to try to raise Iepa and generally growing more frustrated the longer I stayed.

Charlotte had the good sense not to comment as I stomped my way back up to the main chamber, grumbling and complaining to myself about the contrary nature of a maji who only showed up when it was convenient for *her*, and wasn't *she* all kinds of special that she could make *planes* and *create* crap while I had to wait around for her goddeship to freaking pay attention.

Why, yes, I was the Queen of Irritableville.

I should have taken Liam with me. At least he would have been able to read to me. Though even he might have grown annoyed with my behavior by the end of it, so it was best he'd just stayed where he was.

That made me think about Trill and the way she softened around him. My temper jacked up about fifty notches. Which meant by the time I reached the main floor, I was in the kind of mood that could only be alleviated by blowing up something.

I didn't shake free of my angry funk until I was almost to the front door. Charlotte's hiss and her hand on my arm snapped me out of it, just in time to pull me to a stop out of the main entry's line of sight.

I saw Stewart talking to someone, the last light of the day shining into the house over the cold marble floors. His voice was low, apologetic, but very proper. I eased closer, opening my demon ears so I could hear what was up.

"Again, I'm afraid the master of the house is unavailable, sir." Stewart's words were clipped, now as chill as the blood of the vampires before dinnertime. "You may call back in an hour or so. I'm certain Lord DeWinter will be delighted to speak to you then." Though his words were polite, I had the impression there was nothing delightful about this visitor.

"Syd," Charlotte hissed. "Sorcerer."

Oh *hell* no.

Something pushed against the door, as though someone was trying to pry it open despite Stewart's firm grasp on the handle. A voice muttered something, higher pitched than the butler's, though just as icy. My demon caught, "insist" and "stand aside" before she jabbed me with a snarl.

Not like I needed the encouragement. I practically ran to Stewart's side, though I gathered my poise in time to wrench the door out of his hand and glare at the man on the other side.

Pinstriped suit on a not-so-tall body, about my height. Expensive tie. Ostentatious vest. Kerchief in the brightest red. Dark hair slicked back from a broad, deep forehead, receding from a pointed widow's peak. The barest goatee. All of these facts reached me in my first good look, though I already knew it was the same man I'd seen stalking my house earlier.

The Brotherhood.

But it was his pale amber eyes, a washed-out version, nowhere near the intensity of a demon's tone, I noticed the most. Not because I found them appealing, but because the heartless, soulless, emptiness of them told me to be careful.

And since when did I ever do what I was told?

"Miss Hayle." Stewart knew well enough to drop the coven leader address, though I didn't have time to tell him this was no ordinary mortal. He also knew not to show surprise at my sudden appearance, taking it in stride. I felt the presence of others, knew the rest of the human servants had gathered in the darkening hall behind me, sworn to protect the vampires they served.

Hopefully I wouldn't need their help. The sun was almost down. And while Gram's warning not to go after the Brotherhood directly still rang in my head, there was no way I'd allow one of them inside the mansion.

The really pissed-off part of me wanted him to push it.

"Sydlynn Hayle." The man smirked at me, just the barest of a smile, eyes dead, flat. "We meet sooner than expected."

I hated when bad guys had the one up on me. "I take it you have a name somewhere inside that ugly suit?" Oh, Syd, Syd, Syd. Bad girl.

Oddly, my remark didn't raise a negative reaction. Instead, he offered his hand. Charlotte chuffed behind me, baring her teeth at him.

Probably not a good idea to let him touch me.

"Liander Belaisle," he said in his smooth and polished politician's voice, as though I should know exactly who he was.

"Nice to meet you." So not. "I think Stewart just asked you to leave?"

The butler quivered beside me, not out of fear, though I think he was finally understanding there was much more to this man than he'd first assumed.

"And yet, I find myself still wanting to enter." Belaisle's smile widened, showing brilliant white teeth, a tiny diamond glinting from one of his canines. How tacky. He didn't move, body still and calm, but there was a coiled tension to him that told me if I made the first move, he'd be ready for me.

Bring it.

"Sir." My powers of observation were clearly single-minded. I'd been so focused on Belaisle, I hadn't noticed the two tall, broad-shouldered suits flanking him. Both towered over him, one broad, the other whip-thin, as protective of him as Charlotte was of me. So either bodyguards or sorcerers. Or both.

Bad guys and their backup. Sheesh, so original.

Belaisle ignored his companion's subtle prod, though I noted the one on the left's eyes as they lifted to the horizon and the disappearing sun. So, they didn't want to be here when Sebastian and his clan woke up?

Yeah, hardly blamed them.

Belaisle didn't seem to share his two guard's apprehension. Instead, he took a step forward, casually, as though he'd been invited in.

He most definitely was not.

Belaisle rebounded slightly from the wall of family magic I put up between him and the threshold. I felt the power in the mansion respond, reach for me. It knew me, from the trial, from my family ties to the clan. But now I knew it ran deeper than that. The very earth below the house, the chamber, knew me, welcomed me, my maji blood.

Belaisle's pale eyes finally showed emotion. The barest touch of irritation. "You don't want to start something you can't finish, witch."

"Witch, Sidhe, demon, vampire, maji," I said, so sweetly I almost turned my own stomach as I ever so gently poked him with my power, tied together into a knot the size of an index finger. "You were saying?"

Was it wrong how much I was enjoying myself?

Belaisle's stoic expression didn't falter. "I know you have them," he said. "You really wish to begin a war between us over a pair of vagabond children who mean nothing to you? To your coven?" He looked up before meeting my eyes. "To this clan?"

"Sorry," I said. "What are you talking about?"

More frustration from him as the broad-shouldered guard leaned close.

"Sir, we really must—"

Belaisle's hand came up, silencing the man, his irritation snapping like a whip. "Foolish child," he growled. "I will have them no matter your involvement. Protecting them will only lead to your destruction and that of your family."

"Just push me, jerktard," I tapped his chest again with my magic, though it slid around him, not doing any real damage, his sorcery deflecting my power. Still, it felt good to get that little jab in, even if all it did was jerk his chain.

Especially if it jerked his chain.

Something impacted my shield, tore a gash in the center. I clenched, pouring energy into it, alternating green, blue, white, amber as he pushed against me. The stones below his feet groaned, cracked, crumbled as he continued to probe and shove against me like the big bully he was.

We'd see about that.

I let my demon have her head even as I called on Shaylee. She dove into the ground beneath him, his power devouring the heart of the stone he stood on, her Sidhe magic crumbling it faster even as my demon lashed out and hit him with everything she had, the vampire core of me creating a barrier inside for my demon to use as leverage.

I didn't get the spectacular results I'd been aiming for. Instead of flying backwards, body crushed against the side of his shiny black car, blood oozing from his mouth and nose, he staggered back a step.

One step. Damn it.

And yet, it surprised him, shocked him even as his eyes widened, mouth parting, hands clenching into fists at his sides.

It would have been a fight. I know it. And I honestly have no idea if I would have won or lost. Okay, I would have lost, I wasn't too arrogant to admit it. But I didn't get a chance to spin that particular dance. The moment Belaisle recovered, the sun vanished over the tree line leaving a burning red horizon behind.

He appeared beside me in a flicker of shadow, Sebastian's cold hands on my shoulders, flashes of darkness popping up all over the drive and yard, the entire blood clan frozen, menacing, as their master faced down the sorcerer.

"You are not welcome here," Sebastian said, simple, straightforward, backed by nearly a hundred vampires who would happily do his bidding. "Do not darken my threshold again, sorcerer."

Belaisle didn't comment, didn't move, though his companions both shifted, clearly nervous, prepped for anything. But the sorcerer obviously wasn't ready for a confrontation with an entire blood clan, because he smirked again, reaching inside his jacket to pull free a card which he tossed at my feet.

"I'll be seeing you again, Miss Hayle," he said as he turned, walking with casual grace toward his car as though his life wasn't in imminent danger. "I want those children." Belaisle paused by the back door, waited for the thinner guard to open it for him. The man's arrogance was unbelievable. "This is none of your business." He met Sebastian's eyes. "Nor yours, vampire." Belaisle flipped a casual wave my way. "And the next time, you might want to reconsider starting a fight you won't be able to finish."

"Fight?" I crossed my arms over my chest and smiled sweetly. "I thought we were just trading insults. You want a real fight, you let me know."

"We've been willing to overlook your kind for the time being," he said. "But I have the power to change that."

"More threats." I faked a yawn while Sebastian laughed, though he remained tense beside me. "I'm getting a little tired of all this talk, Belaisle. You really are a pompous ass."

Did his cheek just twitch?

Awesomesauce.

He slid into his car, tall and suited slamming the door

on his boss before heading forward to the front passenger's seat. Within a moment, the engine roared to life and the black car cruised down the drive, flanked by staring vampires with nothing good in their intentions.

"You play a dangerous game, Sydlynn Hayle." Sebastian sighed beside me.

"Maybe," I answered, "but he just confirmed something for me."

"That being?" The handsome vampire's eye brow raised, corner of his mouth twitching the sexiest way.

"My idea worked," I said. "Putting the kids he's looking for with Liam. Now I just have to figure out how to kick his sorry sorcerer's ass and we're all set."

"If anyone can, it would be you." Sebastian's laugh made me feel better.

Well, made me feel something.

Down, girl.

15

A quick talk with Sebastian, Sunny and Uncle Frank in on the action, and I had them up to date on the latest.

"So these children Belaisle seeks," Sebastian said, pacing with a glass of wine in his hand. At least, I think it was wine. Ew. "They are somehow vital to the war against the sorcerers."

"It's what the dream warning was about." I hesitated. "I've been trusting this maji," I said, not wanting to show weakness in front of the vampires even though I knew they'd be the last ones to judge me. "Maybe that's a bad idea."

Sunny's arms went around me, hugged me even as Sebastian shook his dark head, eyes meeting mine. "The maji are creators, Sydlynn," he said. "The sorcerers, destroyers. And I believe Belaisle himself was enough proof you're on the right side in this."

Exhale. Relief was a wonderful thing.

"Have you yet spoken to Miriam?" Sebastian set down

his glass, the liquid shining in the light. Definitely wine. Though I still shuddered at the thought of the glass goblet full of a stickier substance. "Surely the High Council must play a part in this."

"If she'll listen." Not like Uncle Frank to be such a downer. But when I met his eyes, I shared his sentiment.

"I've kind of been putting it off." Not on purpose, per se. I'd been a little busy. But yeah, I'd known all along I'd have to fill Mom in at some point. "But you're right, Sebastian. She needs to know."

Here comes Syd with more bad news. I'm sure she'd be thrilled to see me.

I left them then, pausing next to the van while Charlotte looked at me as if she suspected I was about to leave her behind.

Which I was.

"I need you to take the van home." Oh, the resistance. Written all over her body, her face, in the snapping fury in her eyes, the way she tensed, upper body leaning toward me as though prepped to grab me if I tried to run. "Charlotte, please, listen." I handed her the keys, which she ignored. "I'll be fine. I'm going to see Mom. But those kids..." I pressed the keys into her hand, hearing the jangle as she dropped them, letting them fall to the gravel unclaimed. "They are more important than me, if Iepa is to be believed. And I do believe her. They need you, more than I do right now."

She swayed just a little. "You can't leave me," she said, a simple fact, the time of day or a casual comment between friends.

"I'll be right back." I took a step away from her, reaching for the veil. I didn't want to use my power on her, but I would if I had to. And I really needed—okay wanted—to face my mother alone. Not that I had anything against Charlotte, but I never had a second where she wasn't hovering around me, except when I was sleeping and I had the sneaking suspicion she checked in on me in the middle of the night. And though I knew it caused her discomfort, maybe it was time to start pushing her away a little at a time to see if we could stretch her boundaries.

And give me some freedom.

Charlotte quivered. "Don't. Please."

"I'm ordering you to go back to Wilding Springs," I said, "and watch over Trill and Owen."

The weregirl groaned, tongue snaking out to lick her lips, desperation in her eyes. "You swear you'll be right home?"

"There and back again." I crossed my heart, though hope to die didn't appeal to me.

"Go." She gritted her teeth, spinning away from me. "Just go."

She didn't have to tell me twice. And though it wasn't fair and I knew I was causing her anguish, I tore open the veil and set my path to Harvard.

I didn't get to ride the veil alone anymore. Charlotte was my constant companion since she'd bound herself to me, her misguided sense of honor compelling her to be my bodywere after her father failed to fulfill that same role. Now that I was on my own, I felt the pull of the veil much stronger, my demon's need for it roused. Her power pushed against the edges of Demonicon, the rubbery membrane calling me home. I exhaled sharply as I exited into the dark Old Yard of the college, the veil sucking at me, sealing shut with a sigh of disappointment.

A big reason to be thankful for my bodywere, one I hadn't counted on. Apparently, she also served as a buffer. I'd make sure to hug her when I returned home.

Trying not to think of the return trip and wondering if it would be worse the second time around, I entered Massachusetts Hall and climbed on board the elevator, the sigh of the doors closing and the climbing floors feeling like I was heading for some kind of prison. Shaking off my foreboding, I stepped off and into the main lobby outside Mom's quarters, reaching for her.

Only to find the place empty.

Just perfect. Though when I reached out in frustration, I realized she wasn't far. At University Hall, just across the Yard, in a meeting.

Syd. Mom's mind touched mine. *What are you doing here?*

We have to talk. I kept the thread tight, just for her. *It's important.*

She didn't brush me off, to my surprise. *I'll be home soon.*

Okay then. I let myself in, wandered through the dark-paneled rooms, past Meira's bedroom door all the way to the back of the building.

A kitchen? How had I never known Mom had a kitchen? Well, duh, Syd. Though, to be fair, it wasn't like I ate here much. And even when I did, I was confined to the dining room. For all I knew, food was magicked in, befitting a Council Leader.

Snort.

My stomach rumbled its happiness at the find and I was soon hip-deep in her refrigerator, hauling out ingredients.

By the time Mom walked through the door, I had two

plates of fettuccine and chicken served up, garlic bread on the side, a nice salad to go with it. The smile she gave me, her tired expression and the welcoming hug accompanying it told me I'd done something right for once.

Maybe I was getting the hang of this good daughter thing at last.

A glass of white wine in her hand and the first few appreciative bites chewed and swallowed, Mom reached out and squeezed my hand.

"Thank you for this, sweetheart," she said. "I was going to grab a piece of toast and do some paperwork. This is much better."

"Where's Maurice?" Her constant companion as much as Charlotte was mine, the annoying little secretary was nowhere in sight. Wasn't complaining, considering we kind of abhorred each other.

"Still with the Council," Mom said. "I left him to sort the minutes." She winked.

Bless her.

"It's been a massive year," she said, swirling her noodles with her fork. "Working to unite the covens for common goals while speaking to other covens and Councils around the world." She sighed over another sip of wine. "Did I tell you, I'm trying to arrange a world conclave next summer."

She wrinkled her nose with a smile. "Or the one after that. Witches are so slow to act."

I snorted. "Oh, really?"

She swatted my hand with a laugh, my mother, the one I loved and was hoping to see tonight, showing her face. "Brat," she said. "I love you, Syd."

Why did those words choke me up? Probably because I didn't hear them enough.

Or say them enough, for that matter.

"I love you too, Mom," I said. "How are you?" It was a sensitive subject, the whole Dad thing, one I never knew if I should bring up or not.

But Mom didn't shut down, at least. "I'm fine," she said. "I really am, Syd. I was prepared for this, remember?"

"Mom," I said, "I don't care if you knew the exact time and day, it's not something you just get over." I thought of Quaid, of Liam. What would it be like to love and marry and have kids only to watch my mate grow old and die while nothing changed for me?

Shudder. Not going there anytime soon.

Mom must have known I wasn't just talking about her, because she leaned over and kissed my cheek.

"We'll both be okay," she said. "We're Hayles, remember?"

"Right," I said with a little smile, going for the humor in it. "And Hayle witches are too stubborn to fail."

She laughed, a deep, rich sound, before leaning back again. Sighing. Setting down her glass while her blue eyes focused on mine.

"Now," she said, "tell me why you're really here."

Sucked. But, she was still my mom, hadn't retreated from me, wasn't Council Leader Miriam Hayle, so I drew a deep breath and told her everything.

Mom steepled her fingers together, eyes never leaving mine. She asked the odd question but, for the most part, just let me ramble on until I was done, finishing with the confrontation with Belaisle.

"Sorcerers." Mom let her hands fall to the table, toying with the edge of her napkin. "My darling Syd, you have a way of making life so interesting." Her smile was warm, but brittle around the edges. "In a way, he's right, Belaisle. This isn't any of our business."

Um, what? "Sorry?"

"We're witches," she said. "Interfering on purpose in the workings of other magical races isn't our job, Syd." She shook her head as I spluttered at her, unable to come up with anything to say. "Listen to me, sweetheart, please." She grasped my hand again, but this time I wanted to pull away. "I know how you feel, I really do. If I were in your position, I'd probably be in your seat, talking to my Council leader. But Syd, she'd tell me the same thing I'm telling you. We can't get involved. To do so risks a war none of us are ready for."

My hands shook as I slid free of her and clasped them in my lap, clenched against my rising temper. She sounded just like the man I'd confronted. "You don't think the sorcerers are a threat?"

She shook her head, suddenly angry. "No, not at all," she said. "I know they are. But I won't start a confrontation I can't win."

"If helping others isn't witch business, what is?" I pushed my chair back, surging to my feet, resisting the urge to pace. "Besides, there is so much more to this than just simple witch politics. I haven't been 'just' a witch for a long time." Like that was her problem. Okay, well, it was, considering I was a coven leader under her command. Time to remind her. "This was dropped on my doorstep for a reason, and I refuse to walk away from anyone in need." I drew a breath and crossed a line I swore I wouldn't out of fear of the answer. "You told me, when you accepted this role, the Hayle coven would never again have to worry, that no matter what happened we'd always have support from the Council."

I watched her face fall, saw in her eyes how she begged me not to go on, but I couldn't stop. "Council Leader, I'm asking for your help."

Mom sighed, deep and long, head down, before standing herself, lifting her gaze to mine. Her face was blank, calm, eyes guarded. "It's not that easy," she said. "The Council can't help you, coven leader. And I advise you to distance yourself from this matter, for the sake of your coven."

That was that, then. We stood there, face-to-face, neither of us bending. I needed to leave before something broke.

She let me go, not a touch of magic, nor an offer of a motherly hug. I wouldn't have accepted either, so it was just as well.

16

I stepped into the Yard, exhaling a stale breath I hadn't known I'd been holding, feeling the cool of the evening settle around me. I'd done what I could to get through to Mom and though she'd left me high and dry, I felt better for having at least tried.

Now I could act and not have to second-guess myself. Because the threat was real, even in Mom's eyes. Abandoning Trill and Owen to the Brotherhood was totally out of the question. And as I reached for the veil, my demon stretching her power to tear open the outer membrane, I had an epiphany.

How many times had I acted on my own in times of trouble, times when Mom was aware of my actions, but unable to do anything herself? And in at least a few of those instances, I knew my actions were exactly what she needed from me. Was that my mother's modus operandi? Turning me into her hands when she herself was trapped without a way to resolve the issue because of her position?

Not that I minded even if I should have. I'd found I was more of a take action rather than sit around and think it through kind of girl. No matter how deeply I managed to dig myself into a heap of crapola, things managed to turn out. But suspecting now as I did Mom was using me to do her dirty work, I almost rebelled.

Almost. Sighed. Stepped into the veil with a firm grasp on my demon, Shaylee and my vampire backing me up as she hummed her unhappiness and longed for Demonicon. If Mom was manipulating me—ha, if?—at least she was doing so around things I would be acting on anyway. Still, a little collaboration would be nice.

And not like I was completely shocked by my ah-ha moment. Mom had been carefully controlling me my entire life.

Fine. I'd be her action hero. But on my terms.

A second ding-ding sounded in my head as I stepped out of the veil at the edge of our property, as reluctant as before, but unable to hold me thanks to my preparations and support. The veil. Why couldn't Meira use it? Sassafras? Neither of them could use their demon power to ride it as I did. Ahbi Sanghamitra, our demon grandmother could control it, proved that when she trapped Meira and me on Demonicon. But she was Ruler, had all the power of the collected planes behind her, using sheer force to make it do her bidding. But the veil acted different with me, more open, welcoming. Despite Ahbi's attempt to keep me from using the veil when I was visiting, I'd been able to access it, ride it as I did here at home, in a moment of true need.

My maji bloodline. Did it give me more control over the veil because of my ancestors? Had to be. And yet, Meira had the same blood, from Mom. So there had to be more to it. Trill's cryptic remarks came back as I paused after a moment, wrapped up in thought in the darkness of the back yard. She'd said it wasn't my demon power that made it possible. Was she referring to the fact I had maji blood? If so, Meira had to as well, both of us from the same parents. What made me different?

So many questions for which I really needed answers, but was almost afraid to ask.

Almost.

Time to confront Trill and find out what was really happening to me. I didn't feel any more unusual than ever, though admittedly more in balance than I had in my life. But I equated that to growing up, to losing the geas keeping me from using my magic when I returned Gram's power to her. To accepting and finally embracing what I was.

Could there be more to it? Trill certainly seemed to

think so. And now I knew the maji also had an influence over me, I was starting to wonder if the parts coming together inside me were accidental or some kind of grand plan I had no control over.

More manipulation? I wouldn't put it past Iepa. No, I didn't know her well yet, but if I'd learned anything it was those in power didn't hesitate to use the tools they had access to when a job needed doing. And I was really getting sick of being a tool.

I'm not sure why I didn't go to the cavern right away. Wishful thinking, maybe? Instead, I quietly slipped inside the house and down the hall to the kitchen. I waited a moment at the basement door, hand on the knob, debating if I wanted to add a heavy heart to all of the confusion in my mind, but I couldn't seem to resist the pull. Trusting my instincts, I opened the door and went downstairs.

Cool air greeted me, the thrum of the family magic welcoming as I set foot on the concrete floor, a faint glow of blue lighting the pentagram etched and painted on the floor in answer to my presence. I stood in the center of it, drew in my power, let the coven's energy warm me and hug me, instantly lightening my mood.

A slow pivot turned me to face the fabric-draped statue of my father, crystalline feet peeking out from under the woven magic sheet Mom made to cover his effigy when Dad severed their mating and went home to Demonicon. I'd called him a few times in the last six months with no luck, when I was home to do so, but only once since I returned from school for the summer. My efforts had been half-hearted at best, almost fearful. Better to call him quietly and fail then put my heart and soul into it for nothing.

Three steps put me at his side, my hands jerking free the sheet. I looked up into Dad's diamond face, guilt washing over me in a wave. It was my fault he was gone, forced to take Second Seat, a position he never wanted and fought against during his very long life. I'd allowed Ahbi to manipulate me, thus cornering him, doing what so many others had tried to in the past—tear our family apart at last.

I could call him. Maybe he'd come if I really tried. But there was nothing he could do, I knew that already. And yet the vision Iepa showed me had demons fighting side-by-side with witches. Which meant he deserved a warning.

I'd take that excuse.

Nerves tingling as anxiety tried to worm doubt into my magic, I pulled my demon tightly to me, feeling her chuff and squirm.

We have to reach him. Would he answer? Would she

let him? My teeth ground together at the thought of Ahbi. Mom might have manipulated me, but she'd done so out of love, I was certain of it. Ahbi on the other hand, had spent so many centuries as a political creature, I highly doubted she had feelings anymore, outside of worrying about keeping her throne.

Determination cut through my nervousness and sent it packing. I had to try, if only to fill him in, to warn him about what was coming. But more so, to prove to myself I could.

My demon writhed, but in agreement, temper crackling as I held her in check. One last drawn breath and I let her out, my magic calling for Dad.

Tears welled as his effigy instantly flooded with life, my father's spirit stepping across the veil and into his statue. I choked them back, chest tight, throat burning with sobs that wanted to escape as I stepped forward and into his waiting arms.

His warm chest was as strong as I remembered, the softening of his statue to human form almost complete.

"Syd," he whispered into my hair. "Hi, cupcake."

I was laughing and crying all at once, one hand smacking his arm as he grinned down at me over the old nickname. Funny, I didn't really mind it anymore.

"Hey, Dad," I said. "Don't call me cupcake."

We smiled at each other for a moment, a father-daughter instant in time where nothing had changed and I could just be happy to see my Dad. But it couldn't last, I knew it couldn't, as much as I clung to my flash of need to be young and innocent and just a girl who adored her father.

Not in the life I lived.

Dad broke the moment, hands gripping my arms. "I don't have long," he said, eyes full of sadness. "Are you all right? Your sister? Miriam?" So much sorrow in him, and a desperation, as though he'd been waiting for word while trying to pretend he was someone else.

I hugged him quickly again. "Meira's fine, loving school. Mom's... well, Mom is Mom, you know?" Dad smiled, nodded, though I could tell he wanted more. "Dad, you're right, I don't have much time either. But there are things happening you need to know about."

I filled him in as quickly as I could, for once not rambling on in my usual scattered way, proud of myself for managing a succinct breakdown of the past two days or so. Dad listened as Mom had, mostly just listening. When I finished with the conversation I'd had with her, he sighed, lips twisted in a grim line.

"As much as I wish she wasn't," he said, "your mother

is right, Syd. It's not so easy." He frowned, arms crossing over his chest as his mind visibly churned. "I'll warn Ruler about the sorcerers, but it's unlikely she'll listen. We've been busy putting out fires in Demonicon and I know what she'll say."

"It's not your problem." I had a feeling that phrase was going to get old fast. And that I'd better get used to hearing it.

"I believe you," he said. "And I'll take the warning from this maji seriously. But Syd, there's a lot you don't know about the maji. Ask your friend Liam to look into it further. That library of his should turn up Demoniconian history. Specifically about the forming of the planes in the first place." His expression deepened into a scowl. "They may come across as benevolent, but remember they created the planes and the demons who occupied them. I've always believed we were some kind of experiment they chose to run. You might ask her about their real motives when you speak to her again."

Well, that was news. But again I wasn't really surprised. It was just one more layer of proof Iepa had an agenda. As long as our goals remained the same, I'd pay attention. But the moment I even suspected something was hinky, she'd find out what screwing with a Hayle really meant.

"Thanks, Dad," I said. Stopped. Felt guilty again. "Are you okay over there?" His face tightened, shoulders sagging just a little before he straightened and nodded.

"I'm fine, Syd," he said. Which naturally meant he wasn't. "There's been a period of... adjustment. But I'm dealing with it."

Oh, Dad. I could have pressed him, made him talk to me maybe. But the look in his eyes asked me not to and, though I felt like a coward for backing off, I took the easy road and let him be.

The feeling of him shifted, the sharpness of the crystal making up his effigy cutting through a little before Dad's human form returned. I was running out of time. But the act made me think, connected two ideas together, old ones I'd almost forgotten.

"The crystal." I tapped his chest. "The one that turned your effigy from metal to diamond. It's sorcerer magic. It's too bad I can't have it back."

"You're welcome to try," Dad said. "But Sassafras and I tried everything to damage this new form, remember?" Did I. I'd caught the two of them at it and screamed at them for being total idiots before bursting into tears. Sassafras died to send Dad back to Demonicon, all because his old statue had been destroyed. And the pair of morons thought it would be a good experiment to see how strong the new one was.

"I remember." I wrinkled my nose, irritation returning. Dad just laughed. "The crystal had an effect on your power. Made you able to stay here longer?"

Dad nodded slowly. "I feel different when I'm here," he said. "My magic isn't as raw. More defined."

I knew what he meant. The fire-based power of demons had a wildness to it, an almost primal feeling. What had the crystal done to him?

"I wish I could be of further help." He reached for me again, hugging me close, cheek on my hair.

"You have," I whispered into his broad chest, feeling our demon power connect. "You listened. And I just wanted to see my dad."

"You have no idea how good it is to see you." His voice choked off. Dad cleared his throat before gently pushing me away, moisture standing in his eyes. "I have to go."

"I know." I stepped back, felt his power retreating, hugging myself, trapping the remaining warmth from his embrace.

"Syd," Dad said as he faded away, "I love you. Be careful."

Ha. Didn't see that coming.

I bent to retrieve the sheet only to toss it in a half-open cardboard box. Mom might have decided to write him off, but I had a feeling I'd be needing my father again and draping him like he was dead or something just didn't seem right.

The crystal winked at me in the light of the single bulb swaying softly over the pentagram. Hmmm. I'd gotten the one Sassafras used to save Dad from Demetrius Strong, the leader of the Chosen of the Light. A sorcerer. But surely it wasn't the only crystal, nor he the only sorcerer who used such a tool? Demetrius was gone, taken by Batsheva Moromond when she was ousted from the Council Leader seat during Mom's trial, when it was revealed she used blood magic to steal the Council's power. But there had been other sorcerers in his group.

Maybe they knew where he found the crystal. Or had their own.

As much as the idea turned my stomach, I knew what I had to do. I needed a weapon against the Brotherhood and there was only one person I could think of who might lead me to what I needed.

Angela Morgan's nasty little maid, Rosetta, was going to be so happy to see me.

17

Charlotte was waiting for me at the top of the stairs when I emerged from the basement. She touched me with trembling fingers, face pale in the low light of the tiny bulb over the oven, eyes frantic. But she calmed the moment our skin made contact, her hand clenching around mine almost painfully before she settled, taking a step back.

"Here's the keys." She handed them to me, no longer trembling, as though it was no big deal.

I really loved her sometimes.

Together we rode the veil to the library. This time as I entered the slice between planes, I purposely felt for the difference. Yes, it was Charlotte and the power connection she had to me muting the pull of Demonicon. Completely one-sided, formed when she bonded herself to me out of some misplaced sense of honor, it anchored me to her and, thus, to my home plane. My demon didn't complain either, and I considered the possibility Charlotte's connection to me was more than just a bond. Something much more.

I really had to stop worrying about her feelings and figure out what the magic between us was all about.

But later. Yeah, always later.

Liam waited for me with Galleytrot at his side as I passed through the barrier. His arms slid around me, hugging me as he always did, his favorite form of greeting. Shame on me, I didn't resist, loving—yes, loving—the feeling of his arms around me.

I was a horrible, horrible person.

"Did you find out anything?" Liam led me past his room. A glance inside showed Owen curled up with a book, Meira at his side, though the open tome lay across his chest and both of their eyes were closed. I smiled a little, wanting to go to him and brush the hair out of his face, to kiss Meira's cheek, surging protectiveness rumbling inside me. Poor kid, he had to be exhausted. This was probably the first time in a long time he was somewhere safe from the Brotherhood.

My sister's eyes opened. Fixed on me. She slid from the bed and came to my side, taking my hand, covering a yawn with her free one. A glance to the left showed me Trill on Liam's computer, sitting at his desk, Sassafras curled up on his favorite chair, watching her. His amber eyes winked at me as I passed, energy touching mine. I continued following

Liam as the silver Persian hopped down and waddled his way after us.

Galleytrot sank to the floor with a groan, big head falling to his front paws as Liam stopped beside the Gate, glancing back the way we came a moment before focusing on me.

"What did you find out?" His voice was soft, not quite a whisper, and I wondered at his sudden need for secrecy.

"Not much," I said. Hated to admit it, really. Sassafras hissed at me when I mentioned Belaisle and my first encounter with the Brotherhood, tail swishing as I told them what Mom said.

"Damn her," Sass snapped. "What is she thinking?"

I kept my suppositions about Mom's motives to myself. "I managed to reach Dad," I said.

Sassafras perked, amber fire flashing in his gaze while Meira looked momentarily angry. "Harry?" Was that hope in his voice? Longing? Did Sass blame himself as much as I did for Dad's present circumstances? Probably. There was lots of guilt to go around. "What did he say?"

"About what Mom did." I didn't intend for that to come out so glum. "He's going to warn Ahbi, but doesn't expect her to take any action. Oh, he did mention I should ask you," I turned to Liam, "to do some research into the maji's creation of the demon planes. Dad seems to think Iepa isn't to be trusted."

Sassafras snorted while Liam nodded. "Of course she isn't," he said in his most condescending tone.

Smartass cat.

"You've been acting like you know more than we do," I said, focusing on him as his tail twitched in irritation. "Time to 'fess up."

He shifted from one front paw to the other, eyes glowing as he looked away. "The Zornovs were friends once upon a time," he said. "Vasek and his wife Josephine. Your great-great-great grandmother Auburdeen was involved with them. And the Brotherhood."

I knew how much it bothered him to talk about the past, but this was important. "And?"

"It's odd," he said. "Josephine was a sorcerer and Vasek maji. But both were enemies of the Brotherhood. It's a long story," he turned to me at last, "and has little bearing on what's happening now. Except your two families used to care for each other. Fought together." Sassy sighed then, a sad sound full of years of memory. "But from what I knew, the Brotherhood disbanded, thanks to their efforts, and Burdie's."

Interesting. "Obviously not."

Sassafras hissed softly. "Obviously."

"At least now we know Trill and Owen are safe here in the cavern." I found myself glancing back toward the entry, mimicking Liam's tone of voice. "The Brotherhood may be here, but if they can't find what they're looking for, they might just leave."

"They'll never give up." How had Trill snuck up on us like that? One second the entry had been empty, the next she stood there, body tense, Owen's sleepy but unhappy face beside her. "You've just succeeded in trapping us here."

Owen murmured something to her before meeting my eyes with his intense blue gaze. "We're really grateful," he said. "But Trill is right. We can't stay here forever while the Brotherhood tears apart your town looking for us."

Damn, I hadn't warned the family. I reached for Gram, just caught the edge of her mind. But the Sidhe wards were too strong. I'd have to leave to talk to her.

"We need to go." Trill turned, grabbing her brother's arm, the scowl back on her face. "Thanks for nothing."

I went after them, but it was Liam who held them back. The wards at the exit flared, green magic blocking them in. I wasn't sure if he'd be able to keep Trill contained for long while I struggled for a way to convince her to trust me.

Sassafras reached her before I could, standing on his

back legs, front paws on her thigh. "Please listen," he said. "You aren't trapped. You're safe. And we'll find a way to get rid of the Brotherhood. You just have to trust us."

Trill shook her head, anger rising on her face while Owen just slumped, defeat written on his entire body. "You don't know that," she snapped. "They'll find a way to reach us, to breach these defenses." She looked up, met my eyes. "You don't know what you're dealing with."

"I do," I said. "I've faced off with sorcerers before." Was I getting through to her? Did she just relax a little? There was shock on her face, enough to tell me I needed to keep going before she talked herself out of listening at all. "Not the Brotherhood, but the Chosen of the Light. And we defeated their leader, destroyed their order. We can do this, but only if you don't run off and do something stupid."

Great choice of words, Syd. The tightening around her eyes told me instantly I'd gone too far. But Owen was listening. And the despair he'd been trapped in was gone.

"Trill, we have to listen." He pulled against her, drawing her back from the wards. They flashed once and faded, Liam releasing his power. An act of trust I probably wouldn't have shown her.

But it worked. Trill hugged her brother, anger gone, a moment of hope crossing her face before she nodded.

I just hoped the risks I was taking with my coven and Sebastian's blood clan, now targets thanks to my meddling, would be worth it in the end. But though I still didn't know exactly why these two were so important, I had to trust my instincts.

As long as those instincts weren't maji implants to control my actions.

Choosing to believe in the former, I stepped away from the others, motioning for Galleytrot while Liam kindly herded the pair of siblings back into his office. Meira looked back at me, face dark and expression closed and I winced privately.

Thanks for waiting for me to talk to Dad. She shut me off, not letting me back in as she left me there with her guilt-trip doing its job.

She had to know I didn't go looking for Dad without her on purpose. But I guess it would seem that way.

One more conversation I had to have.

Charlotte hovered at my side while the big dog sat on his haunches, red fire flickering in his eyes. "What do you need?"

"To find Rosetta." I quickly sketched out my plan. "I'm hoping she'll lead me to other members of the Chosen. I need one of their sorcerers."

Charlotte twitched a little, but Galleytrot nodded. "You're thinking one of them can help?"

"I need another crystal." The big dog grunted. "If I'm right, having one could give us the advantage we need." I reached out and scratched his big head. "I know you hate to leave Liam right now," I said, "but I need to find her."

"I agree," he said. "As distasteful as she and her sect are. Though you recall there wasn't much left of their order when we scattered them last time."

"I know," I said. They'd taken it on themselves to work with the Dumonts, to kidnap Sassafras when he was still in mortal form. Mom and I made sure they would never have the nerve to come together again. Still, I refused to believe someone as fanatical as Rosetta with her absolute hate for other witches, though she herself had our power, would ever give up entirely. "Do you remember her scent?"

He shook his big head, fur rippling, though not in the negative. "I do," he said. "But it would be better refreshed, if we can manage it."

Only one place to go to give his nose what it needed. I dreaded returning to the Morgan's big house, the memories of my former best friend, Alison, still clinging. How I'd failed her and left her to exist in a half-life of the ghostly monster she'd become. But this was too important for me to let something like grief and heartbreak stop me.

Way to be a trooper, Syd.

The black dog and my wereguard at my side, I paused at the entry to the archive. Liam looked up, Trill back behind the laptop, Meira and Owen looking through the stacks while Sassafras had returned to his seat.

"We're going out," I said, purposely vague. "Hopefully we won't be long."

Liam hesitated before smiling. A strained smile. But when his eyes touched on first Charlotte then Galleytrot, he relaxed a little. Probably because I had so much firepower at my back.

"Keep us posted."

Trill looked up, the light from the screen reflecting on her glasses, hiding her eyes. "I need to see the chamber under the mansion." She crossed her arms over her chest. "I think you might be right. That it could help us. Why else would Iepa lead you there?"

"I'll take you when I get back," I said, using my best Mom tone. Yeah, I pulled out the Mom tone. But the rebellion in Trill's whole body told me I had to do something. "Every time you leave this cavern, there's a chance the Brotherhood could track you. So we'll keep travels to a minimum, got me? Trill, we're just trying to keep you safe." Why didn't she understand that?

"What about your coven?" Trill dropped her arms, hands fisted on either side of the computer. "And the vampires? The longer we stay here, the more danger they are in and you know it."

Ah. My final bright light moment of the day came in a jab of sympathy. Anger hid fear and guilt inside the maji girl. How many people had she seen hurt or killed because of her and her brother? Had they trusted others to keep them safe in the past, only to fail, to fall? It seemed very likely.

"Iepa wouldn't have sent you to us, your Nona wouldn't have, if they didn't think this was the right thing to do." No more Mom. Just me, all gentle, reaching for her with my power.

To my surprise, Trill reached back as her hands unclenched, shoulders shaking a little as she drew a harsh breath. Her maji magic connected with mine, the touch tenuous, but present as she spoke.

I can't live with it, she sent, her mental voice near a sob. *If anything were to happen... I won't be able to forgive myself.*

You're forgetting, I sent back, hugging her gently with my power. *I'm one of you. Maji. And we have to stick together.*

A little smile, wavering and thin, but present. "Okay," she said. "We'll try it your way. But I won't stay trapped here forever."

Fair enough. "We'll be back as soon as we can. Hopefully with a weapon we can use against the Brotherhood."

As I turned to go, I sent a tight link to Liam.

Watch her. Just in case.

I was through the wards before he could answer, but had no doubt he took my warning to heart.

18

The Morgan mansion towered over us in the darkness, empty and lifeless. It was clear from the dirt on the windows, normally polished and cared for, as well as the untidiness of the typically flawless grounds, no one lived here for quite some time. Not since Alison died, I was guessing. With Angela living in New York with her husband, Roger, the big house sat alone and tragic, the bones of a broken family left to rot.

Alison was never far from my thoughts, and I tried many times to track her. But despite my efforts, I was never able to find her, not since she sampled blood for the first time, her echo enhanced by the power of the vampire essence inside me, thanks to Ameline's meddling. I could only imagine Alison found the taste to her liking. And since she no longer pursued me for the power I had inside me, it was clear she didn't think she needed it—or me—anymore.

Talk about give me nightmares. Even the vampires

didn't know what drinking blood would do to a ghost, especially one fed by her magic. Hard to guess when it had never happened before.

Moving on. I had a job to do, and Alison wasn't part of it. Or, at least, I didn't think she was. My skin rippled into gooseflesh as I magically picked the lock to the kitchen door and let myself in, passing over the threshold with the sudden worry this must be where Alison had been hiding out all along.

But no, again, nothing. If she was here, she didn't show herself and, from the snuffling Galleytrot was doing, he wasn't finding much either.

"This family is long gone," he rumbled in the dark of the extravagant kitchen, big paws resting on the marble counter top as he rose up on his hind legs to touch his nose to its surface. "How sad to only catch the oldest of scents where once this house was alive with them."

He had to go there, didn't he? I snuffled a little, but refused to let my sadness get the better of me.

"Rosetta?" It came out like a pointed stick, sharp and precise. But Galleytrot showed no indication I'd hurt his feelings, instead absorbing my grief-fed anger without a word.

He hopped down, head swaying back and forth as he

crossed the kitchen to a small cupboard, like a closet, tall and thin. A pass of his paw flipped it open, revealing a cream-colored sweater inside.

The cable-knit looked familiar. In fact, wasn't it the same sweater we'd used last time to track the traitor witch? Galleytrot buried his face in the fabric, drawing a deep breath before spinning his big body toward me. Red fire burned deep in his eyes, casting a glow around him as he shuddered and growled low in his throat.

"I have her," he said in his voice like rolling thunder. "But she's far, far from here."

"You can't run the whole way," I said. "We take the veil."

He grunted, as though to protest, then nodded. "We could lose her that way, waste time. But I'll do my best."

"Might I suggest," Charlotte said as we left the house, locking it behind us, feeling as though if I left it open I'd be adding to my betrayal, "we try to link Sydlynn to your nose using magic?" I stared at her, Galleytrot too, before laughing.

"Little slow on the uptake." I smacked my forehead with my palm and grinned at the big hound. "I can use air magic to tie into your sense of smell. You should be able to use it to find her no matter where she is."

"Will I be able to smell her in the veil?" He seemed more optimistic, licking Charlotte's hand in thanks.

"I don't know." I shrugged. "There's only one way to find out."

It was a brilliant idea, really. Took us a bit to figure it out, I admit. And the first time I dumped us outside the veil, I received matching glares from Galleytrot and Charlotte while water soaked my jeans from the knees down as we appeared in the cold water of a stream.

"What?" I hopped out and used some water magic to shed the moisture before helping them both dry off the same way. "This is new. Give me a break already."

Turned out Galleytrot couldn't smell inside the veil, but was able to point us in the right direction. After a few tries, we were sailing along nicely, slipping in and out, changing direction as needed.

And we needed to. I'm not sure what Rosetta had been up to since I saw her last, but we visited several houses where she'd obviously taken up residence, all of decreasing attractiveness in gradually depreciating neighborhoods. Then apartments, also growing more run down until we finally emerged on a dark street, one light in the distance the only illumination, the moon long set as the deepest part of the night took hold. I side-stepped a pile of refuse in the short, ugly alley outside a squat building covered in spray-paint artwork, the front windows mostly boarded up, the brick itself covered in graffiti.

"This is the place," Galleytrot muttered. "Even through this offal, I can smell her." He paused, head lifted. "She is here, Syd."

Well, finally. "Where the hell are we?"

Charlotte shrugged, eyes everywhere. "Does it matter?" She'd grown increasingly tense as our surroundings degraded. She now looked like if anyone appeared and even glanced my way they'd be taking their lives into their own hands. "Let's move."

Funny how bossy she became when she thought I might be in trouble.

Galleytrot surged ahead, following his nose into the alley way while Charlotte gently prodded me to keep moving. It was warm out, much warmer than I was used to, humidity levels making me sweat. We had to be somewhere further south. Charlotte's encouragement added to the annoyance I felt as my temperature rose, inside and out. I almost told her to cut it out, but left well enough alone. This wasn't the time to stand around arguing with my bodywere.

That I would save for later.

The black hound disappeared into the shadows, my demon enhancing my vision as I passed from the edge of the light and into the darkness. He was clearly visible ahead, one paw reaching out to impact a steel door, surface running with rust, but firmly bolted.

"Through here."

I made quick work of the lock, letting it swing inward onto a dark hall lit only by the exit light as Galleytrot took the lead again before I could enter. Smelling a conspiracy, I scowled back at Charlotte and wondered when they had the chance to decide I'd be sandwiched between them the entire time.

The quick gleam of guilt in her eyes told me she knew I was on to them.

They were both going to have a very stern talking to when this was over.

Something squealed and dashed over my right foot. I leaped back, a little shriek of horror escaping. Just a rat, yes. But seriously.

Yuckamundo.

At least there was light up ahead, cold fluorescent casting a vile greenish glow on everything. Galleytrot was already moving up the stairs at the end of the hall, nails clicking on the industrial tile, chipped and filthy. My foot slipped a little on a patch of something wet, but I refused to stop and examine what I'd stepped in.

Double yuckorama.

Three flights we climbed, to the top of the building, before emerging into a dankly carpeted hallway, the smell of mold and urine, animal and human mixed together burning my nose, peeling wallpaper barely holding up the plaster, more graffiti mingling with water stains, one section of the ceiling bowed downward as though ready to collapse at any moment. I sidestepped the spot, avoiding whatever was up there, not even wanting to think about it falling on me.

I *so* needed a shower. Just being there made me feel dirty.

A door creaked open beside me and I had a view of a startled face before it slammed shut again. Obviously, the neighbors here had no desire to ask questions. Perfect.

Galleytrot stopped at last at the end of the hall, the final door on the left, and turned to face me, eyes still glowing, eerie red flickering lights calling me onward. I reached his side with Charlotte crowding my back as the big dog sank to his haunches.

"Here," he said, voice low. "She is here. But Syd, she's not alone."

I didn't have to ask if he was sure. And while I would have loved to simply barge my way inside, I didn't. Sure, the neighbors might seem like they wanted no part of anyone else's business, but the last thing I needed was to have police show up and challenge me before I had what I wanted.

Though I hesitated to touch the peeling gray paint on the warped wooden door, someone had to do it.

A firm knock stirred movement inside the apartment. I waited, patience almost gone, as feet shuffled closer. The peephole was black, and I had to assume it no longer worked, because I was sure if Rosette knew who was on the other side of the door, there was no way she'd open it.

Which she did, snatching the handle, popping the door back, glaring at us where she hunched, pale and thin, under a dirty shawl. The moment she saw me, her eyes widened and she back-pedaled, hissing and swearing at me in Spanish, making signs with her fingers as though to ward me away. I ignored her, pushing my way inside, the big dog crowding her out of our path while Charlotte softly closed the door behind us.

It wasn't until Rosetta had backed out of the short hall and into the open space beyond, I caught sight of the others. I recognized a few faces, though, like Rosetta, they were all shadows of themselves, gaunt and desperate, their fear of me as real as my hate for them.

Or the hate I used to hold. As I stood there, eyes flickering from one fallen Chosen member to another, the dozen or so members crouched on rickety, sagging furniture, clutching each other in terror, my animosity faded, converting to regret and pity. Not empathy, I wasn't ready to commiserate with them or anything. But I could at least feel sorry for how things had turned out.

I couldn't show weakness, not yet. If ever. I needed a crystal and being sympathetic would likely get me nowhere. So, mean bitch Syd it was.

"Nice to see you, Rosetta." No need for sarcasm. She got it.

"You have no right to be here." She stammered through her words. "You will leave us in peace now."

I shrugged. "I will," I said, "when I have what I came for."

They shuddered as one, exchanged horrified glances. One woman's eyes flickered to a doorway and back again. Interesting. Were they hiding something?

What were they afraid I was after?

"I need information." I pinned Rosetta with a rope of family magic, not to hurt her, but so I could feel her power and know if she lied to me when she answered. I could also compel her to speak, though the thought of doing so turned my stomach.

She spit on the floor at her feet, making another warding sign with her hands, but the gesture was weak and without power to back it. "I won't tell you anything, evil one."

"You will." Okay, I didn't mean to squeeze her until she squeaked. Honest. But I was getting really freaking tired of being jerked around.

Really, really.

"Tell me about the Brotherhood." I expected some kind of reaction from them, but certainly not the moan of terror, the scrambling of bodies, Rosetta's wail of despair. Galleytrot and Charlotte both moved as the group scattered like rats, most running for a window and the iron fire escape outside, but I stopped them. A handful remained, faces buried in each other's shoulders, their hysteria attacking me in a wave of overwhelming emotion.

"It's the end, don't you see?" Rosetta fell to her knees, wringing her hands. "The end of everything. They will come with their army and destroy us all. All."

Well, as much as she sounded like she was babbling, at least she seemed to be in line with what Iepa showed me.

"You're not tied to them?" I guess I wasn't surprised.

The Chosen hated all magic, though they were magic users themselves.

Rosetta shook her head, turning her face away, bringing her shawl up to cover her weeping. And no matter how I pushed her, what I said, what magic I tried, she refused to speak, just crying and rocking.

Galleytrot snuffled around as I stopped pushing the woman and tried to think. She was clearly broken. And none of the others seemed much better. It was hard to tell if any of them were sorcerers because they all felt equally empty.

Leave it to the black dog to remind me what I'd suspected earlier.

"Someone hides within." He pawed at the door. A closet, had to be, too thin to lead to a room. "This scent... I know it, Syd."

As I turned to join him, Rosetta rose, shrieking incoherently, diving for me with her hands in claws of rage, even as Charlotte smoothly stepped in front of the woman and struck her with the side of her hand.

Rosetta went down in a heap, eyes rolling back in her head, out cold. Charlotte grimaced, bending to wipe her hand on the woman's shawl before turning to the others. They simply stared at us, hopeless and lost, as I grabbed the door handle and tugged it open.

"Sydlynn," Demetrius Strong said, his face still cherubic though in demon form. "How lovely to see you, my dear."

19

He crouched in the back of the small closet, amber eyes alight with fire, body hunched and scrawny. His thin hands made grabbing motions before him as he smiled at me, white teeth flashing. The man who had led the Chosen, the powerful sorcerer who had tried to kill me twice and almost succeeded, was as wasted and pathetic as his followers.

"Demetrius." The last time I'd seen him, he'd fled with Batsheva. "Where's your mistress?" If that old (b)witch was in on this, I'd be more than happy to make sure she ended up minus a head.

He shuddered violently, tears welling in his eyes though his grin, now manic, never faded. "She's gone, gone, gone, gone." He shook like a dog coming out of water, falling to his backside and kicking his feet against the floor, dirty flip-flop sandals flying free. I winced, seeing him crack and break, knew, though he had been mad before, he was now truly insane. His previous madness at least lived behind a veneer of absolute civility, an almost cheerful crazy that creeped me out. This was worse. Not because it was icky, but because it was so gaping and raw, his mind an open wound in front of me, one that would never heal.

He crawled forward on his hands and knees, looking up at me with the rictus of his smile firmly in place, snot and tears mingling on his red cheeks, tracking through dirt and over what looked like old bruises. A scar ran from under his right eye, down the side of his face to curve in a crescent, pulling the corner of his mouth askew. I backed off a pace as he emerged into the light, blinking and smiling and shaking.

"Are you hiding from her?" I could see why, if he'd broken down like this in her care. Batsheva would simply kill him if he was no longer of use to her.

"Evil," he whispered, eyes wide again, innocent almost, as he clutched at my pant leg. Charlotte shoved him off with one foot, her distaste clear on her face. He whimpered and backed away, holding himself as he crouched at my feet, still weeping, still smiling.

"She is evil." Nice he finally saw it, even if he had to go bonkers first. "Where is she?"

He shook his head suddenly, a high-pitched whine coming from his throat. "Nononononononononononono."

Demetrius pointed one finger at me, his black nail cracked and broken. "No more of her. No."

Okay then. I could let Batsheva go for now. But here at least I had a source, if I could break through his insanity, of another crystal. And though my disgust almost did me in, I sank to my haunches next to him and met him on his level.

"Demetrius," I said. "What do you know of the Brotherhood?"

Again fear, but not as powerful. He sank back, a puppy kicked one too many times. "Can't go near them, not ever. Not ever. Not anymore."

So he did know them. "You worked for Belaisle, didn't you?"

He shook his head, a spark of rage in his eyes. "Never. She is evil. He is despair."

Lovely. Someone worse than Batsheva Moromond.

Demetrius reached for me again, slowly this time, his smile coming back, head tilting from side to side as he did. I shooed Charlotte off, let the former Chosen leader stroke the back of my hand with his fingers, the barest touch, feather strokes, though my need for a shower just increased tenfold.

"Please," he whispered, the sound still oddly piercing, sharp and jagged in his need. "Please, will you fix me?"

It took me a moment to understand what he meant. I couldn't heal his mind, could I? But when my demon roared her denial, I knew then she'd figured it out before I had.

She'd punished him for trapping her, for stealing some of her power for his crystal. When we'd defeated Demetrius and left him behind at the mansion for his people to find, he'd been in the physical guise he still wore. Black horns, one chipped, the shine long gone, peeked from his silver hair, his red skin mottled and pale rose in places, the demon version of gray. She'd made him look like her, the only way she had to ensure his people would reject him, maybe even kill him.

But he'd somehow escaped them, and now I knew not all of the Chosen saw him as the enemy. Maybe at first, but the fact he found refuge with the remains of his sect told me they were desperate for leadership, even from someone as shattered as Demetrius.

"You want to be human again?" I thought about it even as my demon turned her back, crossed her arms over her chest and pretty much told me where I could shove my willingness to consider it. I hardly blamed her.

More tears, more snot. Seriously? I was going to stand under hot water until I cooked.

"Lovely, kind, generous one," he continued his light caress. "Fix me?"

"What do I get if I do, Demetrius?" No way was I going to battle with my demon if there wasn't something in it for me. And the feeling I had he knew more than he was saying about the Brotherhood was confirmed when his face compressed, a nasty smirk replacing his openness.

"Anything," he whispered. "Everything."

Quite the offer. But could he, in his condition, deliver?

"I need a crystal," I said. "Like the one you used on me."

His head bobbed immediately, Adam's apple bouncing in time as his throat constricted.

"Yes, yes. I get you anything, all of it, you want it, you have it." He cackled suddenly, falling back, rolling over on his side, giggling and rocking himself while his bare feet scrabbled on the floor. Charlotte firmly grasped my arm and pulled me up, back, putting herself between Demetrius and me.

"Will having one help me against the Brotherhood?" If he could give me the answers I needed, be my secret weapon, this trip would pay off big time.

Demetrius straightened, saw my bodywere between us and whined softly. "Mistress," he said, sing-songing the word and the ones after. "Trust me. I'm not your enemy." He reached for Charlotte who bared her teeth at him. He shrank back, but not far, easing forward again when she stopped. "Let me help you, you be my new Mistress?" Demetrius laughed, a horrible sound full of crazy.

Oh crap.

"I'll make you one, a crystal, the perfect one. Kill Belaisle, kill them all." Demetrius stood up, hopping around in a circle, one foot to the other. "Make my Mistress the most powerful Mistress in the. Whole. Wide. World." He stopped, stared at me with his manic amber eyes. "Fix me?"

I could have lied to him. Said I'd do it. But my heart constricted, my conscience weighing on me. We'd done this to him, as horrid and evil and nuts as he'd been before. This crumpled remnant of what used to be a human being was my responsibility. And if he could deliver what he promised, if I could find a weapon that would ensure we could defend against the Brotherhood, it would be worth it to give this pitiful creature back what he longed for.

Only one problem. My demon. Sigh.

Come on, I sent. *He's suffered enough. And we need him.*

Silence. Cold and yet burning at the same time as she slammed up a wall and drove me back.

You achieved what you wanted. He's in pain, endless pain. And even if we turn him back, he'll never recover. You know that.

Chuffing breath. Absolute fury.

Sometimes being more than one person really sucked.

Consider, the vampire core of me spoke up, surprising me when she did as she addressed my demon. *The transition could be made painful.*

That got her attention. The wall came down at least.

That's kind of sick, don't you think? My stomach rolled around a little at the thought of causing suffering on purpose.

Naturally, it made my demon even happier. Not happy, nope, nope. Just happier.

Even more shocking? *We could ensure when the transformation is complete, every moment is agony,* Shaylee spoke up. Shaylee. Who never spoke up.

And when did she become so bloodthirsty?

Their support was enough, turned out, even though I could only splutter inside my own head while the three of them plotted their nastiness.

My demon turned back and snarled her consent.

We all really need to have a serious talk, I sent to them. *When this is over.*

Still fighting my stomach and the fact I harbored some

seriously cruel people inside me, I refocused on Demetrius and nodded.

He practically fell over himself trying to get to me while Charlotte flung him backward, his weakened body impacting the wall across the room. I shoved her aside and went to him, reaching for his hand, pulling him to his feet while he whined and shivered.

"We need him, damn it." I met her eyes, saw the rebellion in them.

Hell no. The three hardheaded women sharing my existence might have been able to get away with it, but my bodywere didn't get that kind of slack.

"I mean it, Charlotte," I snapped. "Back off."

She did at last, though I caught the moment of hurt as it crossed her face.

Tough cookies, cookie.

"Fix me?" So pathetic. I glanced back at Demetrius whose amber eyes begged me. Yeah, like I'd be turning him back any time soon. No way I trusted his crazy ass, not until I had what I wanted.

"Crystal first," I said. "Fix you after. Deal?"

He bobbed his head, grasped my hand, kissed it.

Now I needed boiling water, an entire jug of soap and bleach.

We left Rosetta and the remains of the Chosen behind, stepping into the veil from the apartment. The little maid hadn't woken yet, and I had no desire to find out what kind of mood she'd be in when she did.

The veil sucked us in, Demetrius clinging to me all the way, stumbling as we emerged into the aging night on the soft grass of the library lawn. The air was so crisp and fresh I took a moment to fill my lungs, sniffing at myself as we walked to the door, finding I still carried an aroma with me.

Screw the soap. Bleach it was.

Though I hesitated to take the ailing sorcerer into Liam's cavern, I didn't want him out of my sight. While Galleytrot chuffed at me, his unhappiness with my choice as clear as Charlotte's, I stepped through the wards and into the cavern with Demetrius still clinging to my hand like a lost and terrified child.

The moment we passed through, I felt it, the sharp spike of fear in Liam's power, tensed as he emerged from the archive with Meira and Owen beside him. My Sidhe friend's face told me what I needed to know, though Owen's tear-streaked cheeks cinched the truth around me like a noose.

I groaned, shaking my head, as Liam spoke.

"I'm sorry, Syd," he said, voice shaking. "I don't know how it happened. One minute she was there, the next..."

"It's my fault," Owen said, voice steady. "I should have been watching her, too."

"Damn it," I said. "How long has Trill been gone?"

I didn't wait for an answer before firing off another. "Where's Sassafras?" I was already turning, heading for the exit.

"He went looking for her." Liam moved as if to join me, hesitated.

"You have to stay," I said. "Galleytrot, watch over them, would you?" I gave Demetrius a gentle push. "Stay here." I met the big dog's eyes. "Keep an eye on him. Don't let him out of your sight."

He growled. "Not even for a moment."

Charlotte beside me, I barged through the wards and leaped into the veil, a heartbeat of fear all it took to exit the slice between planes, landing in the driveway outside the mansion.

Neither of us missed a beat, running for the front door. I opened it with magic, not bothering to knock, freezing as I passed the threshold to the sight of Sebastian standing over Trill, three vampires keeping her contained as he confronted her.

His blue eyes met mine as he looked up, lips a grim slash. "We've uncovered an intruder," he said at his most polished. "I assume she's one of the two you mentioned earlier?"

I glared at Trill who glared right back as I shoved my way between Anastasia and another vamp to confront the girl. "What were you thinking?" My magic lashed out, wrapping her up in shielding until I could barely feel myself let alone her. "How did you find this place?" Charlotte quivered beside me and I could only guess what I was forced to do also affected the bond she had with me, but I wasn't in a position to go easy on anyone.

Least of all a stupid maji girl who just put everyone I cared about at risk.

"I'm not sorry." Trill's voice quavered, telling me otherwise. "I had to come." A slip of paper in her hand told me she'd found the address, probably on Liam's computer.

Stupid, Syd. Really stupid.

"Alone and unprotected." My desire to smack her silly had returned with a vengeance.

"Yes," Trill said. Took a breath. "No offense, but I have no real way of knowing if I can trust you."

Um, what? "Excuse me?" Charlotte growled beside me. "Still? Really? What the hell is your problem?"

Trill didn't answer, just crossed her arms over her chest after an angry adjustment of her glasses.

"Considering you're so worried about putting my coven and my vampire family at risk," I snarled, "this wasn't exactly the smartest move you could have made."

She had the good grace to flinch at that, at least.

Sheesh.

"This little stunt of yours could very well have told the sorcerers exactly where to find your brother, have you thought of that?" What would it take to get through to her?

"I left Owen behind so he would be safe." A moment of fear, gone as fast as it came.

"Did you not hear what I told you when I left you there?" Shaking her was imminent. Like, any second now I'd be rattling her teeth together. "You were both safe as long as you stayed put. But your leaving likely revealed the entrance to the cavern. And the location of your brother." I punched my hip to keep from using my fist on her in my frustration. "Not to mention my friends. I took you in, protected you, even when it meant danger for my family and myself. And you. Don't. Trust. Me." I spun away from her, had to. Stalked off a step. Drew a breath. Caught my temper between my teeth before turning back. "I want the two of you out of Wilding Springs. I'm done playing nanny to a spoiled girl who refuses to accept help when it's offered. And since my assistance is clearly not wanted, you can go back and pick up Owen and get the hell out of my town."

Trill shook, hands clenched at her sides. If she had any plans to come after me...

Tears. Were those tears trickling out from under the shine of her glasses? Were her lips trembling as much as her body? I held myself clenched and tight, unwilling to back off, but starting to feel like a bitch.

"I did it for Owen." She crumbled, hugging herself while Sebastian kindly held her up. "I have to protect my brother."

Sigh. "That's no excuse, Trill." Okay, maybe it was. Would I have done the same, pursued, hunted, Meira at my side? Would I take stupid risks to protect my sister?

Um, yeah.

Damn it.

"He's the important one." Trill pulled herself together, shaking off the handsome vampire leader, wiping at her face with both palms. "I don't care what Nona says, the stupid light and shadow business." Her hands chopped downward as though cutting off the very idea. "Owen is the key, not me."

I gestured to Sebastian, who, in turn, waved off his

vampires, though Anastasia glared at Trill as she flickered into shadow and vanished. Trill didn't move as I approached, just stood there shaking, but holding her ground.

"You never explained what it meant." Anger ebbing, I reached for her, half-expecting her to reject me, but instead she took my hand.

"I know," she said. Followed by a whispered, "I'm sorry."

The only problem with having a temper was the guilt after. And how well I knew that lesson. Oh well. I refused to let it get to me too badly. She was the one who screwed up. Nice to know I wasn't the only one who could.

"Come on," I said. "Since you're here, and now that you're shielded, you can at least see what the fuss is about." I met Sebastian's eyes, caught his nod.

We'll watch, witch girl, he sent. *But dawn approaches.*

Crappy crap on a crap-covered cracker.

Trill missed our exchange, still holding my hand as I guided her quickly down the hall and to the room with the secret stairs.

"There's some stupid maji prophecy," Trill said as we made our way down the tunnel to the maji chamber. "About a light and a shadow—a maji and a sorcerer, born of the same blood. The maji is to be the salvation of the world, but he will be her downfall."

I could see why she didn't want to pay attention to something like that. Not when the meaning was clear enough. She had a job to do, and Owen would betray her. Though I knew, as I'd already agreed with upstairs, if it was Meira and me I'd be just as stubborn about it as Trill.

"He's my brother." Trill stumbled a little as she passed over the threshold into the maji chamber. "I love him. I will do anything I can to protect him." She met my eyes, despair and hopelessness making my heart hurt. "He can't be my shadow."

How much did this suck? Instead of answering, wishing I had some comfort to offer, I led Trill down the winding stone stairs. She didn't seem to notice or care where we were going, head bowed, cold fingers still clasping mine, the odd tear escaping from behind her glasses, which she attacked with a fierceness that worried me.

The moment we touched the last step, everything changed. I felt her energy shift, quiet, the pull of something drawing both of us onward. And as much as it made me nervous, we needed answers and it seemed whatever solutions were to be offered, I required Trill's presence to receive them.

I stayed with her, Charlotte close behind, as Trill approached the slab in the middle of the room and climbed up on it, lying prone, her dark hair spreading around her. I heard her sigh, could almost see the air leaving her lungs as her maji power reached outward—

21

—*the battleground. I rise above it, Trill at my side, Iepa hovering before us, infinitely sad.*

I know you doubt, *the maji says,* and I can hardly blame you. But please believe, no matter the mistakes my people have made in the past, this one we wish to unmake.

A line of demons fall, the ground crumbling beneath them, swallowing them as they scream in agony. Witches shift to save them, earth magic joining with Sidhe.

Your father is correct, *Iepa says.* Not all of us have the best of intentions. Like all races. The formation of the demon planes, the division of their race, was never meant to go on for so long. An experiment? Yes. We've tried for time unknowing to perfect our creations.

Witches die under a cloud of poisoned smoke, choking, lifeless even as the Sidhe retreat from the advancing sorcerers. We're losing, badly.

This can't happen. The very earth protests, heaving and

bucking beneath the feet of the enemy, but for those who fall, ten more take their place.

Are there sorcerers on every plane? *I need to focus, to ask the right questions before Iepa chooses to send us back and leave us on our own again.*

Not yet, *she tells me.* But once they have the light to show them the way, there will be no plane free of their taint. Or their influence.

Trill gasps beside me. That's what's coming? What the prophecy means?

In a way, *Iepa says.* You are the light, Trillia. It is your brother who will betray you and give you over to them. And when that happens, you will become a tool of the sorcerers and they will have what they need to cross the veil.

Trill weeps openly, clutching her chest as though Iepa has torn her heart from it.

Things are moving faster now, *Iepa tells me.* Because of recent events, it is possible the time-table of those you call the Brotherhood could be brought out in the open too soon. If that were to happen, all would be lost.

Helpful. Tell me what to do, then. *All of my frustration rises to the surface as my demon roars her fury, Shaylee writhes with rage and even my vampire core burns with cold white fire while the family magic inside me calls for action.* I can't act unless I know what to do.

You must keep them safe, *Iepa says.* The light and the shadow both. That is your task for now. Only they can decide the fate of all planes, Sydlynn Hayle. And you are now responsible for them.

More freaking riddles? I'm done. *I pull back, shaking my head.* I'm not some pawn in your game, maji. If you want my help, you have to tell me more.

Her face falls into sadness as infinite as the Universe. Alas, *she whispers,* even I don't know everything. But what I know, you know, I swear it.

Something jerks against me, pulling me away, this time not with my consent. I reach for Trill, feel her fingers tighten in mine again, hear Iepa call out one last time.

You must be ready—

—someone was screaming, a name I thought, but it took me a moment to break free of the hold Iepa's vision had over me. As I spun, Trill beside me, half-falling from the stone slab, her arms outstretched toward the exit and the stairs, my body compressed and shifted, power crushing me.

Instinct took over, shields snapping into place, reinforced even as I finally realized, in the split second I needed to adjust, it was Trill's high-pitched cry I heard.

"OWEN!"

The chamber was crowded, or felt that way. Hadn't we been alone only a moment before? No longer, not with Liam and Galleytrot staring in horror, Meira holding Sassafras, grim, tears on her cheeks though she stood her ground. Even Sebastian hovered near, his vampire body glowing white.

None of it mattered. None of them. Not while the young sorcerer stood at the entry with his eyes pitch black, mouth gaping, a hole of nothing while his power pulled me toward him.

Even through my shields, past layers of demon and Sidhe magic, blowing away witch and vampire too. Until I struggled to remain standing, my eyes dimming, the air itself, once aglow with the light of the maji now being devoured by the boy at the door.

Liam flung himself at Owen as I fell to one knee, trying to fight back, no longer thinking offensively, but simply about surviving whatever was happening to him. I could hear it now, the rushing sound of life leaving, of light and goodness being swallowed by the dark.

My Sidhe friend seemed to hang motionless for a moment as time slowed down, stilled, quieted. It was almost a shock when it sped up again, accompanied by Liam's flying form, tossed back like a rag doll from the black engulfing more and more of Owen. Trill continued to scream, but I didn't have the energy to focus on her. Not when Sebastian, face set and power flaring, made a grab for the boy, only to cry out and retreat, panting, skin shriveled and wasted for a heartbeat before it returned to normal.

This couldn't be it, the moment of betrayal. Could it? I'd been caught with my pants around my proverbial ankles, lost in some fiction woven by the maji while the world was falling apart around me. After everything I'd done, every evil I'd faced, I couldn't believe I was about to fall to a boy who I was trying to save.

My demon whimpered, struggling against his power draw where once she roared. Shaylee passed out a moment later while the vampire core of me retreated, hiding herself away. I hardly blamed her, though the family magic stayed by me, pumping out of me, a ruptured energetic artery. I could feel the coven reaching for me, trying to support me, but I shoved them away, blocked myself off. If I was going to fall, so be it. Gram had the other half of the family's power. At least some of it would survive.

Diminished, weak and failing, I collapsed against the pedestal, Trill's hand touching mine.

Wait, she was whole, untouched. I could feel her power inside. More. Better.

I could feel mine. The maji in me, stirring, waking, rising to the surface.

Desperate, I dove into Trill's mind. *We have to stop him.*

She met my eyes, all thought gone, her body shimmering with rainbow light though she didn't act, her mind empty of all but terror and loss. What was wrong with her?

Fine. I'd do it on my own.

There wasn't much, but it would have to be enough.

I teased the maji energy forward, felt around the edges of this creation magic I'd never known lived inside me. Welcomed the stir of the vampire essence as she answered to the warming maji power until strength returned. Enough I could kneel. Stand. Stagger a step forward. Another.

Owen's body shook, a thin cloud of black mist formed around him, thickening by the moment as my friends, magic all, withered and fell as I had. Sparkling energy shone over my shoulder and I turned, caught sight of Trill as she slid free of the pedestal, face now a mask of calm as though some kind of switch had flipped. She approached slowly, a glittering torch of iridescence, the light reaching for the shadow.

This cannot be! Iepa's mental voice reached mine. *You must stop them, Sydlynn Hayle, or your world is ended now!*

She didn't have to tell me twice. No time for prayer the power I'd found would be enough. Instead, I put myself between them, both hands plunging into the black cloud consuming everything, including Owen, and pushed him back, using every ounce of power and muscle I had.

He held his ground, a rock, a mountain, the mist tugging at me, suctioning to my skin, my hair and clothing. Vile, filthy, hungry, it pulled me close, wanting to swallow me whole.

I pushed harder.

Owen's feet slid over the rock, the pressure finally winning as I dug and begged and wept for more strength. Just a little more—

His collapse caught me off guard, sending me tumbling forward on top of him as his feet slid back over the joint of stone marking the entry to the room. Owen crumpled completely, black cloud dissipating in a reeking puff of charred smoke and burning rubber, the scent of destruction and death gone so quickly it felt like I'd dreamed it all. In a rush that made me high and giddy, all of my magic returned, flooding me with so much power I found myself giggling on the edge of hysteria.

Trill fell to her knees next to me, trying to pull me from her brother's unconscious form, but I shoved her away.

"Don't even think about touching him." I didn't mean to be harsh, but we'd almost lost everything, at least according to Iepa's warning, and I wasn't about to allow the two of them a second round.

Liam limped to me, lifted Owen into his arms while favoring his right ankle. "I'm okay," he said. "But we need to get him out of here." Liam paused, distress making him seem very young. "Syd, I'm sorry. This is my fault. I should never have brought Owen here."

I shook my head, letting my power settle, feeling someone rattling against my shields with increasing insistence. Yeah, knew who that was. But I wasn't in the mood to have Gram yell her head off at me.

I'm fine. I flashed her a tight show of what just happened, through a barely-there break in my wards. She tried to worm her way in but I was quicker. *Just let me handle this.*

After a moment, she backed off. Amazing. Or, it meant I was in a whole heap of trouble and she was saving it for when she could get her hands on me.

Lovely.

I turned to Sebastian as Liam began to climb, only to see fury flicker across his face. Why was he angry? Yes, this could have been a disaster, but we'd taken care of it.

If only. "They're here." Before he could explain his cryptic comment, Sebastian flickered into shadow and vanished.

Thing was, he didn't need to explain. I knew exactly who "they" were.

I ran after him, racing up the stairs past Liam, Trill hanging from my Sidhe friend, her eyes locked on her still unconscious brother while Meira and Sassafras chased me, Charlotte bringing up the rear with one hand firmly grasping the back of Demetrius's neck.

Funny, I hadn't seen him during the whole Owen meltdown. Part of me snapped in anger. Surely he, as a sorcerer, could have stopped the boy. And yet, was the old Chosen leader in any mental state to even comprehend what just happened?

No time to deal with him just then. Not when I finally left the maji chamber and reached for the veil, leaping into it for a mere blink before storming out at the front door of the mansion to stand at Sebastian's side.

Where the Brotherhood stood waiting.

23

Belaisle smiled at me, hands folded neatly before him, impeccable suit perfectly tailored to his short, slim frame. He looked more like a smarmy executive out to rip people off than the dangerous leader of the Brotherhood. But it was the empty feeling of him, the way his cold amber eyes showed only a shark's interest in prey that gave me the willies.

"I thought I told you," Sebastian said, deep voice pushing power ahead of it, "you aren't welcome in my house."

Belaisle shrugged a little, stroked the shining black goatee on his chin as though he hadn't just been told to remove his nasty ass from the vampire's turf.

"I'll leave," he said, "when my property is handed over."

My eyes flickered to the horizon and the dying night. We were running out of time. Soon the vampires would be helpless, unable to fight, leaving Belaisle and his Brotherhood to do what they wanted.

Over my dead body.

Gram, I sent. *I need the coven here, now, at the mansion. Tell them to be ready to fight.*

A mental hug as hard as a blow and she was gone.

Okay then. At least I wouldn't be leaving Sebastian and his blood clan unprotected. But it did mean I was putting my family at risk. More than risk. It was pretty obvious Belaisle and his people wouldn't hesitate to do whatever it took to get what they wanted.

How could I throw my coven into battle with sorcerers when there was little chance they could win?

Agony, as hot as a blazing sun, tore through me at the thought of losing even one of my family to the Brotherhood. And yet, what choice did I have?

Being leader really bit all kinds of nasty.

"You're coven won't be able to stop me." How did he know? Duh, Syd. Must have been obvious. Not a mind reader, just an asshole.

"Maybe if you run now, Belaisle, I won't have to humiliate you in front of all your little friends." There were times my mouth got me into trouble. And times when it got me out.

Wasn't sure which this was going to be, but I couldn't seem to rein it in.

Even if I wanted to.

Belaisle's gaze left me, went over my shoulder. I glanced back, wanted to curse. Trill stood there, staring, body shaking even as the sorcerer held his hand out to her.

"You know why we're here," he said to her and only to her. "It's time to come with us now, Trillia."

Did she waver? I reached for her, took her hand. She seemed to snap out of some kind of trance, but pulled away from me, stepping back, refusing to look up even as Belaisle's arm dropped.

"Don't be foolish, girl," he said. "You've run out of places to hide. And you certainly don't want a repeat of what happened last time you allowed strangers to interfere."

So my supposition was right. She'd tried to find help before with what had to be tragic consequences from the burden on her face.

"Why can't you just leave us alone?" Her words came out in barely a whisper, but Belaisle clearly heard her because he laughed.

"You have a great destiny," he said, for the first time coming alive, though the greedy need flowing from him in waves toward her triggered my protectiveness again. "You and your brother."

"No." Owen shoved himself between his sister and

Belaisle, his body pressing back against hers, scowl so deep it aged him years. I'd completely missed him waking. "Leave her out of it."

"Would that I could," Belaisle said, lips curving downward into a sad face before he snapped his fingers. "I'm done talking. We can finish our conversation on the way home."

They were on the move, the small group of sorcerers, in answer to his unspoken call. Only about a dozen, men and women, but none seemed afraid, not even the two I'd faced down tonight. Was it really only hours ago?

Vampires appeared behind them, a rush of shadows closing in, trapping the sorcerers in a half circle between them and the cold stone of the house. But I knew better. While some of the sorcerers might fall, there were enough of them, their destructive magic somehow able to defeat the most powerful of us, the kids were in serious danger.

Go. Sebastian's mind snapped in mine. *Take them.*

No way was I leaving. *The coven is coming,* I shot back. *When they get here—*

They will be too late to save the children. His power pushed against me as he reached outward to his clan. I could feel his magic, the pulse of it, wondered for a moment why he shared so much with me, such an intimate view of himself.

But he wasn't sharing, not on purpose. Thanks to the vampire core of me, he was a wide-open book. He caught my eyes, shock in his before he carefully walled me off.

Syd, please, he sent. *If these children are as important as you say, they must be protected. At all costs.*

Syd. Uncle Frank's mind touched mine, joined by Sunny's. I caught sight of them then, standing behind Belaisle, Sunny's gorgeous face twisted, fangs showing, my handsome uncle glowing with white power. *Take them and get the hell out of here.*

Hesitation held me still while the sorcerers continued their slow advance. I could feel the wall of empty coming before them, the touch of their power, now familiar thanks to Owen's little performance downstairs. We had no defense, no way to stop them. Their power seemed to work no matter what we did against them, that emptiness devouring everything—

Wait. What did Trill say to Liam in the Gate room? About sorcery drawing on the internal power of objects for source energy… or stealing from others. I suddenly understood what it meant.

They destroy to feed their magic. I sent the message to Sebastian, to his vampires, to my friends at my back and my grandmother and our whole family as hope surged in a rush of adrenaline so powerful I had to fight my need to invent a happy dance of my own. *But they have to have a source to make it work. They use your shields against you, drawing on the power you're using to protect yourself. Do you understand?*

Gram's grim answer was another hug while Sebastian flashed his very white, very sharp fangs.

Brilliant, he sent. *Which means we vampires are ideally built to combat them.* His clan's answering joy was almost horrible as they began their own advance.

Belaisle must have sensed the change in the air, a little frown creasing his forehead, because he snapped his fingers again and his people paused. "Surely you won't allow it to come to open battle, Trill? Owen? You know how this will end."

I grinned at him, letting out the exultation, feeling my demon winding up, the earth magic Shaylee commanded sending tremors into the ground at my feet while my vampire watched and waited.

"We could solve this ourselves," I said. "You and me, Belaisle."

Oh, please.

He snorted softly, though he didn't seem overly confident. "Why would I do such a thing?"

"He will never." Demetrius slunk out from behind me, stepping close to the entry, just past the threshold. He hissed at Belaisle who started back a step.

Scared of Demetrius? Really.

But only for a moment, it seemed. Belaisle recovered, smirking his oily little smile, stroking the fuzzy pet he had on his chin. "How far you've fallen, old friend."

Demetrius howled like an animal, dropping to a crouch to pound the ground with both fists like a furious caveman. "No friend!" His words were a shriek, cutting the air with razor sharpness. "Never friend." He shuffled forward further, toes touching the wooden casement marking the line between the front step and the house. So the threshold had a meaning, did it? Were the sorcerers somehow unable to enter, much like uninvited vampires?

Because of the maji?

No time to figure it out. Belaisle flicked his fingers at Demetrius as if dismissing him. "You've ended where you began," he said, disdain making the madman twitch and moan, "as nothing."

We were so running out of time. The sky was lighter, not much, but enough. And I could feel the nervousness of the clan through Sebastian, through my uncle and his girlfriend.

Belaisle turned his head, let his gaze linger in the east before he returned to face me, smile widening.

"Just a few more minutes," he said. "Your dear vampires will be asleep in their coffins, or burned by the sun. And your precious coven? Too far away to do any good." He yawned, checked his watch while my demon chewed and fought for freedom, throwing images of his bloody head in our hands.

You're right. We have to go. I touched Sebastian's hand. *They should leave if we do.*

And if they don't? Gram wasn't letting us keep her out of the decision. *We're almost there.* I could feel her tension, panic. *Just a little more time. But you're right. You need to go now.*

Belaisle snapped his fingers again. "I have the mansion surrounded," he said. "Just hand over the children and we'll be on our way. If not, we'll burn this place to the ground and hunt and kill every member of your family."

Now or never. *Remember what I said*, I sent out again, to the family, to the vampires. *They draw power. Don't give them anything to feed from.* Damn it, I still paused, unsure. I'd never run from a fight before, not when so much was at stake. And this felt like running.

Cold emptiness shoved me backward, eating at my

shields. Time to take my own advice. I dropped my wards, all of them, let the sorcery pass over me, through me, forcing all of my magic to fall passive.

Oh. My. Swearword.

Did it actually work?

Trill cried out beside me, clutching her chest and I knew my time was up.

Heart clenched against what felt like cowardice, I grabbed her arm and Owen's hand. Multiple fingers grasped me from all directions, Demetrius turning just in time to hook his hand around my calf, the others clinging to my clothing as I ripped open the path between planes and slipped into the veil.

24

The library loomed above us in the early morning as I dumped my following onto the grass just past the parking lot. My power wrapped around Trill and Owen as we emerged, blocking off the natural pulse of their magic as we dashed as a group toward the door and down into the Sidhe cavern.

The moment Trill and Owen were safely behind the glowing green wards, I ran out into the hall, Liam hot on my heels. He grabbed my arm, turned me back to face him while Meira joined him, taking my other hand.

"You can't go back." My sister's tone told me she was far more levelheaded about the whole mess than I was. Clearly. Her steady gaze had nothing on the manic need coursing through my veins to go back to the mansion and kick Belaisle's skinny little ass. "Gram will handle it. Syd." She jerked her grip on me, just painful enough to catch my attention. "We need you here."

I shook my head, trying to pull free of her. "You're as strong as I am," I said.

"No, Syd," she said softly, letting me go. "I'm not. And we both know it."

No regret from her, not a trace of blame, despite the anger she'd shown earlier when I'd called Dad alone.

"Meems..." My entire body ached to leave, to charge into battle, though the need was fading as I caught my breath, tried to be rational, if only for her sake. To come up with a logical reason why I should leave them behind to fight.

Yeah, I had nothing.

Liam pulled me into his arms, but I didn't soften, though I quickly returned his hug before sliding free. "I'm sorry. I should never have let Owen talk me into taking him to the mansion." The boy looked guilty himself, though Trill just glared at me. Back to the old attitude, were we? "I made things worse. But you did everything you could. And if there was any doubt before how dangerous those two are, I'd say it's pretty much gone, wouldn't you?"

I shuddered a little at the memory of Owen, the hungry blackness, Trill's answering maji power.

"How did you stop him?" Meira bent to pick up Sassafras who spoke as she did. I hadn't seen him join us, but then again I wasn't exactly being very observant at the moment.

"I found it, buried." Again with a shudder, this one leaving me cold. "The power of the maji. Like Trill. But it's been dormant, I guess, because of my witch magic. And, for all I know, because of Gram's little stunt." Not fair, I knew it. Gram had done what she could to keep our family safe. But when she hid most of her magic inside me before fighting the Purity coven, she'd walled off my connection to my demon, thanks to a geas she implanted to ensure I wouldn't want to keep her power. The result was history. I'd spent my entire childhood, from baby to the age of sixteen, hating my magic and just wanting to get rid of it. Gram spent those years struggling to remember, in the grips of insanity the final battle with the Puritys reduced her to, what it was I had of hers she needed back.

Talk about a mess. Now I wondered what else was lost to me. And what I'd find if I really went looking.

Meira hugged Sassafras close. "We have the bloodline," she said, matter of fact. "So it makes sense. Does that mean the only counter to sorcerers is maji magic?"

"I hope not," I said. "Because if that's the case, we're in serious trouble." The power I'd uncovered had barely been enough to keep me upright, let alone fight the Brotherhood. Which meant even if we could find and train all of those with maji blood, there was a very good chance we'd still lose.

"Trill and Owen are the answer to this," Liam said. "We have to protect them, Syd."

I didn't answer, reaching for Gram, feeling, as the vampire core inside me shivered, the sun rise. *The clan?*

Gone. She grunted mentally and I caught an image of Belaisle backing away from her, his people retreating.

You beat them? Awesome. Way to go Gram. But she was already denying it, allowing me to use her eyes to watch them climb into their black cars and retreat while the coven members Gram brought with her sagged, exhausted, though from what I could tell none of them looked seriously hurt.

No, she sent. *Not even close.* Grim, those words. *They chose to leave. The kids?*

Safe, I sent back. *As far as I know, the Brotherhood can't find them here.*

As far as I knew.

I'm alerting your mother, Gram sent. *This was an open attack on our coven and the vampire clan. The sorcerers have finally crossed a line.* She paused, voice tired, hugging me. *I just hope we're ready for them, Syd. Because if we're not, I have a feeling there won't be much we can do to stop them.*

Happy thoughts.

We needed a weapon. And I was done running.

I marched back through the wards, stomping up to Demetrius who crouched by one of the walls, looking around with terror in his eyes.

"Don't like it," he muttered. "Too much dirt."

"Get used to it," I snapped, in no mood to deal with his loose screws. "Listen up. We need a crystal. And you're going to get me one."

"And you fix me?" That hopefulness had returned, the spark of it in his amber eyes.

My demon didn't fight me this time. Even she knew how much trouble we were in.

"Yes," I said. "But after, remember? The crystal, Demetrius. Now."

"We go," he bobbed his head, reaching for my hand. I stepped out of his range, backing away. "You trust me, we go. I know what you seek."

I paused. We had no idea if it would even help, aside from Demetrius's crazy talk. And if he knew, would he lie, considering his normal appearance hung in the balance?

More, why was he willing to help against his own people? He was a sorcerer too, after all.

I had to know before this went any further. "You could just turn us in." I watched him carefully as his eyes flew wide and he shook his head back and forth, parted lips wobbling with the movement. "You're one of them."

"NEVER!" Demetrius pounded the ground with both fists, body shaking with violent rejection. "NEVER ONE OF THEM!"

Touched a nerve, did I? Not like he was in much mental condition to lie to me, as far as I could tell. I just had to risk it.

"Will it work?" I stopped him as he settled from his mood swing. "Will the crystal help me defeat Belaisle?"

Demetrius hissed, rubbed his ears with both palms as though the very sound of the man's name hurt his head. But when he met my eyes, his were full of hate.

"Yes," he said. Giggled. "Oh yes. He won't stand a chance against you."

I'd just have to take his word for it.

I was almost to the wards when Trill grabbed me. And boy, oh boy, was I sick of being grabbed.

"You're not going without me," she said. Like there was a chance in hell that was going to happen. I choked out a laugh, not even bothering to pull away, or answer for that matter. She seemed to retreat into herself, hand sliding free of my arm. "I have to go with you." Desperation. Need. A fire I hadn't seen in her before, fed by fear.

Had Belaisle some kind of hold over her I didn't know

about? She'd seemed ready to go to him when he called her. But no, it couldn't be. She was the light.

It was her brother I had to worry about.

"You do know my family and the vampires risked everything to protect you so you and your brother could get away?" There were times I came across more harshly than intended. This wasn't one of those. Cold fury sat in a gathering caldera deep inside my chest, just waiting for a chance to explode. "And now you want me to take you out again so the Brotherhood can take another shot at you?"

She shook her head, backed away, face crumpling, but I wasn't done, not by a long shot. "You two," I jabbed a finger toward Owen who came to his sister's side, scowling at me, his anger coming to answer mine, "aren't going anywhere until we figure out a way to defeat the Brotherhood."

Her rebellion was gone, leaving behind a horrible grief, but his was just beginning. "It's not our fault." Like I thought it was. "Stop yelling at my sister."

"When she develops some sense," I shot back, "maybe I'll consider it. In case you're forgetting, Owen, your sister left you behind in her little adventure to betray us all to Belaisle." Trill flinched. This time Owen's face fell too, his only defense fading as guilt replaced anger. "Just stay put and let me handle it."

Trill met my eyes. "I'm sorry," she said. "I really am, Syd."

Yeah. Whatever.

I turned away from them both, Charlotte at my side, taking Demetrius's arm. Now look who was being grabby? I stopped at Meira's side, Sassafras still in her arms.

"I need you two to watch them." Not that I didn't trust Liam, but he was sweet and thoughtful and a bit of a sucker. My sister and my demon cat especially, knew better than to be so trusting. Meira nodded, Sassy's amber eyes burning as his tail thrashed against her side.

"Let me come too," he said.

"Not this time." I backed off. "Meira needs you."

Sassafras grumbled softly, but agreed.

"We'll be back as soon as we can," I said, trying to smile at Liam who looked like I'd kicked him. Even Galleytrot sank to the floor, eyes downcast, ears drooping. "Hopefully with the means to put an end to this, once and for all."

Big words, Syd. Considering I was forced to trust a mentally crippled sorcerer whose only desire not so long ago was to burn me at the stake with the fate of our world?

I had to be out of my mind.

I guess it was going around.

25

I had to see Gram, even if it was only for a moment or two before running off on yet another mad mission. Yes, I could tell from our mental connection she was fine, but after putting her and the rest of the coven in harm's way, I needed to see for myself.

A quick stop at the house found it dark, but only because she was in the basement. And she wasn't alone. I felt them all reach for me as I walked into the kitchen, their relief, the hug of the family magic pulling me close and helping to calm me down way more than anything I could have accomplished on my own.

I left Demetrius at the table with Charlotte to watch over him and descended the stairs into the crowd of witches circling the pentagram. My grandmother stood in the center of it, mismatched sweater and very loud pink pants worn as casually as the highest fashion. I knew part of her peculiar behavior was a mask, a way for her to hide from the world just how much of her still lurked inside, but even I had no idea if the brief jaunts back into nutty old lady were authentic or part of a show she put on for our benefit.

Gram was all business this morning as I eased through the crowd at the bottom of the stairs, letting them touch me, feel my magic, opening to them. And as I joined Gram, turning to face back the way I'd come, I sent out my thanks, surprised to find tears standing in my eyes.

"My coven," I said, throat aching, but voice strong. "Your bravery and strength bring honor to the Hayle name and I am so very grateful I have you to count on every day."

They swelled with pride, almost as one, their relief and optimism passing from face to face, from magic to magic until I felt like the whole room hugged us all.

How I hated to bring them down. But there was so much left to do and while I didn't want to crush their hope, they had to know the truth.

Knowing time was short, and I needed more than anything to escape the house, the coven, and allow Demetrius to fulfill his part of our bargain, I took my time filling in the family. They deserved no less and needed to know, after all we'd been through, after they'd stood behind me, beside me, learned to trust and follow me despite the pressure they were under. Pride and commitment to them drove my tears away and actually brought my own positive thoughts back, despite knowing how far we had yet to go.

They listened without question, nodding, whispering acknowledgment, each and every one of them, from the twins with their withered apple faces and matching twinsets, holding hands while their determination held me up, to the smallest child, their magic wrapped up in mine.

"I'm assuming my plan worked?" I turned to Gram as I finished. "I tried it myself, dropped my shields. The sorcerer seemed to have no effect on me when I did."

She nodded, grunted, balancing on one foot while she tapped out a beat on her crossed arms with her dancing fingertips. "It did," she said. "Goes against all instinct, girl. But it worked." The coven agreed, their eager, familiar faces so dear to me. There had been a time I wanted nothing to do with them, a time the mere touch of their power near me made me sick, want to run. But now I knew how Mom felt, why she wanted this for me.

Family was everything.

"I refuse to put you in danger again." At least, not until I knew if I could come up with something better.

"We're not going anywhere," Estelle said, her twin nodding beside her. As she spoke, her magic stroked mine. Yes. Estelle. For once I didn't have to guess if it was her or her sister Esther. "This coven has survived more hardship than any other, and we're stronger for it." The family agreed with words and magic. "You have saved us from ruin time and again, Sydlynn Hayle. No matter what you need of us, we are yours. Now and forever."

Okay, weepy time. I really had to find a way to get past all this crying business. And yet, as the family pressed close, hands reaching out, smiles all around despite their worry, no matter the conflict we faced, I knew I wasn't alone.

"Go home," I said, sending them love. "Ward your homes and keep an eye open. Belaisle isn't stupid enough to come after us again, not without a clear target." Please, oh please, let that be true. They accepted the kind of lie with the same solid support I'd already felt before coming to me one at a time for a kiss on the cheek, a hug, a kind word, before filing out.

My coven. My family.

Hell yeah.

I'd never been so proud.

When it was just Gram and I, she hooked her arm through mine, pulling me against her side.

"You'll do," she whispered. Poked the end of my nose with her index finger. "I guess."

I needed that laugh.

Charlotte stood over Demetrius who huddled in the corner, almost under the table he'd slunk so low in the wooden chair. His amber eyes peered over the edge, focused on Gram as we emerged into the morning light.

"Well, well," she said. "Demetrius Strong. It's been a while."

Whoa. Hang on.

"You two know each other?" But she was nuts when he was sniffing around as leader of the Chosen, and he was already in demon form and outcast when Gram got her marbles back.

"Ethpeal," he cackled softly, sliding upward in his chair as though rising from the earth. "Hello, Ethie."

Major creepy ickle. But Gram just chuckled back.

"Looks like you got yourself into a bit of a pickle, old salt." Was that evil in her eyes?

He writhed in his seat, eyes turning to me. "She said she'd fix me. Said, Ethie."

Gram caught me staring out of the corner of her eye and winked. "Well then, if that's what she said." She turned to the refrigerator as if it was just another morning, a big smile on her face. "Who wants breakfast?"

"We can't." I turned to Charlotte, nodded. She reached

for Demetrius who slunk from her, climbing to his feet on his own.

"Yes," Gram said while she rooted for ingredients. "You can."

Was she serious? Really?

"Gram—"

"The kids are safe," she said, dropping a carton of eggs and a sleeve of bacon on the counter, kicking the fridge door shut with one spotted sock. Green and purple today. Nice blend with the pink pants. "And you haven't slept in what, almost two days?"

When she put it that way... "Fine, breakfast."

She smiled and patted my cheek, fingers cold from the bacon package. "You know better than to argue, girl," she growled. "I always get my way."

Charlotte's lips twitched. Yeah, she was laughing at me.

Mumble, grumble.

At least I had the time to finally take a shower, though the stink of the Chosen's miserable apartment was long gone at least so I forewent the bleaching of my entire body for a good scrubbing with soap and a scratchy loofa. I briefly considered throwing Demetrius in after I was done, but the effort it would take to clean him up would mean I'd have to shower again.

He could stay dirty.

I descended to the happy smells of morning, wondering how I could possibly just sit down and eat while my mind churned with the need to keep moving. But the sight of Gram standing over my plate, tapping her foot on the tile floor with a wicked looking spatula in her hands made me sit and do as I was told.

She wasn't past smacking me with her weapon of choice, just to prove a point.

And I had to admit, by the time I was done, wiping up the last of the yolk with a chunk of homemade bread, I felt much better. Clean, full and human again.

Well, sorta. Witch, Sidhe, demon and vampire. And maji. Aw, hell.

"Did you talk to Mom?" The remainder of my orange juice chased breakfast as I sat back and tossed my napkin on my plate with a yawn. No sleepy. Not yet. A jolt of power shook me out of the food-induced need for a nap—a good night's sleep, to be honest—and back to reality.

"I did." Gram's mouth narrowed to a slash. "She's not happy."

"With me?" I shrugged. "Let her be pissed."

She sighed. "She's sending Enforcers," Gram said. "But I don't know if they'll be much good."

"We can handle it." At least Mom was doing something. "When they arrive, just fill them in on the shielding thing and have them patrol town. Keep an eye on the family."

Gram's faded blue eyes blinked slowly at me. "While you run off and do something stupid, is that it?"

I grinned at her, leaning close to kiss her cheek. "It's what you'd do."

Gram actually had the nerve to look innocent and indignant. "I beg your pardon." It only took a moment for her eyes to sparkle and her familiar cackle to make me laugh. "You know too many of my secrets."

"Me too." Demetrius smiled at us, chewing, eyes narrow and full of mischief, focused on Gram. "Don't I, Ethie? Don't I?"

Yes, we had to go, but I had time to ask some questions. "Gram—"

She was on her feet already, clearing the table with magic, shoving me toward the door as I stood to face her.

"Out," she grumbled. "Save the world again, girl. Then we talk."

I'd heard that song before. "You better believe it."

The veil welcomed us, Charlotte with a firm grip on Demetrius, as we skipped into the slice between worlds, exiting at the edge of town near where our old coven site used to be. Memories tugged at me, but this was no time to think about the past and the girl I'd been.

"Tell me where to go, Demetrius." I pinned him with a scowl. "No tricks."

"No, no tricks, not from me, nonono." He bounced on his toes, clapping his hands together. "Not far, they aren't far, all the pretty crystals you could ever want. Ever."

"Show me." I'd been playing around with my veil riding, the Galleytrot sniffing thing buoying my spirits, and since I always wondered if I could travel somewhere just from an image of it, this was as good a time as any to find out.

"Here." He threw the picture at me, the sight of yet another mansion, but this one ultra-modern, all glass and cold concrete and white stucco surrounded by grounds manicured to within an inch of hideous. I ground my teeth against the intrusion, but took it before cutting him out.

"Okay," I said. "I'm going to give this a try." I didn't need the look of concern briefly touching Charlotte's face, thanks. "Just hold on as usual, and don't let go." She could have a little freaking faith already.

I grasped for the veil, the image of the house in question firmly in my mind. My demon grunted, shrugged and pulled us in, two heartbeats passing before she dumped us out again into a small grove of trees.

Damn it. The boonies. And no house in sight. I sighed as I scanned the horizon before me, the stretch of forest and winding road, blue sky. Great.

Just great.

"Sorry," I said. "I guess it didn't work after all." I was so sure it would.

Charlotte tapped on my shoulder. I turned to find her looking in the other direction with a little grin on her face.

"Sorry I doubted," she said.

There, behind us, at the bottom of the low rise we stood on, was the very house.

Okay then. *You have a terrible sense of humor,* I snapped at my demon.

She just muttered at me, though her tone was definitely on the side of giddy.

Bratski.

26

I was still trying to decide if marching down to the house was the best course of action when I felt someone reach for me. It was only the barest flicker of a touch, hardly there at all. And if I hadn't been out in the open, mind focused and power gathered, I probably would have missed it.

Reaching back for whoever it was gave me nothing.

"There, see?" Demetrius did a little dance before me. "Told you. Get a crystal now. Then fix me!"

"Hang on." I waited for a repeat connection. Whoever it was, there hadn't even been enough contact for me to identify the power source. Was I imagining things?

Nope, there it was again. I dove after the thin, fragile thread of demon magic, finding Sassafras, Meira boosting him. His power latched onto mine, but so weak, as though he were too far for me to reach.

Or behind the Sidhe wards.

My heart stopped, pounded once as the thread

strengthened and suddenly surged to life, my demon cat yelling my name.

Sass. I cut him off. *What's wrong?* Please, please, tell me they listened. That Trill didn't do what I now feared she'd done, and this time not alone.

They're gone. His mental tone was furious, magic lashing around him while Meira steadied the link, though her power was equally as angry. *Tricked the lot of us. Even me, Syd. Even Galleytrot.* He shuddered. *That maji power of hers, she used it to make false forms, smell, vision, everything. They only just faded now.*

I was trying to talk to Owen, but he was ignoring me. Meira's temper had always been moderate, nothing like mine, but I wouldn't have wanted to be the younger Zornov at that moment. *Turned out he wasn't really there at all.*

Syd! Liam's mental voice reached me as he too stepped outside the protections of the cavern. *I'm sorry, Syd. We lost them.*

My decision was made for me before I even realized I had a choice. *Liam, you and Galleytrot track them. Find them. Meira, you and Sass go home and help Gram. There are Enforcers coming to protect the family. I want everyone out looking for those two.*

I cut off communication, glaring at the house below

while Charlotte waited, as patient as ever, though Demetrius squirmed for attention like a love-starved puppy.

"The kids are gone," I snapped to my wereguard. One of her arched eyebrows rose, but she didn't comment. "Trill and Owen have forced our hand, it seems. Our only choice now is to get a crystal and hope it's enough."

Demetrius slunk low to the ground as I spoke. "He'll find them," he whispered. "We're doomed."

I resisted the urge to kick him. "Just do what you promised," I snapped. "And get me that crystal. We'll worry about the Zornovs later."

Damn her. Damn her.

I was going to wring her neck.

"Come," Demetrius waved at me. "They aren't home yet. Perfect, perfect."

"Wait." I stopped, stared at the house, the empty driveway, the walls of glass shining in the sun. "Whose house is this?"

"His." Demetrius giggled madly, wiggling and squiggling until following his movements made me nauseated. "Himself, of course."

Belaisle.

Could my day get any better?

"You've brought us to the snake's nest?" Charlotte

grabbed him, faster than he was though he tried to dodge out of her way, shaking him by his collar so hard the fabric ripped. "Are you—" She didn't finish, for obvious reasons.

"Yes," I sighed. "He is insane, Charlotte."

She dropped him, backing away a step. "We have to get out of here," she said, voice low and soft like it always sounded when she knew I was in danger.

"I have to have that crystal," I said.

"So send him in after it." She crossed her arms over her chest.

Bossy. "You actually trust him to go in there and steal a crystal on his own with no supervision?" Demetrius crouched in the grass, poking at his big toe and humming to himself. "Seriously."

Charlotte hesitated. "I'll go with him then," she said.

"No." I took a step toward Demetrius who leaped up, ready and eager. "I'm going in."

"I don't trust him." She glared at the wreck of a man.

He whined softly, ducked his head, amber eyes pleading. "You can trust me," he said. "You can, you can, you can. Always trust me."

"You're forgetting the time you kidnapped me and blocked my powers." Sarcasm. My tool of choice. "Or tied me to a stake and tried to burn me alive." That was a fun time, yup, yup. "Or drugged me and stuffed me in the back of a van so you could kill me?" His face crumpled as I went on. "Sure I can trust you, Demetrius. You've done nothing but prove that to me."

He fell on his face, pressing his lips to the tips of my shoes. I pulled back, but he followed, creeping on his hands and knees. "Forgive me, please." He rolled over on his back, stared up at me, all innocence and need. "That was different, was then, before I knew you, knew the truth. Knew everything."

"Such as?" He was babbling. And yet... what did he know that might have changed his mind?

"Mistress," he said. "Just trust, I promise."

Best I was going to get from a looney toon. I turned to Charlotte and her clear protest. "You can stay here if you don't like it."

Charlotte had the good sense not to comment. Because there was no way what came out of her mouth in reply would be anywhere near polite.

Our approach was surprisingly simple. We just strolled down the hill and headed for the house. Demetrius didn't seem concerned and, after Charlotte carefully sniffed her way along, neither did she.

Any attempt I made to check the place out with magic

met with a wall of emptiness, so I was relying on the pair of them to make sure we were clear.

Nervous times.

Charlotte paused once, jerking me behind a tree, when someone emerged from the front door and climbed into a car, black, naturally, before driving off. Demetrius gave me two thumbs up, grinning like a fool.

"All gone," he whispered so loud I'm sure they heard him in the next state. "Just the servants left."

And that was a good thing? Seemed to be, according to him. We bypassed the rock garden as I tried not to allow my gaze to linger on the carefully pruned shrub resembling a giant octopus as we made our way around the back.

"No security?" When the Chosen were running things, Demetrius had the mansion the vampires now occupied wired with lights and surrounded by his people, but the man in demon guise shook his head.

"Nothing mundane. Just sorcery." He moved on before I could stop him, feet silent on the grass, softly padding on the concrete walk as his flip-flops impacted the ground. I hissed at him, but followed, feeling very exposed, though at least Charlotte seemed calm.

Her I trusted. Him? Yeah, not so much.

"Here." He set his hands on a window casing, the vinyl

panel sliding upward, the tall, wide hole almost as big as a doorway. When he let it go, it stuck open, the plastic melted and bonded together, holding the window in place.

Again he moved without waiting, sliding through the gap and into the house. I went after him, biting back curses, only to stop, frozen by horror, as my powers went away.

Just like that. Gone. No demon, no Shaylee, no vampire. No family magic. Not a blessed thing.

Panic? Me? Well, it's not like I hadn't felt anything like this before. After all, I'd been demonless, my witch magic smothered by Gram's, basically rendered inert and latent.

Hadn't liked it then, either. Way less now. My skin did a goosebump shimmy, air gasping from my lungs as I lunged forward and jerked Demetrius to me with a claw-like grip I was sure would leave a bruise.

"My magic." I could barely choke it out past the absolute sense of loss kicking me in the guts over and over again.

He whined, but nodded. "Shielding," he said.

So they hadn't stolen my power? "You're sure?" Because I'd have to kill someone. Probably him. With my bare hands.

Demetrius didn't know smiling at me was the worst possible choice. Was too crazy to understand his faux pas. It was times like this I was so grateful for Charlotte. She carefully pried my hands from around his neck, calm and soothing, putting herself between us.

"We have to go," she said.

I looked back over my shoulder, longing tearing me apart. I could just leave, trust her to bring back what we came for. She'd offered, after all. Leaving was a great idea.

If Demetrius could be trusted...

I had to know.

My demon roared at me as I stepped outside, Shaylee shrieking like a banshee while my vampire calmly told me in no uncertain terms she would never, ever forgive me if I went back inside that horrible house.

It took every single scrap of resolve I had to turn around and climb back through the window.

The quiet made me want to weep, to collapse in a ball and hug myself, but I couldn't. Maybe later. "Let's go."

It occurred to me as we wound our way deeper inside it was probably the worst possible choice I could have made. I was useless to the both of them if something happened, my power gone. Sure, I could do a little damage in a fight with my feet and fists, but I wasn't Charlotte by any means. She could kill someone with a sideways glance. I'd be lucky to break my hand on their jaw.

The more I thought about it, the more reasonable it

seemed for me to turn around and go back outside, to hide in the bushes and wait for my faithful wereguard to make sure the deed was done. I could count on her, of course I could.

What the hell was I thinking?

Charlotte's hand settled on my arm and I let out an involuntary squeak before she covered my mouth with her hand. A wide-hipped woman in a maid's outfit swayed her way past us where we hovered in a partially opened doorway and let her go. I shook myself, tried to pull my act together. We overlooked some kind of foyer and only then did I kick myself for running on autopilot.

Get a grip, Syd.

Demetrius waved at us to follow, drifting along as though he owned the place, the sound of his flip-flops so loud I wanted to strangle him again. But I figured Charlotte would just rescue him and waste my effort, so I crept beside her instead with my hands in fists, waiting for the worst.

It never came. Instead, Demetrius led us to another door, on the other side of a massive spiral staircase, the steel and concrete winding its way up to the second floor. I bypassed it, slipping to his side as he tapped the handle with his fingertips and let us inside.

Light flooded the room. I heard Charlotte close the

door behind us while my eyes traveled upward, taking in the massive glass dome over a large wooden desk, the giant skylight setting the room aglow with sunlight. Demetrius had no such need for sightseeing, instead heading right for a glass case in the center of the space. I joined him, drawn to the glinting facets of cut crystals as he jerked open the curio door and turned to me.

"Ta da!" He held up both hands, a proud jeweler showing off his wares. "You see? You trust me, always."

So far, so not in the custody of the Brotherhood. I took it as a good sign. "Now what?"

His face crumpled from happiness to petulance. "Choose," he said.

Oh. Right. I looked inside, hands shaking a little. The cabinet was more museum display case than anything, four glass shelves holding an array of crystals. "These are all weapons?" Maybe I should just take them all.

But Demetrius shook his head, voice that of a teacher with an exceptionally slow student. "Only one will fit you," he said. "Like mine fit me." Tears welled in his eyes. "Choose, and wisely."

No pressure or anything. "So the Brotherhood has tested all of these against their people?" It seemed odd no one was a match. Some of them were lovely.

He shrugged. "Not all can use them," he said. "Only those with power over stone. But Belaisle hoards what he can't bend to his will."

We definitely had to talk later. If we got out of here all right. And survived the Brotherhood. And found Trill and Owen.

Focus, Syd.

The blue one on the second shelf called my name, but I worried it was the color drawing me in. Oblong, about the length of my palm and relatively flat, it was the only one with smooth sides, no edges. I reached for it, saw him nod, smile before he cackled and grabbed it just as my fingers touched it.

"Watch." He held it up in front of me while his free hand took mine. "Feel."

And I suddenly did feel, magic again. But this was foreign, dark and angry magic, demanding, destructive. It wound through Demetrius and into my hand, up my arm, into the crystal. I wanted to pull away, but couldn't, the draw of his sorcery tying me to him. To the blue stone. It burned with an internal flame, multi-toned, reminding me of the iridescence of the maji power, pulsing in time with my heartbeat while it absorbed what it needed, drawing from my very spirit until it finally flared one last time and went silent.

Demetrius clapped his hands, leaving the crystal in my grip, spinning in a circle. "Done!" He hugged me, the stench of him, something I'd grown accustomed to, so powerful all of a sudden I gagged from the close contact.

Like I had time for another shower.

Crystal acquired. Time to skeedaddle.

But Demetrius had other ideas. "Fix me." His amber eyes went cold as I slid the crystal into the pocket of my jeans.

"When we get out of here," I said, turning to go, already a whole house ahead in my heart, the need for my magic's touch returning with a vengeance.

He grabbed my arm, turned me to him. This time his demon face snapped with anger, the scar on his right cheek taut with fury. "FIX ME!"

Okay, if we'd gone undetected so far, we'd be caught for sure, now. Charlotte cursed in her home dialect and dashed for the door, peeking out to be sure we were okay while I grabbed Demetrius's shoulders and shook him.

Just a little. Honest.

"My power," I whispered though it was really a silly thing to do, considering. "I can't change you back until we're outside the shielding." He relaxed a little, but his doubt didn't leave him. "You asked me to trust you," I said. "It's your turn now."

He sighed, deep and harsh, but nodded. "Please," he said. "Please."

"I promise," I said, really meaning it for the first time. He'd done his part. And I would make sure he had what he wanted in return.

It was the least I could do.

Luck, so far on our side, seemed to be holding. Charlotte nodded as we approached, giving the all clear as Demetrius, now happy again, led us out on his noisy shoes. The staircase passed to our left, the doorway we'd come through on our way to the office still ajar. Home free.

Oh, Syd. Silly Syd. Since when?

Charlotte grabbed my arm shoved me physically through the door, just as the large front entry swung open. I crouched next to her, breathing hard, and watched from the crack she'd left open as Liander Belaisle and his two main goons walked in.

They weren't alone. Not by a long shot. Trill and Owen were with them.

Marvelous. Now what?

"Show these two to their room." Belaisle gestured over his shoulder as he began to walk toward the office we'd just left. Trill hugged her brother with one arm while the pair of sorcerers half bowed to their leader.

Trill. I'd forgotten my maji power in all of this. But no, I couldn't feel it either. I still had to try.

Her head snapped up, eyes locking on mine behind the glare on her glasses. She froze for an instant as I winced.

Hang tight, I sent, hoping the message made it through. *We'll get you out of here somehow.*

She didn't respond. At least not to me. Instead, she turned toward where Belaisle was disappearing behind the staircase.

"Sydlynn is here," she said, pointing at my hiding place. "And she's powerless."

27

Angry? What was angry? Raging? Had nothing on me. More like a pyroclastic meltdown with a side order of *hell no*.

I was not pacing the thick, cream carpet of a second floor bedroom with my hands so tightly fisted I couldn't feel them anymore. Nor was my wereguard prone on the matching comforter with some kind of liquid metal shoved in her mouth and wrapped around her head, the same oozing stuff pinning her arms and legs so tightly all she could do was tremble and stare at me with desperate eyes.

No, we were not trapped, prisoners, turned in by the very two kids I'd done everything I possibly could in my power to keep safe.

Hell. No.

Maybe if I'd had access to my magic, things would have turned out differently, though part of me doubted it. Not after Trill's blatant betrayal pinpointed our location. Charlotte tried to save me, diving in my way, yelling for me to run even as Demetrius's keening echoed in my head as he rushed the two sorcerers coming my way.

I couldn't leave them, but how could I stay? Belaisle reappeared, smiled. Hit me with something I couldn't see but, could I feel it, oh boy, yes. Like a freight train taking out a brick wall while the whole world exploded.

Nighty-night, Syd.

At least when I woke, I was intact. No broken anything. Just a headache and a whole lot of pent up anger I then took out on various furnishings now lying scattered in pieces on the soft, deep carpet.

Even without power, I could still manage to make a mess.

Charlotte's bindings worried me, especially at first. She struggled so hard I thought she might hurt herself. But the moment I touched her shoulder, my tantrum over, she calmed, though the despair in her eyes never left her, not for the entire hour I paced back and forth, checking on her over and over again, trying to pry the nasty stuff from her lips only to have it try to wind its way around my fingers.

I still had no clue what happened to Demetrius. I could only image he was either gone, escaped, or also in Belaisle's custody. And while I really didn't like the crazy demon-man, I'd lost my hate for him.

Besides, I still owed him and I meant to pay that debt.

No windows. Just one door, locked. No amount of pounding on it seemed to elicit a response, not even when I beat on the polished surface with the splintered leg of a rather expensive looking chair. Hit something hard enough against a wall and it will break apart eventually.

So I had a weapon, just in case. The heft of the length of solid wood felt good in my hands. But who was I kidding? Another blow like the one that took me down and I'd be in pain-riddled snoozeland all over again.

The same metal holding Charlotte sealed the edges of the door. So I couldn't even peek out from underneath. Yes, I tried. And the lock was modern, no keyhole to use for spying. Frustration central. At least the vampire mansion had the good grace to offer old-fashioned options.

I decided right then and there I hated modern homes and if I had the chance, I'd take this one apart personally.

Charlotte grunted, body twisting, giving me just enough notice to turn with my chunk of wood at the ready as the door seal sighed open. I leaped for the exit, chair leg at the attack, only to stagger back as Owen fell through, practically into my arms, the pair of us landing hard on the floor. I looked up just in time to see Trill stagger her way inside, flinging my weapon toward the door with all my strength.

Too late, the thing thudded shut, my badly-aimed throw bouncing the heavy leg sideways and almost hitting Trill.

"Watch it," she snapped.

Oh no she *didn't*.

I pushed Owen aside, ignoring his cry of pain as I leaped to my feet and lunged at her. Wanted to grab her, shake her to pieces, scream my head off. Didn't. Went for cold instead, knowing if I opened that can of very antagonistic worms I'd regret it when she was dead.

Well. Maybe.

"What. The. Hell."

Trill's anger was gone as she stepped back away from me, rubbing her arm. Someone must have been gripping it tightly because she winced when she touched it. Either that or her expression was for me.

"You're not supposed to be here." Bitter, angry, yes. But sad, too. Enough I didn't freak out.

Proud of me?

"There had better be a damned good reason why you tossed your only chance for protection to the wolves." I spun on Charlotte who glared. "No offense intended."

Owen stood before sinking to the edge of the bed, hugging himself, not looking at his sister. "I can't believe you did this, Trill. Syd is our friend."

So she acted alone. At least I'd only have one murder on my conscience.

Steady, girl. Steady.

Trill turned from us, facing the wall, shoulders shaking. "You don't understand," she wailed. "I didn't have a choice."

Her brother was on his feet, flying across the room, slamming both fists into her back before I knew his guilt turned to anger. "You did!" He shoved her, hard, Trill impacting the wall with one shoulder, sagging against it, slowly sinking to the floor with her face still turned away, the rocking of her shoulders, the way she clutched her hands to her face telling me, while they were silent, her tears came in giant sobs. "You told me we were going to run, but you led us right to him. Right to him!" Owen stood over her, face mottled red as he yelled at her. "You betrayed all of us, Trill. You betrayed *me*. And now it's all over." He sagged himself, deflating, his internal rage balloon emptying as he spun and put his back to her, so much hurt in him I stepped forward and hugged him to me, though he didn't hug me back. "I can't believe you gave up."

Trill pushed herself to her feet, wiping at her face, glasses dangling from one hand. "I told you," she whispered. "I didn't have a choice. And I meant it."

"Then give me a good reason." Owen pulled away from me, a shot of anger left. "Just one."

She nodded, head bobbing, hope gone. "Owen." She met his eyes at last, hers nearly black with grief. "They have Nona."

28

Not even I could stay mad after that. The thought of Belaisle having Gram in his clutches made me weak with fear. I could only imagine how the Zornovs felt. I'd grown up supported and loved and sheltered whether I liked it or not.

All they had was each other. And their Nona.

"You weren't supposed to be here." Trill shrugged, without anger, without much of anything resembling emotion considering the bombshell she'd just dropped. Though I could only assume some kind of firestorm waited to be born. "Belaisle said if anyone interfered, he'd kill Nona. That we had to cooperate or she was dead." Trill wrung her hands together, voice still calm while her body struggled to express something, anything. "I had to turn you in when your power touched mine." She met my eyes, glasses a little fogged around the edges from the remains of her tears. "You would have ruined everything."

Deep breath. Let it out. And my bubbling fury with

it. All of it, down to the ground, until I felt clean, purified by it. "I understand," I said. "I really do. And it's likely I'd have done the same thing if we had to trade places."

Trill just bobbed her head, though part of me wondered if she heard me. I could only imagine she was doing to herself what her brother had, accusing, beating. What I used to do.

Okay, what I still did. Sometimes. More often than I should.

"Is that why you ran off the second time?" Made sense. I was sure she'd gotten the hint the first time around.

Trill sagged, misery taking over at last. "Yes," she said, harsh, broken. "At the mansion, he reached me, told me about Nona. Let me feel her." She shook her head as she suddenly flared with anger all over again. Personally, I liked it better than giving up. "How could I just let her die?"

Probably wouldn't help to tell her thanks to what she'd done, she'd doomed the whole plane to a horrible ending. I may have been through enough to toughen me up, but even I struggled with the idea of letting someone I loved die in order to save the rest of the world.

Gram again. No crying.

Wait a minute. Gram. "Trill, why could I reach when all of my other magicks are mute?"

She shrugged, snuffled. "I don't know."

Argh. "Yes you do," I said. "Think."

Again the lift of her shoulders, the tip of her head. "Because the maji made the sorcerers too," she said. "Maybe that means our power supersedes theirs."

You have got to be kidding me. "They did what?" Of all the idiotic, irresponsible, short-sighted—

Trill tossed her hands in the air. "I didn't do it," she snapped.

Count to ten.

"Does that mean I might be able to use the maji power to reach my family?" I hadn't even tried, considered it a waste of time.

Panic surged as she rushed toward me, hands gripping my sweater. "Please," she said, more tears trickling. "You can't. They'll kill her."

I turned to Owen who hugged his knees to his chest. "Well?"

His jaw tightened and he turned away from his sister. "Do it," he said.

"Owen!" Trill let me go, face wide open in shock. "You can't mean it. This is Nona!"

"Who taught us who we are is more important than what we feel." He didn't bother to raise his head when he snapped back at her. "Syd, just do it. We can't let Belaisle have access to Trill."

Not like I needed their permission, but it was nice to know he and I were on the same page. "I promise we will do everything we can to rescue your grandmother," I said. "Just, for once, please, can you trust I know what I'm doing?"

Would be a stretch since I was playing it by ear with a bad case of tone deaf. But Trill finally nodded, turning away, neither of the siblings meeting my eyes. Charlotte glared, nodded as I drew a breath and looked inside.

It took a moment to find it, the part of me that was maji. When I'd contacted Trill, tried to warn her, I'd done it on instinct, my usual mode of communication when I wanted to keep information secret. This was more of an exploration and search for power, enough boost to reach past the shielding and someone I knew.

And hopefully who wanted to help. Catching the edge of, say, Ameline's mind wouldn't do me much good. In fact, the ice-hearted sociopath would likely cheer the sorcerers on. And anyone in the Dumont family would be a total waste of time.

Okay, so focus. First, a test. I reached for Liam, keeping the feeling of him in my mind, my heart. Nothing.

Fair enough. This time, I tried for Meira. Her combination of being my sister and a fellow demon might make the difference. Nothing. I could try Mom, but I was tired of screwing around.

Gram. This was so hard. I had no frame of reference, no way of knowing if what I was doing was simply bouncing back from the shields and hitting me or reaching my target. The feeling of the maji power was so foreign, I was lost for a moment, willing her to hear me, more than using magic.

Flutter.

Gram?

Flash—*S*—flicker. *Syd*—spark.

And then, nothing.

I gasped for air, remembering to breathe as I dropped my focus, bending in half, hands on my knees, feeling as if I'd just finished running a marathon.

"Did it work?" Owen didn't sound like he really wanted to know.

"I think so." I flexed my hands, feeling the blood rush into them as I relaxed the fists I'd seemed to be holding tight a lot lately. "I don't know." I slid my hands into my pockets, felt the smooth surface of the crystal against my hand.

Started to swear. Didn't stop for quite some time while I stomped my foot in impotent rage. Owen stared at me like I'd lost my mind, Trill the same, though Charlotte's eyes narrowed as she watched me pull the stone from my pocket.

"I'm an idiot." I held it up, curses cutting off as I showed it to them. "We might have all the help we need right here." I really needed to stop getting hit in the head. It had to be doing some permanent damage.

Owen's eyes lit up as he leaped from the bed and came to me, reaching for the crystal before he smiled a little. "May I?"

I dropped it in his hand. "Knock yourself out. Or better yet, get us out of here."

He studied it, fingers sliding over the polished surface. "You did it," he said. "And stone. I can work with stone." He beamed at me before his face fell a little, but not in sadness again, thank goodness. More in curiosity. "Syd," he said, "did you say you used one of these before?"

"Sort of," I said. "To channel power."

He drew a breath, suddenly tense, lips quivering in excitement. "You're right, Trill," he said. "I didn't think you were, but she has it too."

Trill joined us, eyes locked on the crystal while I scowled at the pair of them. "I have what?"

Owen ignored me, grinning like none of this had even

happened. "This is a power source, yes," he said. "But it also amplifies the user's ability."

I told them quickly about my demon, how Demetrius trapped her in the first crystal. How her power remained though she wasn't diminished. How I'd used it to send the Wild Hunt back into slumber and how, ultimately, Sassafras used it to save Dad, the transformation of his effigy.

"No wonder the effigy is indestructible," Trill said, focused again, without the anger. I had to believe this was the real Trill I was finally seeing, the mask of her temper gone. "All that creation magic channeled through the crystal?"

Owen laughed. "Amazing," he said. "But it wasn't Sassafras's power that made it work. It already had hers in it."

How was anything they were saying not in code? And wait a second. "Hang on," I said. "Creation magic? Sassy killed himself. He used blood magic."

Trill wrinkled her nose. "You witches call it that." She touched one fingertip to the stone before dropping her hand again. "To the maji, using our blood is the purest form of creation, the very source of all energy, of life itself." She fixed me with her brown eyes. "And if you're going to be of any use to us at this point, you're going to have to use it too."

29

I credited the fact my powers were cut off, since I didn't feel a surge of nausea at her words. And yes, I'd heard the geas thing before and was fairly certain it was true. That sorcerers forced a witch to use her power to convince every witch thereafter the use of blood—creation—magic was evil and the very worst crime someone could commit.

Still. The idea I'd have to use it... she couldn't be serious.

Trill must have seen my reluctance. She scrunched her nose at me, glasses twitching, before she sighed and crossed her arms over her chest. "This is how things are," she said, her no-nonsense attitude reminding me of Sassafras. "Crash course, pay attention." Owen shook his head with a little smile. He might have been used to her, but she was pushing her limits with me. If I hadn't needed the information, we'd be having a serious talk about her abrasive nature.

"The maji created everything," she said. "From witches to the Sidhe." I still struggled with the mythos, but let her go on. "From demons," knew that already, "to yes, even the sorcerers." Which made the maji some kind of master race. Why did that give me the creeps? "They even created the planes we live on, and the veils to keep those planes apart." This was all starting to sound even more like religious dogma, but I held my judgment until I could do my own research. And yet, I couldn't argue the maji did have their hands in a lot of different pies. "Though they were—and are—very powerful, they are, like us, only human. At least, in the sense they aren't perfect." Trill paused, let her arms drop. "I'm doing this wrong. Nona tells it better than I do."

Owen just smiled at her. "Keep going, sis," he said. "Syd gets the point."

I nodded for her to continue. "I don't need the fancy version," I said. "Facts do me just fine."

"Okay," Trill said. "The maji made mistakes on other planes and had to leave ours while they were still working on things. From what Nona told me, they meant to come back, but couldn't." More likely didn't. Or were distracted by something shiny. I was growing more annoyed with the almighty maji by the moment. "They left their half-bloods behind, sons and daughters born of our races, to keep things going. But here on our plane, and I'm sure on others," Trill pushed her glasses back with one finger, "the blood thinned over the centuries and much of the knowledge of what maji could do was lost."

"Iepa mentioned they were trying to perfect creation." Shudder. "A few kept the histories." I thought of the chambers under the mansion. "Right?"

Trill actually smiled. "Exactly. Nona's family was one of those."

As mine was supposed to be? Maybe. I nodded again for her to go on while my mind churned.

"With most of the maji spread throughout the population and with no idea who they were or what they were capable of, the sorcerers finally rose up and began their plot to kill off or control each of the bloodlines. They were the last creation of the maji before they left our plane, and the most daring of their inventions. Without the full maji here to control them, the destructive nature of sorcerous power gave them an edge over all of the other races. They used their influence and the lust for control—a byproduct of their magic—to seek out other races here on this plane and find ways to either destroy them or use them for their own gain. Both openly," I thought of the Inquisition, "and covertly, they have been hunting us and destroying our lineage."

"So why haven't those who know better done anything

about it?" I began to pace, aware it was my tick in face of anxiety, but needing the physical outlet.

When Trill didn't answer, I stopped, met her eyes. Only to see hers were downcast and Owen just looked sad.

"We're supposed to," Trill said.

"But?" I looked back and forth between them.

"It's my task," Trill finally said, body shaking as she gripped her elbows in both hands, as if trying to hold herself together. "My destiny. It's why I'm the light."

Whoa. "You're some kind of general?" I guess someone had to be. But Trill?

"I'm the strongest maji born in centuries," she said. "Carefully created, bred to be as close to full power as possible. It's my line that is the purest and has been kept that way, nurtured, until now."

And I thought my life had been predetermined. "Which is the real reason the sorcerers want you."

She nodded, clearly miserable, shoulders slumping forward. "And I handed myself over to them."

"We need to raise an army," Owen said, breaking the sadness hovering around his sister. Her lips wavered as she tried a smile at him, though I knew now there was no "we" about these two. Not after what I'd seen of his power and reaction to the maji chamber. Still, she needed all the support she could get right now. "An army of maji."

"You don't have to fight alone." I had to talk to Mom again. "Other races will help. Maybe not all of them, but I know my coven won't stand by and allow the Brotherhood to commit genocide now that we know it's happening. Why didn't the maji come to us in the first place?" Frustration warred with sorrow. "We could have stood together long ago."

The old argument of fearful witches.

None of our business.

Trill shrugged, probably thinking what I was, but her reply fed my cynicism. "Passing the buck. Turning a blind eye. Who really knows?"

"Doesn't matter now," Owen said. "As long as we can change things before it's too late."

"You're sure others will help?" Trill actually sounded hopeful. Did she really think they were alone in wanting to protect our home? I guess it must have felt that way her whole life. No wonder she didn't trust me, thinking only the maji cared, and just a handful of them at that. Time to reeducate her on the goals and dreams of the rest of us.

Then again, after everything I'd been through, the

rejections I'd faced time and time again when I needed help, I may have been pushing my optimism just a teensy little bit.

Not this time.

"I think I can speak for a number of races," I said without a trace of sarcasm as my multiple personalities supported me, "in saying there are always those who refuse to accept tyranny. When we get out of here, I'll be speaking to all of them personally." Well, hopefully. Both on the getting out of here and the communication. Might be hard to reach a few of them—the Sidhe for example—but I was willing to try. "Once they know this plane isn't the only one at risk," I said, "I know they'll act."

I turned to face Owen. "I have questions for you too," I said. "About what happened in the maji chamber. Your power attacked us. I take it that wasn't your idea?"

He hugged his knees, lips turned down as he met my eyes with his brilliant blue gaze. "No," he said. "I don't remember doing anything. Liam and Galleytrot were ahead of me. I felt weird when I was walking down the stairs, kind of tingly. But it wasn't until I crossed over into the room everything went crazy. I was pulling power into me and couldn't stop it." A tear formed in one eye, trickling down his cheek before he dashed it away with his hand.

"I just want to help," he whispered. "But I can't if I'm a sorcerer. If I'm meant to betray Trill."

"Don't say that." She sat next to him, away from Charlotte.

"I can't help it," he said. "We've known our whole lives. And now that we've seen proof of what I'm capable, I know I have to get away from you."

Trill tried to hug him, but Owen pulled away, backed off, standing next to me. "I can't be with you anymore, Trill. You may have turned us over for what you thought was the right reason, but I'll betray you without even having a choice and ruin everything."

"I disagree," I said. They both looked at me, startled, and hopeful. "Personally, if you're going to betray her, I'd rather keep you close by so we can watch you."

His face fell, shoulders rolling forward as he collapsed a little. "A prisoner."

Trill opened her mouth to protest, but I laughed first. "Silly," I said. "An ally. Think about it." They both watched me carefully as I went on, the idea forming as I spoke. "I'd rather have a sorcerer on our side who could tell us what to expect and help us figure out ways to counter the Brotherhood, even if that sorcerer is part of some prophesy. Because, I'll tell you, things are rarely exactly as you think they are." Boy, had my life proven that one over and over again. "And trying to guess what will happen just distracts from the more important things. Like getting the hell out of here."

Trill rose and came to hug Owen who allowed it this time. When she met my gaze, hers was level and calm.

"You're right," she said. "So what's the plan?"

Because I was the queen of plans.

Yeah, right.

Pacing, it turned out, might be great for letting out extra energy, but it did nothing to quiet my mind. It did do wonders for distracting me from what was important, though. Like the fact we were about to have visitors. If it wasn't for Charlotte's sudden rise in anxiety, I would have been caught completely flat footed. As it was, I barely had time to spin and lunge for the door before it opened and closed again, a large tray of food slid inside in record time before the way out was resealed against us.

Though my stomach ached with hunger, I refused to eat, not trusting what the sorcerers might have done to the food. That didn't stop Owen and Trill from helping themselves. To avoid temptation, I crossed to Charlotte and sat next to her, one hand on her shoulder. She seemed to calm under my touch as I fingered the crystal in my pocket.

And shook myself. "Owen," I held up the rock, glowing blue in the light, "can you free Charlotte with this?"

He stood, half a sandwich in one hand, mouth working around the other, frowning as he chewed. A long swallow later and he shrugged, reaching for the crystal. "I can try," he said as he knelt next to the weregirl, a sheepish smile on his face. "I should have thought of it before."

Whether she would hold a grudge or not remained to be seen. And anyway, if she'd be pissed at someone, it would be me.

His face scrunched up as he focused, the crystal pulsing in his hand, but after a moment he shook his head and handed it back. "I can feel the rock in tune with me," he said, "but something is keeping me from using it. There's a block on it, you know? Like whoever made it didn't want it used until they decided it was the right time."

Demetrius. I was going to kill him when I caught up with him. And I'd enjoy every second of his death.

From the glare in Charlotte's wolf eyes, I'd be fighting her for the honor.

"So can you just use your sorcery and get rid of it?" I waited and hoped, but knew before I asked he'd already tried.

"Whoever created this," he said, "I'm cut off from it. The metal is feeding on itself, in some kind of power loop. The crystal would give me enough boost to cut through, but I'm not strong enough without it and it's blocked." He gently patted Charlotte's shoulder. "I'm sorry."

I sagged to the floor, back against the bed, staring into space as I pondered. "Tell me more about creation magic," I said as Trill chased a mouthful with a gulp of water.

"You're lack of ability is what's wrong with modern magic," she said. "There's no balance. Magic can't be in proper harmony when one branch of it is avoided, ignored, reviled."

I found myself nodding slowly. "Makes sense." Now if only she could tell me how to convince my mother, the Council and every other witch on the planet. Especially when I knew the moment I cleared the shields and had access to my magic again, the old revulsion would come rushing back.

How had Ameline and Batsheva managed to break the geas? I'd just have to track them down and ask them.

They could join Demetrius in line once I was done asking questions.

"How am I going to convince every witch blood magic isn't worthy of a death sentence, but is a part of their power they need to bring balance to the world?" I shook my head, the weight of the task pushing down on my chest, making it hard to breathe. "And that sorcerers are the reason for our problems, magic users witches can't even feel?"

"There's more," Trill said, though I could tell she was trying to stay calm, a certain level of gloom hovered around her. "The sorcerers have their own version of creation magic. But theirs is aimed at total destruction."

Naturally. Things were just getting better and better, weren't they?

"Sorcery taps into the innate power inside objects," Owen said over his own bottle of water. "Where witches and others draw their magic from the elements, sorcerers pull power from inside objects, destroying them as that power is used up. Each sorcerer has different gifts, depending on what items they can access. Like stone, wood, metals, etc. Only a rare few can use all of them."

"Are you one?" His nod made me sigh. Of course. "And Belaisle?"

Owen shrugged. "I don't know," he said. "But I will assume, since he's the leader here, that's the case. Usually those with the most power rule."

He was right about that. "And this sucking of energy?" I thought about the defense I'd finally come up with, dropping our shields so the sorcerers would have nothing to feed their magic. "That's part of it?"

Owen set his bottle down, looking a little ill. "Nice way of putting it," he said. "But yes. We siphon power from objects, but also from others. The power you have to offer is much greater than some inanimate object."

"Vampires," I said.

"More like thieves," he said. And didn't look happy about admitting it.

Okay then.

"If witches had access to all aspects of their power," Trill said, "their creation magic could bring them in balance and help deflect that aspect of sorcery. But when you are out of balance, there are holes in your magic, places where a sorcerer can worm his way in, open cracks power can be leeched from."

Shudder.

"Nona's been warning us our whole lives," Owen said. "About the fight that's coming. But even she couldn't tell us what we were supposed to do, outside the fact Trill is meant to lead the army of maji."

"And the Brotherhood?" I eyed the last bottle of water with some longing though I refused to give in to my thirst. "From what Sassy said, I take it they aren't a new organization?"

"This incarnation of them might be," Owen said. "But they've been around for a long time."

"Are there good sorcerers?" I wasn't sure why the thought struck me, but there had to be, right? Not everyone could agree with Belaisle and his aim to take over everything.

Owen crossed his legs, peeling the label from his bottle as he thought about it. "I guess there must be," he said at last. "But we've never met any." He looked up, held out one hand. "Can I see the crystal again? I might be able to shatter the hold on it if I try hard enough."

I held back. "This is the only one we have," I said. "What if you break it?"

He laughed, a bright and delighted sound, more like the Owen I'd first met, sweet and almost carefree despite his circumstances. "I promise," he said. "I won't."

Good enough for me.

"Besides," I said as I tossed it to him, "that's what trust is all about. Sharing information." I stared hard at Trill whose ears turned red. Was I laying it on thick? Hell yeah. Served her right. "Trusting each other is the only way we're going to get out of here."

Point taken. She even nodded.

If only her acknowledgment made me feel better.

Man, I was slow on the uptake. Just as Owen opened his mouth to comment, Charlotte started her writhing dance as the door unsealed and swung inward. I leaped to my feet, not ready, as the big sorcerer with the crew cut and the CIA look gestured toward me.

"Mr. Belaisle wants to see you," he said.

I cast a flickering glance at Owen, catching him easing the stone into his pocket. Probably for the best he kept it while I spoke to the big boss. No way did I want Belaisle to know I had it. That was, if Demetrius hadn't already told him.

I could only assume that wasn't the case. Belaisle would have taken it from me long ago if he knew I had anything of power in my possession. Feeling slightly in control with that single upper hand, locked up as it was in Owen's pocket, I followed Big and Grumpy out of the room to the sound of Charlotte howling behind her gag, the echoing pain of it only cutting off when the door sealed shut behind me.

This trip through the house was a little different. No sneaking, for one thing. Though the view wasn't much better, in my opinion. Seen one multi-million dollar mansion, seen 'em all.

And, not a shocker, I ended up back in the central office with the big skylight and the cabinet full of crystals. My heart did an "oh noes" when I entered and found Belaisle standing in front of it, hands clasped behind his back, staring through the glass at the collection.

He knew.

We were screwed.

But when he turned to face me, his silken, well-oiled smile on his lips, he simply gestured for the goon to leave us as he crossed to his desk, an ornate and oppressive piece of posturing furniture, perching himself on the edge of it with flair.

Sigh.

"Welcome to my home, Miss Hayle," he said. "How lovely for you to visit. I hope you're enjoying your stay?"

Arrogant ass. "Not so much," I said, my best casual chic mustered at the last moment despite the fact I wanted to jerk the ugly clump of hair from his chin and feed it to him.

Syd. Temper.

His smile didn't waver. "You can imagine my surprise to find you here. How resourceful. Tell me, did you really trust that horrid old troll to lead you to me?" He snorted softly into one hand, a flashing gold and emerald ring the size of a dinner plate catching the light as he did. Belaisle was nothing if not a show off. "I'm honestly shocked to discover Demetrius Strong is even still alive. Especially after what you did to him." He clapped slowly, three times. "Bravo on destroying what remained of his very damaged mind."

"I'm happy to oblige," I said. "Care for a sample?"

He waggled one finger at me, tsking. "Now, Sydlynn. Be nice. I've been nothing but hospitable since I discovered you in my house, unwelcome. What would you have done to me in the same position?"

I hated to admit it, but he was right.

"You'd be dead now," I said with a smile. "So I guess that proves I'm smarter than you."

Way to prod the dude with all the power. But from the way he flinched slightly, I made my point.

Wasn't done, either.

"Did you have fun?" I crossed my arms over my chest. "Playing with the family?"

His sudden snarl erased the film of genteel he'd adopted. Belaisle stood abruptly and crossed to me, getting in my personal space.

"Your weakling coven and pathetic blood suckers are no match for my Brotherhood."

"Sounds like you're trying to convince me," I said, flicking an imaginary piece of dust from his lapel. "Or yourself, maybe?"

This was too much fun. Too much.

Really, I shouldn't have been giggling inside. Serious business and all that.

Belaisle swung away from me, body tense. "We'll see who comes out on top when we have the time to wipe you out."

"Oh, right," I drawled, letting humor into my voice, knowing I was shoving him as hard as I could, but unable to stop myself. "You're too busy taking over the world first. Well, just so you know, Belaisle? Now that we're aware—thanks for that, by the way—we won't be standing around waiting for you to get your act together before we kick your sorry asses from the pedestal of arrogance you've built yourselves."

Boo-ya.

He didn't answer. Hmmm. I was used to my brand of bad guys boasting their ways into corners they couldn't dig themselves out of. Belaisle simply returned to sit on his desk, though his smirk was long gone.

"Perhaps you and your coven are willing to step into something that you can't handle," he said, "but what about the rest of the witches? Are you so sure they will side with you against us, when it's only your word, and that of a pair of silly children, against us?" He stood, began to pace. I wasn't the only one, it seemed, though, as he did, his mood lifted. "You seem to think we've become so focused on our goal we've forgotten how important it is to ensure our success."

I didn't like the sound of that. "If you've hurt any witches—"

He laughed at me then, good mood returned. "Hurt? Harmed? You're a fool, Sydlynn Hayle. You win more wars with sugar to lure your bait than attacking with fire."

"You're still recruiting witches?" My mind skipped, shuddered, started running a mile a minute until I dragged it back under control. But yes, of course, it made total sense...

Belaisle's eyes gleamed, his posture relaxing. "I'm sorry to say, you now know too much. Well, you did before now, but any further guessing will only take you closer to answers I can't afford you to have. Which means, my dear, as much as it pains me," yeah, I could see it really pained him, "you're going to have to meet with an unfortunate accident."

It was almost funny. I guess he had no idea about my little immortality issue. Made me feel a little better on one hand, but very, very anxious on the other.

I had to talk to Mom and find out who was working with the Brotherhood.

Idiots.

"You realize my coven knows exactly where I am," I said. Bluffing? Not sure. Gram might have had enough to go on. "Do your worst and see where it gets you."

He nodded slowly. "Ah, yes. Well. If you're not fearful of losing your own life, there are always other means of keeping you quiet. After all, not everyone in your family has access to the power you do."

He did *not* just threaten the people I cared about.

Did *not*.

"Your mother is in a precarious situation." Belaisle toyed with the giant ring on his hand. "And your grandmother, with all that unprotected traipsing around the countryside she does. She really should be more careful." Red fury bloomed inside me, burned a hole in my chest, made my whole body sizzle and vibrate. "And your little sister. Meira, isn't it?" Something cracked around me for a moment, the shell casing of power holding me confined shattering for a single moment as molten rage drove knives of hate into my heart. "Our files tell us she has many young friends in the witch world. Some of them we know quite well."

My demon howled in the distance, the touch of her welcome. I reached for her, felt the touch of her power and welcomed the tint of amber fire over my vision as she rose to greet me.

Belaisle shrieked suddenly, a little girl sound of fright, face bone white as he dropped his posturing and slid sideways, scrambling behind his desk, one hand pointing at me, shaking.

"Bruno! Emil!" The door behind me slammed open as Belaisle cowered.

She fought to stay with me as more emptiness smothered me, forcing us apart, the feeling of her cut off despite my absolute need. I was left panting, bent in half, still staring at the Brotherhood leader with absolute fury, ready to tear him apart with my bare hands and eat his bloody heart.

Laughing all the while.

He regained his composure almost immediately, but I knew then he was a coward, held it to me like a gift, grinned at him with all my teeth bared and my contempt tearing a window open into my soul.

"Take her somewhere quiet and kill her." He turned his back on me, a slight tremor in his voice. "I don't care how, but make it look like an accident."

The two bullies approached, though I could feel their matching fear. When they tried to grab my arms, I yanked free and took a further step. Belaisle spun back to me, fear flickering in his eyes.

"I'll see you soon," I said, blowing him a kiss. "For dinner."

He blanched as I turned and strode out, the two sorcerers piling on more weight until I stumbled from it, unable to continue my forward momentum without them carrying me.

Kill me, huh? We'd just see about that.

32

My imminent death should have given me more concern than it did. If only I could die. These schmucks were obviously totally unaware. Turned out Belaisle's files weren't quite as accurate as he thought they were.

Creep.

The pair guided me toward the back of the house, near where we'd entered in the first place. I needed to figure out a way to break free of their magic, only able to use wishful thinking they might slip up and take me outside.

Even they weren't that stupid. Or arrogant. Or any combination of the two.

Was still worth hoping though.

Instead, they led me into the large, stainless-steel kitchen and toward what had to be the basement door.

"How you want to run this?" Bruno, had to be. The big lug-like sorcerer goon's voice made me shiver, my head still so heavy my eyes were forced to observe the floor under me as they half-carried me along between them.

Emil, his long and lanky partner, shrugged, the feeling of his action running up my arm he clutched too tightly. "Drowning?"

Bruno must have been pondering, because he didn't say anything until his hand reached for the door handle. "I hate the drowning ones. All that gurgling." A goon with a delicate stomach? "How about fire?"

Flinch. Memories of being burned at the stake ran through my body in an electric current of denial, limbs jerking in response.

Emil chuckled, a nasty sound full of bile. "Fitting, yeah? She's a witch, right?"

Bruno didn't answer, just laughed along with his brother idiot, the door almost hitting me in the face as he pulled it open. Blackness stared back, a row of wooden stairs under my sagging head, my feet making thudding sounds on the risers as they dragged me down into the cool damp of the basement.

Now, Ahbi told me I was immortal. Dad, too. Sassafras. And I had no reason to doubt them. But as Bruno and Emil placed me in a wooden chair at the back of the basement, a small, filthy window letting in the only light, the scent of gasoline strong in my nose as a can was brought forward, the cap twisted off, I had my doubts.

I might have been immortal, but would I heal? Or survive the burning with scars for the rest of my very, very long life? Images of Uncle Frank's half-melted face, the result of being left in the sun, churned terror in my guts, irrational fear taking over as panic tried to drive my limbs to move.

Something scuffed near me, a polished shoe, a pant-leg clad in a designer suit. A stream of liquid poured out around me, forming a puddle on the concrete as the sorcerer circled me, creating a ring of combustible fluid before lifting the canister to waist height.

"Time to fry," Emil said.

Panic set in. Mind-warping, heart-attack-inducing, agony-filled panic that drove every single coherent thought from my brain as the metallic clink of a lighter being flipped open took up my entire Universe with one soft snick.

This could not be happening again.

Grunt. Thud. Scuffle. Another grunt, this one ending in a sigh. Emil half-turned, the can of gas falling to the floor to gurgle out its contents as he lunged out of my line of sight. The pressure on me decreased enough I could raise my head, peer into the darkness.

Bruno lay crumpled against one wall, blood oozing from his nose and the side of his mouth. Two figures fought in the black, just out of sight, enough I knew someone was on my side. I fought the remainder of the sorcery holding me down, felt the edges tear as Emil crumpled and fell, toppling backward into the puddle of gas.

I found my feet, able to move again, grasping the wooden chair for support, ready to use it as a weapon. Two pinpoints of amber fire stared at me from the shadows as Demetrius oozed out of the darkness and smiled at me, white teeth flashing in the dimness.

"Saved you," he said. "Fix me?"

33

The temptation to just leave, run, get the hell out of there was so powerful I was shocked at my own lack of courage. Mind you, I'd been through a lot, thanks, what with having no contact with my magic and almost being burned alive and all. But it wasn't like me to cut and run.

Time to slice myself off a little piece of slack. I drew one deep breath after another while Demetrius forced chunks of stone into the sorcerer's mouths, the rock seeping outward like Charlotte's gag, more of the concrete slices forming bonds at ankle and wrist. I could hear him whispering, muttering to himself, while the two men groaned before falling totally silent.

"Would kill them," Demetrius said softly to me as he turned and smiled the expression of a happy child, "but Belaisle will do much worse."

I was all for that.

"Need to go." He grabbed my hand, started to tug on me, leading me to the stairs. "Out, out, out."

Our hustle to the kitchen helped me burn off my panic, shook me loose of the fear I'd almost succumbed to. Enough that when he tried to steer me toward the door I resisted, pulled back, though my heart longed for the fading day outside.

"The others," I whispered. "We have to take them with us."

Demetrius grumbled. "Out," he said.

"Yes," I said. "With the others."

He was going to fight me on this, I could tell by the way his face scrunched up, his eyes spitting flames of amber.

"Fix you," I said. "When we save the others."

That got me what I wanted. Demetrius snarled at me, but bobbed a nod and darted for the interior door.

He was going to get us caught.

I really needed to practice what I preached and learn to be more trusting. He was a sorcerer after all, no matter the health of his twisted mind. Once again he led me, cautiously but quickly, through the mansion until we were winding our way up the spiral stairs to the second floor. The house was oddly quiet and I could only imagine Belaisle had his people out and about, doing their dirty duty, undermining the fabric of magic use on our plane.

My imagination was running away with me.

I didn't even recognize the door, but Demetrius had no problems choosing the correct one. He unsealed it with a touch and, within moments, we were back inside my prison, Owen gaping at us while Charlotte's wolf eyes faded to human. I gaped at them, trying to understand why Owen was sitting on her where she lay, almost to the door, gouges cut out of the carpet under the heels of her boots.

"She went after you," Owen said with what sounded like apology in his voice. "I tried to stop her, but she's really strong."

I crouched next to her, holding out my hand to Owen. "The crystal." He dropped it in my palm before I spun on Demetrius. "You want me to fix you?" I thrust the stone at him. "Fix this first."

He turned sideways, away from me, eyes darting all over the room. "I made it," he said, "for you."

"You made sure I couldn't use it," I snapped back, so far down the end of my rope I'd be strangling him with the remains any second now. "Undo whatever you did or our deal is off."

Demetrius lunged for it, took it in his hand, eyes full of sorrow. "Needed to be sure," he said. "Needed to be fixed first." He squeezed it in his fist, the blue light dancing between his fingers before he handed it back to me with so much anguish in his face I knew he'd done as I asked. The moment the crystal touched my skin he buried his face in his hands and sobbed.

Didn't matter. I wasn't paying him any attention. Not while my demon suddenly howled to life, Shaylee screeching at the top of her lungs, the vampire essence surging outward and into the crystal.

Whole. I was whole. *What are you doing?* I reached for the magic my vampire core was giving up, but she buffeted me aside.

What is necessary, she sent. *You used to trust me. Don't let that faith waver now.*

Trust again. I felt along the edges of her, how she wasn't reduced, not in the least, by what she'd done.

But the crystal now pulsed with life, the magic of the maji, humming happily in my hand with dog-like adoration.

I reached for Charlotte and her bonds, pressing the crystal to her gag, tried to sever the magic holding her captive. But no matter what I told the crystal heart thudding away in my hand, it didn't understand. It tried, even cried gemstone tears inside its shell, a tiny soul wanting to do what I asked.

I just didn't know what to tell it.

"Owen." I pressed the stone into his hand, gritting my teeth against the inevitable loss letting go of the crystal meant for me. "You try. I'm getting nowhere."

Horrible, horrible emptiness. My hand spasmed as I released the crystal, the blankness returning. And now I had an extra burden. It felt as though I'd let another life leave me. Like I needed even more identities but no, this was different. My vampire created another vampire, a life, one I was now responsible for.

Lovely.

Owen seemed tense, unhappy, but he moved to do as I asked. His eyes flew wide as the crystal pulsed in his hand. "Incredible," he said. "All this power." His gaze met mine. "You scare me sometimes, Syd, you know that?"

I didn't get to respond. Demetrius hissed at us, turning to grab my arm.

Owen looked up in shock as the door began to unseal. He had just enough time to shove the crystal into his pocket—no, I needed it!—and push me toward the crazy man before the last of the seal died away. Demetrius shoved me under the bed as I heard the door handle snick.

"You're next." A new voice. I couldn't see anything.

"I'm coming." Owen.

"Leave my brother alone." Trill was back. Good to know. I wanted to risk a peek, go after Owen for the crystal and access to my power, but Charlotte was still bound and I needed her fully operational if I was going to take on the sorcerers.

I heard Trill grunt and the door bang shut, the hiss of magic as it sealed up again. Demetrius squirmed his way free, me pushing him out of the way, to find Trill staring at the door with clenched fists at her sides.

"Free her." I pointed at Charlotte, dragging Demetrius forward, hands shaking in shock at the loss of my power again. "Owen has the crystal so you're all I've got."

He bobbed his head and went to work while Trill turned to face me.

"You're all right." Her voice was dull, washed out. "He said he killed you."

"I had help." I pointed at Demetrius. Owen might not have been able to break the hold on the metal gag and bonds, but the wily old sorcerer didn't seem to have the same problem. I watched in sick fascination as Charlotte's gag began to dissolve, retreating, falling away as powder from all three points until my bodywere was on her hands and knees, coughing up the last of the goop as it rained down in flakes the moment it touched air.

"We don't have much time." I knew Belaisle would soon start to wonder where Bruno and Emil were.

"He wouldn't let me talk to Nona." Trill wrung her hands together, tone still dead and lost. "I begged him but he laughed at me."

There wasn't much I could say.

"What if she's dead?" A wail crept into the girl's voice. "Because of me? And now we're in their custody because I let them manipulate me over her and she's already dead?"

I reached for her, but not just out of sympathy. She had to pull it together if we were going to escape. But it wasn't my touch that calmed her down.

Charlotte hacked up the last of the gag and fixed the girl with a glare, wiping her mouth with the back of her hand as she crouched, eyes flashing to wolf and back again. "What if they never had her in the first place?"

Trill froze and, to be honest, I did too.

Oh, hell no.

"I don't smell the woman you speak of," my bodywere said, climbing to her feet, flexing her hands as if they pained her. Which I imagined they did, considering how tight her bonds were. "Her scent clung to you when you first arrived, fading with time. But that smell, it's nowhere in this house."

"I heard Nona's voice." Trill's eyes pleaded with Charlotte behind her glasses.

"Voices can be faked," I said as gently as I could.

"No one of your bloodline has been near this house," Charlotte growled with absolute certainty. "Your grandmother was never here."

34

I caught Trill before she could crumple, tears pouring down her face.

"This is all my fault," she said.

I wasn't about to argue with her, but I kept my mouth shut considering the timing.

Demetrius was at the door, unsealing it, amber eyes fixed on me. "Come," he said. "Time to fix me."

No argument from me. Except we were still shy one of our number.

"I can't just leave Owen." Trill tried to pull away from me, ending up in Charlotte's reach.

From the expression on her face, the weregirl didn't care a scrap what Trill wanted and I couldn't bring myself to blame her. Charlotte had just endured a very bad day and the wolf in her seemed ready to act on her own whether we were part of her exit or not.

"We're leaving." Charlotte's hand clamped down on Trill's arm. "Now."

The girl dug in, tears turning to fury. "I need to know Nona's not here," she snapped. "You could be lying so we'll leave. Your loyalty isn't exactly a big secret or anything."

Oh boy. Charlotte's normally calm demeanor snapped in half, a dried up and dusty wall her wolf was tired of hiding behind. Her alter persona emerged, face lengthening into a snout, eyes huge and full of cold rage.

"I said," she growled in a voice that echoed with the howl of a wild animal, harsh with an accent, "we're leaving." She snuffled the girl whose anger faded to fear at the sight of the werewolf begging for release. "And I swear to you, maji child, if you betray us again, your light will be extinguished once and for all, without your brother's help."

Trill squeaked a protest, but that's all she managed as Charlotte dragged her to the door and snarled at Demetrius.

"Lead the way," she rumbled, face returning to human. "But the same warning stands, old man. I'll kill you without a moment's thought."

He snarled back, but grunted and spun back to his work.

I probably should have told Charlotte to back off, but I just didn't have the heart.

She'd earned a little fun.

We'd just reached the top of the staircase when Demetrius stopped, dropping to a crouch, looking through the iron railing at the entry below. I slid up beside him, Charlotte, now fully human again, still clutching Trill so hard the girl winced from the contact.

"Your place is with us." Belaisle stood below, at the base of the stairs, Owen before him with two guards flanking him. No sign the sorcerer had any idea I was free, so at least we had something. Without the crystal and my power, I couldn't act against Belaisle. But I wasn't willing to leave the boy behind in the care of the Brotherhood either. All I could do was hover there and hope Owen would come to us.

I'd just have to deal with Belaisle later.

"I'll never join you," Owen said, voice strong, sure. "You can threaten me all you want, threaten my sister and the people who have helped us, but we know our duty. We'll stop you, somehow."

So much courage. I found myself grinning even though Owen's stand was pretty empty. Trill stared down at her brother with a fierce kind of love and loyalty and I wondered how their grandmother managed to instill so much faith in the two of them, faith in each other, considering their destiny.

Belaisle finally waved at Owen. "Take him back to his sister," he said. "If they don't comply with my orders, kill her."

Owen's face settled into a mask of anger. "You won't kill her," he said. "She's too valuable."

"You're wrong," Belaisle snapped back. "Neither of you has any value. Believe it. And with her dead, the last hope of the maji dies with her." He laughed. "You think we can't find another with maji blood to part the veil for us? Foolish boy and your pathetic prophesy."

Belaisle turned, swept really, away, heading for his office with his perfectly coiffed hair and impeccable pinstripe suit. We'd see how cocky and collected he'd be the second I was out of this cursed place.

The thought of facing him with my full power made my mouth water.

Charlotte hissed at me, retreating from the sightline of the stairs and I half-turned to follow her. We could retreat to the room now, pounce on the guards, maybe take them out before they could warn Belaisle. Make a clean break and tear this place apart from the outside.

At least, that's what my brain wanted to happen.

The reality wasn't under my control.

His amber eyes alight with flame and a howl of fury on his lips, Demetrius Strong took matters into his own hands, flinging himself forward to attack the approaching sorcerers.

The first went down without a sound, mouth gaping open as the former Chosen leader landed on him, legs wrapped around his chest, arms flung around his neck, gaping mouth flashing those very white teeth. Owen didn't hesitate, lunging forward toward us, Trill grasping his hands and pulling him after her as Charlotte spun and landed a bone-crunching kick to the second guard's chest.

No, I wasn't kidding. Bone definitely crunched under the heel of her heavy boot, ribs at the very least, if not the man's sternum, giving way to the ferocity of her attack. I let her have her head, the wolf half emerging again, foam dripping from her fangs as her snout elongated, talons hooking from her stretched and knobbed hands.

"Get them out." She snarled those three words just before she threw herself at the third guard who was already turning to retreat, his feet tangled in the toppling man she'd just disabled while Demetrius's power sucked the life out of his captive.

The sight held me for a moment, watching as the Brotherhood sorcerer's face withered, his skin shrinking and wrinkling, eyes bulging from his desiccated face. I only broke free of the horrible sight when the first man Charlotte attacked finally crashed his way to the marble floor below with a heavy thud and the ring of metal as his boot struck the railing hard enough to make it sing.

Time to go. I reached for Charlotte to pull her along with me only to find myself falling away from her as she spun and grasped my arm, thrusting me backward away from Demetrius and the lifeless corpse he released. I caught a glimpse of movement at the bottom of the stairs, a rush of suited bodies, locking eyes with Belaisle just before Charlotte's iron grip pulled me past the corner and out of the line of sight.

So much for a quiet getaway. I wrenched my arm free of the weregirl, spinning to race beside her, Demetrius on our heels while the spiral staircase echoed with shouts and pursuing footfalls.

As we turned a second corner, taking a left down a narrow hallway, I spotted Trill and Owen at the end of it, both frozen. They turned toward us, Trill's face scrunched in anxiety. As I looked up and past her, I realized why.

No exit. Just a large window overlooking trees, a very tall floor up from the garden below. We were trapped.

Charlotte seemed to think otherwise. She didn't pause or hesitate, grasping my arm again before she dove between the two kids with her feet out in front of her. I'd been slowing down, losing momentum, but her powerful grip carried me forward with her as the glass shattered under the pressure of her blow.

I was flying, out and slightly upward in a slow arc. At least, it seemed slow. Everything hung in the evening air, the soft tinkling of breaking glass playing music around me, Charlotte's snarl counter-point. Fear took me, shook me hard, collapsed my lungs, forced my mind to the past—

—*falling and falling, the shining mountain flashing past me, the red-tinted stone of the Parade below as I plunged to the ground*—

—my demon screamed as we cleared the threshold of the shields and tore open the edge of the veil, pouring Charlotte and I into it. My feet touched ground a heartbeat later as that same tear deposited the pair of us on the grass outside the house, glass raining down in a sharp-edged shower as I looked up to see the gaping gazes of our three companions as they leaned out the window to stare at us.

"Don't." I clenched my teeth and balled my hands into fists, wincing at the pain in my right where a shard of glass slit the skin. "Ever." I reached upward, jerked my hands apart, opening a rift in the veil just outside the window. "Do anything." I held on tight as the three tumbled forward into the gap. "Like that." My demon writhed and howled, so agitated I could hardly contain her. "Ever. Again." I turned on Charlotte as Trill and Owen collapsed at my feet out of the gap my demon made, Demetrius sliding free to crouch next to them. My wereguard stared me down, the wolf in her eyes defiant.

"We'll see," she said.

Speechless rage saved her life. That and the shouting from above, from the back of the house, all around us. I threw up a shield on instinct before swearing softly and letting it fall again, knowing my wards were worse than useless.

Belaisle and a pack of his sorcerers ran around the corner of the house, skidding to a halt in the dew-wet grass, glaring under the light of the white overhangs scattered through the garden. They must have arrived back at the mansion after Demetrius freed me, though with the perpetually empty feeling of the house, there was no way of knowing how many of the Brotherhood to expect. "I don't know what you think you will gain from this," Belaisle said, panting to catch his breath. "Return the children."

Like I'd stolen them or something. The anger I'd aimed at Charlotte found a new playground, fed by the pent-up frustration of the last few hours. I let my demon out, heard her shrieking even as Shaylee reached deep into the earth and released her fury, the ground shaking so hard the sorcerers staggered and even Owen reached for his sister for support. My vampire remained silent, but just as upset, making me wonder what trick she had up her sleeve.

Though I knew I could do little to damage the sorcerers, my show seemed to have the desired impact. Maybe Belaisle's people weren't used to opposition, or perhaps they doubted their own abilities. For whatever reason, they shrank back from me, tripping over each other to retreat, though a sharp order from their leader brought them, anxious and on guard, back again.

"I believe I owe you a killing," I said. "Since your effort failed, it's my turn." I let my demon's power circle him, snuffling at his scent, lapping amber flames around his legs. He flinched, but didn't move, so at least I knew I was getting through to him, no matter his abilities.

Epiphany. Shielding didn't just give them power. It gave them power over us.

I laughed in his face, patting his cheek with the flames, a stray wisp snaking out toward his goatee.

"Might want to put that out," I said as the hair began to smoke.

Belaisle cried out, slapping at his own face, the tip of his beard crumbling in his hand. When he met my gaze again, I knew I'd finally pushed him to his edge.

Bring it.

Before I could test my theory further, Owen leaped in front of me, the crystal pulsing in his hand like a baby star, fingers reaching for me as he did. I suffered the touch of sorcery, the devouring magic pulling me into Owen's world while Belaisle's eyes flew wide before narrowing.

"Thieves," he snarled. "So this is the way of witches?"

Owen spun on two of the Brotherhood easing their way closer, despite their fear, pulling me along with him. The black mist formed around them, the same mist I'd seen in the maji chamber, only this time it was thicker, more like fog, clinging to their legs and arms, wrenching them forward. Both men sagged to their knees, eyes wide and full of black, mouths hanging open as Owen's had. Only it was he who took their power, flowing faster and faster into him, through me, until he stood inside a roiling ball of black, my body struggling to gag, spit out the churning shadow. My arm disappeared into the cloud, only his shoulders and head exposed, and the crystal held up before us.

"Stop him!" Belaisle's order was ignored as his people backed off. They were even more afraid of Owen than they were of me.

"Now you see!" Owen turned from the two sorcerers, his power leaving them be as they sagged to the ground with a pair of matching sighs. They weren't wasted like Demetrius's opponent had been, at least. "You see what I am? Why I will never join you."

Belaisle reached for him, face falling into a parody of welcome. "But this is the very reason you're meant to be one of us, Owen, my boy." He eased forward a step, compulsion in his words even I felt through the connection with Owen. "You are to be our greatest warrior, our most powerful leader. You will be worshipped and loved for all ages and nothing will stop you from having what you want."

Owen swayed a little. What hold did Belaisle have over him? I squeezed his hand, strengthened our connection, and Owen stilled.

"Liar," Owen said, holding the crystal out. "You want me to join you? I want you to join me." Belaisle coughed softly. No, choked. Black mist poured out of his mouth, rushing toward us. Three sorcerers threw themselves in their leader's path, taking his place, disrupting Owen's focus. The boy backed off as Belaisle leaned over his knees, gagging and panting for air.

"Kill them." His words were a wheezing gasp. "Kill them all!"

They might have been afraid of me, terrified of Owen, but there were dozens of them and more appearing from the darkness around us by the moment.

Enough.

Gram, I sent, feeling her latch onto me in desperation. *We need help.*

Just come home, she shot back.

I could have. Just torn open the veil and rode it with my small group, escaping. For now. But Belaisle wouldn't stop and I needed him to know chasing us, pursuing us further, was a very bad idea.

Just help, I snapped at her. *Or stay out of the way.*

The family magic surged in answer as the coven cried out in fury.

The air beside me shuddered as Sebastian appeared, Gram in his arms, Uncle Frank and Sunny on his other side. I could feel the clan arriving, the coven with them, circling the Brotherhood, penning them in.

Remember, I sent, *they can't hurt you if you don't shield. And doing so means your power works on them.*

Joy, fierce and hot as the family called up their magic while the clan flickered in and out of shadow, white spirit magic crackling like lightning.

Trill spun on me, glasses crooked on her nose, brown eyes full of fear. She was going to do something stupid, I could totally tell, but Owen was already being pulled out of my grip, his hand no longer locked in mine as she grasped her brother in her arms and shoved the two of them between Belaisle and me.

"Where is she?"

Damned fool girl, what was she doing? But the smirk on Belaisle's face told me. Still full of himself, still thinking he could win. The pulsing light of the crystal faded, cooled, and I understood at last why Owen had taken my hand.

My crystal. His power. Rather a wicked combination.

As for Belaisle, I was a little surprised at his continuing arrogance. Either he was unaware I'd discovered the secret to fighting his kind or he just didn't have the brain capacity to believe he could lose.

About to prove him wrong.

"Where's who?" Belaisle took a slow step forward, his people closing in. Only now they were split in focus as the coven and the clan pushed against them with magic and rage.

"Bastard!" Trill threw the word at him, as sharp as any knife. "Where is our Nona?"

"Your precious Nona." Belaisle brushed at one sleeve as though he wasn't standing in the middle of a fight he was about to lose. "Ah, yes. The old woman. I recall now. She died badly, I'm afraid."

Trill shuddered, Owen's black mist falling to pool at his feet as the star inside the crystal faded to a pinpoint of light.

"You killed her?" So much pain in those three words. I actually worried Trill was broken.

And I needed her functioning.

I needn't have worried she'd fall apart, not after years of heartache and running. But what she did do shocked me so much I didn't fight, didn't think to, as she turned and grasped my hand, the same one Owen held, our connected grip slippery with the blood still oozing from my cut and tapped into my magic.

Not the same. At. All. Weird. Awful. Painful. Stomach clenching—

Awesome. We locked together, her power to mine, creation magic feeding us, swelling between us in a storm of magic.

Owen's power made me sick. Hers filled me with joy.

Like this, Trill sent, spinning out a shield, but not a shield, not like anything I'd ever made before.

But felt? Used? Oh yes.

I followed her, added my power and experience with

such materials as the two of us created a plane wall, a veil of our own in a half-circle dome with our little group inside.

The. Most. Incredible. Thing. Ever.

Ever.

This is what magic is meant to be, Trill sent, her heart singing in tune with mine, no matter what we faced, the music of our magic filling us to the brim.

Yes. Of course.

Belaisle and his sorcerers attacked, throwing power at us, drawing on the veil, or trying to. But there was nothing for them to feed from, quite to the contrary. The rubbery slickness deflected their magic, sending it flowing away to be absorbed by the world around them, their effort wasted as Owen lifted the crystal and opened his own magic, taking my other hand, the blackness surrounding him surging to new life.

Light and shadow came together. In me.

"Are you really ready for this?" Belaisle staggered as Owen's power snaked out, dividing into multiple branches, touching more and more sorcerers as he poured magic into the crystal and sucked even greater amounts back to it. "Sydlynn Hayle, are you ready for war?"

I smiled at him, laughed, couldn't help myself. Felt the balance of my power as the creation magic tied tightly to all parts of me, destruction her happy sibling. "Are you, Belaisle? I'm starting to think you're having second thoughts about me."

So. Freaking. Awesome.

And then the stupid Enforcers had to show up and ruin everything.

Black-robed witches were suddenly everywhere, filling the sky overhead, blue power crackling as they slammed up a dome of magic around the entire group of us, coven, clan and Brotherhood.

As if they could ever contain me. Yeah, right. Still, seeing them had an effect, at least. I pulled free of Trill, our veiled dome collapsing, Owen's magic leaving me as I stepped away from him as well, the realization of what I'd done erasing all the good feelings.

Blood magic. No matter its real name or purpose, it was still an offense punishable by death.

Oh, crap.

Way to break the law with hundreds of witnesses, Syd.

"You will cease your conflict, under orders of the Council of North American Witches." Pender settled to the ground, striding forward with three other Enforcers at his back while the rest continued to circle above us. Power touched me, power I knew intimately, but I didn't have time to wonder why he was there, his delicious magic on the wrong side.

"Your Council has no sway over me or my people," Belaisle snapped, pulling the ragged edges of his arrogance around him.

"Nor mine," Sebastian said.

"Perhaps not," Pender said, "but I am authorized to end this conflict one way or another. And if that means arresting all of you and sorting it out later, I'll do so."

"Try it," Belaisle said. "The battle you end here will mean the beginning of a war. Unless."

Pender paused. "Unless?"

"You allow us to leave." Belaisle actually backed up a pace. "Neither of our people are prepared to begin something we can't finish."

Hell no. "You let them go," I snarled, surging forward, "and you're only making things worse for us later."

Pender fixed me with a glare. "Done," he said. "Though our Council Leader has a message for you."

Belaisle snarled something under his breath, but nodded.

"The next time you interfere with coven business or attack witches or vampires in her territory, she will see to it personally you and your little Brotherhood will be disbanded permanently."

Mom and her empty threats. Except now I knew how to beat them. Still, as my temper cooled a little, maybe she was right. First things first—finding all of the Brotherhood's nests so we could wipe them all out at once.

"Please." Trill let go of her brother, holding out her bloodied hand. Pender stared at it for a long moment while the girl focused on Belaisle. "Where is Nona?"

He looked like he was going to stay silent, but finally blurted, "I don't know." My, my, how sullen and bitter he sounded. "She was never in our custody." A gleam, a moment of triumph as he finished. "But we're very close to finding your brother."

"Liar!" Owen surged ahead, Trill catching him and holding him back, though she seemed floored by Belaisle's words. "He's dead."

"He died with our father." Trill hugged Owen to her, their hurt locking together, building walls no outsider could break through.

"If you say so." Belaisle's feral gaze settled on me. "You can have the brats for now," he said as his people gathered behind him while the coven and clan chose their side, falling in ranks behind me. "But don't get too comfortable." He sniffed, ran his arrogant gaze over Pender. "At least I'll know where to find them when I'm ready for them."

I glared at Pender who ignored me. Just here to break up the fight, huh? Yeah, nice backup there.

"Consider this a benevolent gesture," Belaisle said, heavy ring flashing as he gestured toward me grandly. "But don't push me. And stay out of my way from now on." His smirk returned. "Maybe your witches will survive another century or so before our new order is imposed."

"You're really going to just let him leave?" I prodded Pender with my power. "After he's threatening us openly like this?"

The leader of the Enforcers didn't waver. "I have my orders," he said. "And you, Leader Hayle, have yours."

I stood there, shaking and overflowing with frustration, hardly containing myself or the rage of my alternate identities as Pender dropped the blue shielding and let the sorcerers walk away.

Belaisle, I sent in a tight whip of magic. *I have my own warnings. Stay away from my family and from Wilding Springs. And if I ever see your ugly ass again, you're a dead man.*

Impotent, empty, but I had to. I turned my back on Pender, met Gram's gaze. Her eyes flickered from the retreating Brotherhood to me, speculation in her eyes. And anger.

Oh, yes. And anger.

"Shall we go home?" I tore open the veil with a snarl from my demon, Charlotte's hand taking one of mine, Trill's in the other. "I trust you can return my family the way you brought them, Sebastian?"

He nodded slowly, a frown creasing his handsome face. "Coven leader," he said.

I felt Pender approach, his mind reaching for mine, but I wasn't in the mood. Demetrius's hand hooked around my ankle as I dove into the veil and rudely slammed it shut behind me.

Mom's mind was closed to mine, no matter how hard I tried to reach her. I stood in the back yard where I'd stopped my forward motion from the park after dumping all of us near the edge of our property, the whoosh and sigh of vampires arriving and departing with coven members echoing behind me.

Give me the silent treatment, would she? We'd just see about that.

As much as I agree with you, Gram cut through my irritation as she strolled to my side, striped socks soaked by the early-evening rain I'd missed, *give your mother a little slack. And go see her in person if you're planning on reaming her a new one.*

Brilliant idea.

"We have to go." Trill pulled away from us, hovering with Owen at her side, the glow of the crystal still shining in his hand. "You heard Belaisle. They'll be coming after us. And if they don't have Nona," a single bright spark, that, "we have to get to her before they can track her down for real."

"On your own?" Sebastian strode from the dark, holding out his hands to her. "When there are those of us who would risk everything to protect you?"

Had already.

"Remember what I said?" I let my temper cool, saving the really good yelling for Mom later. "About trust? And letting us help you build your army? We're all in this together, Trill." Even now, more than ever, considering how our magicks worked so well together.

If Mom would just turn us loose, maybe we could send the Brotherhood packing.

Trill hesitated at least, didn't bolt off like I figured she would. "I wish I knew what to do," she whispered at last.

My anger swiftly refocused to the one person who could give us answers. "Come with me," I said, offering her my hand. "Iepa has a lot of explaining to do."

We left Owen behind for obvious reasons, Gram in charge of putting coffee on and settling the coven in the basement for a debrief while Sebastian accompanied us back to the mansion. As much as I would have loved to watch the coven make small talk with the large group of vampires their leader left behind as a show of solidarity, the sheer ridiculousness of it appealing to my rather odd funny bone, I was much more looking forward to yelling at someone.

And the maji woman who had orchestrated all of this would do.

With the remainder of the clan on guard around the mansion just in case Belaisle didn't honor the orders of my mother—I was sure he gave her edicts about as much weight as I did—I descended into the chamber below with Trill on one side and Sebastian on the other, Charlotte trailing along behind.

As usual.

Sebastian seemed pensive, quieter than normal, and the attraction typically affecting us both had worn dull enough I noticed. I reached for his hand, felt his fingers tighten on mine and remembered, pulling away again to examine the injury that fed Trill's power.

The cut was gone. Healed, as though it never existed. Trill noticed me looking from where she followed behind, her voice echoing softly as she spoke.

"Creation magic," she said. "Tied to the power of the maji. You're almost there, Syd."

But where exactly was I going?

The floor of the bottom chamber seemed to hum under

our feet as we crossed the threshold. The slab itself glowed with iridescent power, calling us closer. I went with Trill, Sebastian holding back, as the maji girl walked forward, eyes locked on the empty bed of stone. Her gaze lifted, pinpoints of the same rainbow power now glowing inside her brown eyes as she reached for my hand with one while pressing her fingertips to the stone with the other.

Without thinking, I mimicked her motion—

38

—I gasp for air as fire explodes around me, a line of demons falling back, their power recoiling from the group of sorcerers rushing in to kill them. Fear takes over as I lash out with my magic, calling for the creation power I'd felt before, only to find it hollow and echoing, the full brunt of its ability lost to me though I have access to just enough to save my life when the sorcerers turn the demon's own magic on them, burning them alive.

I stagger free, no sign of Trill or Iepa, the battle raging on around me. My feet skid in blood, over the bodies of fallen Sidhe, their endless lives now done, witches collapsed among them, demons, vampires sagging to ash blowing in the air, making my eyes sting, tears rushing to flow and clear them.

My mind can't fathom the sound, white noise pressing against my ears, pounding inside my head, the roar of an angry ocean surging in waves of death around me. I spot Trill, crouched and weeping, and rush to her, bending over her, pulling her to her feet and out of the way of a bolt of *lightning as it sizzles its way past us and into a cluster of vampires.*

I turn away, I can't watch as the odd bolts of electricity tear the undead soldiers apart.

You know what you must do. *Iepa appears, tears on her face, quiet pain almost an insult in this place of dying. But she's not talking to me, not even close.* You were born to lead the maji, Trillia Zornov, and unless you begin your task, begin to gather your army now, this, *Iepa's arms rise as she turns and gestures around her,* will come to pass. And everything will be destroyed.

Trill shakes her head while Iepa's eyes lock on mine.

Denying your fate will not make this go away, *she says.*

I find myself laughing, clutched in the arms of hilarity fed by hopelessness, bending in half to hug my ribs as I half-sob, half-cackle. I know what running from my destiny feels like. I can totally empathize. But Iepa is right.

We all have to grow up sometime.

You, Sydlynn, are almost complete. Your time will come, the time when you must stand with Trillia and be her connection to all that is.

That made a whole lot of sense. I don't know what you mean. *I wish I did.*

You must accept your creation power, *Iepa says,* despite

the false prejudice of your people. *I feel my body begin to rise as she gathers us to her, drawing on her power to raise us above the battle again. I'm happy to be out of it, and yet it's almost worse in a way. I can now see clearly, from our elevation, just how many of our people are gone.*

And how many of the Brotherhood remain to fight.

You will both be needed when the day comes to battle. *Iepa's magic hugs me, calls to me, feels so familiar I want to weep for its loss when she releases me.* Sydlynn, you have done your duty for now, protecting Trill from the Brotherhood. But she needs to move on if she is to fulfill her destiny. And you have your own job to do.

Trill bows her head. I will obey, *she says.*

I feel myself moving, away from the battle, the cool air and smell of stone reaching me as we cross back to the real world.

But not without a warning. Trill, Iepa says. You have thought Owen was your shadow because he is your brother and that is the prophecy. But Belaisle is right. There is another—

Demetrius crouched in one corner of the kitchen, keeping out of the way as I said goodbye to the last of the coven, sending them home with smiles and hugs and many thanks, their vampire transportation met with the same level of gratitude. I had many more smiles in return from the undead clan than I expected and wondered if maybe the old class boundaries were finally breaking down.

Would be nice. I liked it when everyone got along.

It wasn't until Anastasia pressed a cold kiss to my cheek and swept off with the twins Demetrius finally wormed his way out from under the table and came to me, a soft whine escaping his throat, Adam's apple bobbing in time with the rise and fall of his cry.

Charlotte moved to block him immediately, but I waved her off, taking a seat at the table with Gram watching from where she leaned against the counter, her favorite green mug in her hands, cooling tea untouched as she observed.

Sassafras leaped up beside me, Meira coming to watch

as I gestured for Demetrius to join us. He perched on the edge of a chair, amber eyes begging me while his hands folded and refolded on the table before him.

"Fix me." Not a question, not a demand. A request.

"Are you sure you should?" Meira ignored him, a hard edge to her voice. After all, he'd had Nicholas kidnap her from her own room and shattered Dad's statue, forcing all of us into a chain of events that drove Dad to the Second Seat on Demonicon. I didn't blame her for being angry, or Sassafras for the swish of his silver tail, or Charlotte for the way she stared down at the pitiful wreckage of a man with distaste. I knew the weregirl would happily take him out back and do away with him if I asked her to. Even bury the body deep enough no one would ever find it.

But looking into his eyes, feeling his need, allowing my demon to reach out to him and snuffle his power, more, the core of his spirit, even she relented with a soft sigh.

"I'm sure," I said. "Give me your hand."

I had no idea what I was doing. After all, my demon did the original deed while outside my person. But I was sure she'd take over when the moment came, and personal contact seemed reasonable.

He reached for me, chipped black nails, more claw-like than human, slid over my skin, the heat of his fingertips scalding with fever. Eager but flinching, turning his head away, Demetrius trusted me and opened his power wide and empty.

Good enough for me. My demon slid inside, around him, pulling out what she'd left behind, drawing it back to her, absorbing that which made him like her on the surface. But only on the surface.

I watched in fascination as his skin paled, eyes fading through the color wheel from amber to yellow to green and finally, the piercing blue I remembered, while his demon horns retreated into his silver hair, the cherubic smile returning to his face as his pale skin settled to a more natural tone.

The scar remained, but was far less noticeable, his delight pulling it wide enough it dimpled his cheek. Demetrius examined his free hand carefully, looked down at his chest inside the filthy t-shirt he wore. His fingers slid over his hair, feeling for horns, came up empty. The beaming excitement he fixed on me was enough to make me smile back.

Demetrius Strong, once my enemy, never my friend, clutched my hand to his face and wept.

"Thank you," he whispered, blue eyes full of tears. "You fixed me."

"I promised," I said. "A Hayle always keeps her promises."

He bobbed his head, pulled me closer. "I'm not your enemy," he said. "And I'll prove it to you, someday." More coherent already, the man in him emerging now the demon was gone. But how much of him remained and what would his recovery mean for me? "For now, a warning." He glanced sideways at Gram. "She won't give up," he said. "Not ever. Even now she plots against you."

"Who?" Sassy's tail twitched though I didn't need the answer to know who he meant.

"Batsheva." Her name was a terrible whisper. "But when the time comes, I will do what I can to make sure you have warning. And help from her side."

I wasn't holding my breath, but I nodded before retrieving my hand. "Thank you."

He lurched to his feet, eyeing Charlotte as he headed for the door as though expecting us to stop him. And I probably should have. He had a great deal to answer for, insane or not. But Gram's slow nod to me was all the encouragement I needed to let him slink out the kitchen door and away into the night.

"Syd," Sassafras said.

"You're nuts," Meira growled. "I would have tortured him for everything he knows."

I grinned at my feral sister, my furious demon cat.

"One disaster at a time," I said.

I retreated to the basement as Trill and Owen came downstairs, both showered and dressed. I needed to do the same, but wanted a moment alone.

They helped Meira make dinner, my sister the perfect hostess I'd never be, as Gram and Sassafras joined me downstairs, my bodywere hovering at the top to give us privacy.

I filled them both in on what happened with Trill at the mansion, Iepa's warnings and how I was to break the most sacred of our laws if we were to defeat the Brotherhood.

Already had.

"No one said a word." Sassafras paced around the outside edge of the pentagram. "Not one of the Enforcers, none of the family. You used blood magic tonight, Syd. And no one said anything."

Hard to forget about that, as much as I wanted to. I absently rubbed at the spot where window glass had opened the way for Trill's power—and mine—and tried not to panic.

"They won't," Gram said, eyes narrowed to slits as she tapped her toes on the floor. She'd changed her wet socks, now in purple feather slippers that left little bits of themselves behind as she tippy-tapped. "And I can venture a guess why."

We both stared at her, me hoping for something that would keep me from the stake. And the flames. And Mom's disapproval.

Didn't know which would be worse, honestly.

"It didn't feel like blood magic." She looked back and forth between us. Sassy thought about it. Shook his head.

"You're right," he said. "It felt different."

"Balance." I breathed outward, mentally sending thanks to Iepa, even though I was still miffed with her. "When all of my power was used as it was supposed to be used, I had balance."

"So no one knows." Gram hugged herself, did a little jig. "And no one will find out." A pointed nail jabbed at the two of us, two sharp stabs into the air. "Ever."

I wished it was that simple. "Gram, I have to talk to Mom about this. We need to find a way to break the geas or next time the Brotherhood will win."

It wasn't their magic I feared now. Just their numbers. And the witchly unwillingness to listen to reason even when it meant extinction.

"Agreed," Gram said. "But slowly, girl. And carefully. Or we'll start our own little internal war, won't we? And the Brotherhood wouldn't be happier if we starting tearing ourselves apart, doing their job for them."

"While they continue to recruit witches to betray us from inside our covens." Gram paled, lips tight in anger, Sassafras thudding his tail against the floor so hard I worried he might hurt himself.

Not much to say after that. I joined the family for our very late dinner, but retired to the shower myself and my bed just after midnight. I could hear everyone downstairs, the kids settling on the couch, Trill arguing with Meira they weren't taking her room, Gram's grumbling as she put her own foot down.

My family. My home. What wouldn't I do to protect them?

Including using blood magic?

The house had just settled when I felt his touch on my mind. I moved silently, slowly, not my usual break-neck, headlong flight down the stairs to the back door. Didn't matter. He was waiting for me anyway, in his black robe, dark eyes troubled.

"You were there." Silly, I'd felt him, behind Pender, the weight of his need for me to be a good girl and play by the rules. Like I'd not recognize him or something.

"I'm sorry," Quaid said. "I couldn't help." He sounded truly agonized over it. "We had our orders."

"You shouldn't have been involved," I said. "You're in training, not a full Enforcer."

"Your mother didn't have many of us to choose from." He shifted, uncomfortable. "Aside from Pender, we were all trainees."

Interesting. "And the rest of her army?"

"Doing what they're supposed to do," he said. Snapped. "Following the Brotherhood."

So Mom took my warning seriously.

"Well, thanks for dropping by." I couldn't bring myself to even open my power to him. Not because he'd lied to me about Payten. Not because he'd stood by when we could have struck a big blow on the Brotherhood. But because he chose the wrong damned side.

I have no idea how we would have parted if Trill and Owen hadn't chosen that moment to sneak through the back door and into the yard, freezing as they saw us standing there.

"Hi," I said. "Nice night for a walk."

The backpacks Meira gave them from her stash were hung over their shoulders, bulging with stuff. Owen looked guilty, ducking his head, but Trill just faced me down.

"You know we have to go." She shifted her hand on the strap of her bag. "Iepa was clear about my task."

I nodded slowly, sadly, feeling tired and suddenly much older than my nineteen years. I'd lived lifetimes already, it seemed. How would I survive living forever?

"I still think you should stay," I said. "Let us help you find Nona. Do more research into the family lines." Liam's department. "And we're supposed to work together." Had. And it was amazing.

"We are," Trill said. "But she also said it was time to go. And she's right." Trill reached out and hooked one arm around Owen, pulling him against her. "I've denied my fate for too long. I have a job to do." She smiled, a little smile, but enough Owen did too. "I promise we'll see you soon."

I joined them, hugging first Trill and then her brother, resigned to letting them walk away though my heart begged me not to. Yes, she was irritating at times. And yes, he was a sorcerer and dangerous no matter how much he wanted things to be different. But it felt like I was allowing them to go into trouble alone.

Just went against everything I'd been taught. Family. It was all about family, wasn't it?

"Where will you go?" I ruffled Owen's hair, kissed his forehead while he hugged me hard.

"To find Nona," Trill said.

"And our brother," Owen finished for her. "He disappeared years ago, with our father. We were sure they were both gone. But now..." Owen's brilliant eyes brimmed with hope. "We need to find him." His hand slid over mine as he pulled away, the shining blue crystal settling in my palm. "Thanks for letting me borrow it."

I tried to give it back, despite the surge of power I felt as it reconnected with the magic inside me, but Owen shook his head, closing my fingers over it.

"It was made for you," he said. "I can't use it without you. Besides, you're going to need it to access your sorcery."

Um. What?

Trill rolled her eyes. "Just dump it on her, why don't you?" She pushed her glasses up her nose before shrugging. "You need to know," she said. "The rest of it."

Wasn't sure I wanted to. But since when was my life boring or anything?

"You wouldn't have been able to use it, or the other one, unless you were a sorcerer too," Trill said. "And I already knew you were anyway. Remember what I said? How you were so close?"

I nodded, feeling Quaid drift closer, listening, though

I wasn't sure I wanted him privy to whatever was about to hit me like a ton of bricks in the chest.

"You're maji." Trill was almost breathless when she said it.

"Yes," I said. "I knew that already. Remember?"

"No, Syd," Owen said, squeezing my hand around the crystal. "Not just one of the bloodline, though yes, you have their blood. You are *becoming* maji."

Hang on just a dang minute—

"You would be full maji by now if you hadn't had your growth stunted." Trill sighed. "But your evolution is almost done. You only have two pieces missing, two last magicks to assimilate."

"Your creation magic." Owen stepped away, to stand next to Trill.

"And your sorcery." They linked hands, the light and the shadow, watching me.

"Someday," Trill whispered, "you will join them, the ranks of the Undying. And you will be a creator like no other."

Tears seemed appropriate. Yelling and screaming even. Not this horrible tightness in my chest, the feeling of inevitable endlessness I had no control over.

Destiny could leave me the hell alone.

I watched them leave, silent but tied together, my heart heavy, my soul twisting in loneliness. Undying. Never ending.

Forever.

Until the parts of me, my demon, Sidhe and vampire all reached out and drew me close, winding their way around me.

Not alone. Not alone.

Never.

Hands settled on my shoulders, turned me around. I allowed him to hold me, to tie his power to me, to feel him and his love for me. The knots inside me eased at last, released.

I pulled away finally and looked up at him, into his eyes, detaching gently from the warmth of his magic.

"Watch over them," I said. "If you can. And keep them safe."

Quaid tensed, but nodded at last, bending to kiss me gently before turning away and leaving me there in the dark.

I stood so long, so quiet, the light went out, leaving me in the black, feet rooted to the earth, grasping for the feeling of belonging.

Even longer still before I turned and went inside, wiping away the last of my tears, closing the door softly behind me.

40

Life, as life was wont to do, went back to (ab)normal.

Thanks to Gram's constant vigilance and training the rest of the coven, we were covered on the watching for sorcerers department, at least in Wilding Springs. And with no sign of them over the next little while, I felt the coven relax and accept this disaster as they had all the others.

I just wished I could be so blasé about it.

When I finally managed to corner Mom and talk to her, it was by her choice. She and her Enforcers swept into town to pick me up before winging off to the Brotherhood's mansion, Mom refusing to speak to me about it or even tell me where I was being taken until I found myself standing in what was once a garden, staring in horror at the smoking pile of ash and melted glass that had been the huge house.

Belaisle made sure to leave behind a little gift as a further warning not to pursue him. Mom ordered the white cat nailed to the stake taken down and the upside down pentagram erased from the top of it.

At least the shaken look on her face told me she wasn't going to let him get away with it. Followed by her very firm orders to track and locate every single sorcerer on the continent and report back to her.

Okay then.

When Mom started muttering words like "infiltration" and "task force", I figured my part in the mess was done.

Well, until I could figure out how to bypass her orders not to engage any sorcerers in battle until she gave the go ahead.

Quaid had been silent. I could only hope he was able to keep an eye on the kids, though it was doubtful. He had his own responsibilities and it was unfair of me to ask him to toss everything aside to do me a favor. Even one as important as their survival.

They weren't my problem anymore. Weren't. Iepa made that clear.

So why did I worry about them every day?

Discrete inquiries into finding their grandmother got me nowhere and I didn't trust myself past initial probing with magic not to do damage—like accidentally turning her over to the Brotherhood with my snooping—so I left well enough alone and tried to focus.

Liam was so into studying the maji he thought,

breathed and talked about nothing else. I found myself avoiding him and his obsession though I felt bad about it, considering everything he learned was really for me. And his own driving need for knowledge.

He was such a geek, I couldn't help but adore him.

I had a lot to figure out, after all. Like how to use the crystal Demetrius made me. Last time had been trial by fire, desperation. Now I had time to focus and play around, it seemed impossible to understand what I was trying to do. The little vampire soul inside the crystal adored me, that much was awesome. It cooed and hummed and sang to me sometimes. But when it came to drawing out my ability, I was lost.

I needed a teacher. Not likely the enemy were going to oblige. Besides with so much power inside me, it was hard to tell what I was doing and with which at times, especially with the sweet voice of the crystal distracting me almost constantly.

I'd just have to wing it.

Demetrius was long gone and the miserable little apartment Rosetta and her fellow Chosen lived in long empty. I knew I could have chased them down. Galleytrot was more than willing to try. But for the time being I'd be better off finding a teacher who didn't want to either sacrifice me because I was evil or kill me because I wasn't part of the company line.

Go figure.

On the family front, Gram wasn't easing up on her pressure for me to find a second. Yeah, I had tons of time to think about something like that. I kept putting her off, though I knew it wasn't fair.

I just needed my grandmother around me for a while longer.

Meira was still a little cold with me, even after we both went downstairs together to call Dad and I let her have most of his time and attention. Guess there were things she held against me no matter how hard I tried to let her be her own person.

Wasn't looking forward to her teens.

At least Uncle Frank and Sunny's wedding wasn't being pushed back because of my recent dive into disaster. Their joy was enough to distract me from the feeling I was being drawn away from everything and everyone I loved by fate or destiny or some such tripe that made me nuts in the middle of the night and wouldn't let me sleep.

Being Sunny's maid of honor was a lot of fun, though I could have done without the endless dress fittings. And if she brought me one more pair of shoes to try on, I'd have to kill her.

School. Really? Sigh. I had two months before I had to

think about it, yet. But Sashenka hadn't given up on having me come to visit, so that was something to look forward to.

Charlotte refused to even discuss pushing the limits of her bond and gave me the icy shoulder every time I brought it up. So my little plan to work out some freedom died before it even had a chance to breathe.

One cool thing came out of all this. Feeling drawn to the maji cave, I returned there with the crystal. The slab waited for me, glowing softly. I hesitated to touch it this time, not wanting to have one of those waking dreams Iepa seemed so fond of. But this time, when I did, the most remarkable thing happened.

In slow and lazy lines, the glow of maji power flowing like ink, each of the family trees updated themselves until I was staring at my name, now in English, Meira's beside me, space left yet for the families we would have.

Keeper of the family history? Couldn't be more connected than that.

Like what you read? Find more at

pattilarsen.com or
purelyparanormalpress.com

Now, try the first chapter of
Book Twelve of the Hayle Coven Novels

The giant wave crashed over my head about a second after I turned to see it coming. Blue water closed around me, the fading sun shining through, dispersed as I went deeper, shoved down to thud against the sandy bottom as inertia took over. My lungs spasmed, body begging for air I hadn't had time to draw before going under. The brightly-painted surfboard rocketed to the surface without me, tether line jerking on my ankle as my body tried to figure out which way was up while the foaming rush of water drove me down and rolled me forward, head-first into the gritty bottom.

I suppose I should have panicked, considering. Anyone else would have, I'm sure of it. But even in that moment of mortal terror, my logical mind shrugged.

Immortality had its benefits.

My demon wasn't quite so calm about the whole thing. She started to shriek the moment we went under, clawing for freedom while Shaylee screamed at me in counter-point. I barely had time to catch myself as I began to flip, butt over end before my demon shredded the edge of the veil and threw us all into it.

Sometimes sharing my body with three other consciousnesses was a bit of a pain in the ass.

I hit the dry beach hard as she dropped us free only feet from the surf, coughing up the bit of water I'd managed to inhale. The sound of screaming, yeah, I was familiar with screaming, headed my way, my name being called in panic.

Strong hands grasped me, flipped me over, a pair of arctic blue eyes fading from human to wolf staring into mine told me I was in a world of trouble. Charlotte growled softly under her breath, my ever-faithful bodywere recovering from yet another freak out I caused her.

Hardly my fault. Surfing had been Sashenka's idea.

My college roommate and best friend fell to her knees beside me, her concern clear on her face as she reached for me around Charlotte, even when the weregirl snapped at her with her teeth as a warning to stay back. I pushed Charlotte aside and sat up, spluttering out a mouthful of sand, looking down in disgust at the mess of me.

"I'm fine," I said.

Seriously, how embarrassing. Sashenka's surfer friends had come to crowd around and check on me too. And while I really wasn't interested in any of the guys, my love life about as complicated as I was willing to have it, it still kicked my ego hard in the soft place knowing how much of an idiot I'd made of myself.

No more surfing. My demon chuffed her full agreement.

The gang backed off with cheery comments: "Great ride, Sydilicious!" "Watch those big ones, Syderino!", before running off to leap once more into the brink of yet another gigantic wave.

I tried all week to learn to surf, and though I'd even thrown in a little water magic as a cheat, I just had to admit there wasn't an athletic bone in my body. Outside soccer. And I'd given it up years ago.

Sashenka stayed with me, her hand lifting the severed tether, surfboard nowhere to be seen. "Tallah's going to kill you," she grinned. "That was her favorite board."

I grinned back, wiping at the abrasive sand covering most of my body. "Good thing I'm immortal then, huh?"

Charlotte was not taking this well. "That's no excuse to pull a stupid stunt," she snarled. Her accent was stronger than normal, a sure sign she was losing her temper.

"I didn't purposely try to drown, Charlotte," I said. "The wave just took me by surprise."

Her eyes narrowed, the wolf in them restless and full of anxiety. "You might be immortal, but if you get hurt doing something like this again, I'll kill you myself." She stood and stalked off, grumbling and muttering to herself in her native language. Had to be swearwords.

Had to be.

I sent Sashenka off to keep surfing, taking a quick dip to clean off the sand before lying back in the dying daylight to watch the others ride the waves. I wasn't sure why, but as I did I thought of Trill and Owen. The Zornovs had been gone about two months with no word from them. And though I knew they had their own destinies to deal with, that Trill was hopefully busy building a maji army now that we knew the Brotherhood was planning a world and plane-wide takeover, I still worried about them.

All alone.

There was a time when family didn't mean much to me, my desire to get out of the witch lifestyle and leave it all behind the driving force in my life. But since I'd regained control and taken over half-leadership of the coven, family meant more to me than I expected. And now that I knew I was immortal, thanks to my demon blood, the Sidhe princess and vampire essence living inside me, being part of something bigger was even more important.

I didn't even want to think about what Trill said, how I was turning into maji—not just one of the blood line, but an actual maji like the meddling Iepa—nor consider what being a creator would mean. Hard enough knowing I'd outlive every person I loved. Well, almost. I had a few undead and demon family members who shared my longevity. And yet, I couldn't help but worry about them, too.

They were long lived, yes. But I was immortal. Never grow old, never die.

Ever.

Shudder.

Made me want to curl up under the covers sometimes and hide from the world. Or hug my family so close to me they'd never be free. The truth was so big, the reality of it overwhelming. I just couldn't deal.

So I shoved it down and pretended nothing changed even though I knew everything had.

Besides, most people would kill to have what I did. And here I was, complaining? Maybe if being immortal came with a quiet, peaceful lifestyle, I'd be less anxious. But mine tended to the 'nothing, nothing, nothing, save the world before it explodes, nothing' variety.

Sashenka and Charlotte finally returned, the Hensley second carrying her board, my bodywere lugging the one I'd lost in the surf.

"Saved by the werewolf," Sashenka grinned, bumping shoulders with Charlotte who looked startled at the contact. "Tallah will forgive you now."

I climbed to my feet, grinning at the weregirl. Not very often did someone catch her off guard. "Thanks for saving me," I said with a perfectly straight face.

Sashenka had to go and ruin it by giggling.

Charlotte shoved the board into my arms and snarled, stalking up the beach to the house, body tense and motions jerky and abrupt, a far cry from her normal flowing walk.

"I didn't mean to make her angry." Sashenka and her empathy. I winked and hefted the board, following Charlotte's path with my best friend beside me.

"Trust me," I said, "she's having fun. She gets to punish me for all of this later."

Sashenka's laughter shattered the last of my pensive mood and, waving together at her friends, we headed home.

About the Author

Everything you need to know about me is in this one statement: I've wanted to be a writer since I was a little girl, and now I'm doing it. How cool is that, being able to follow your dream and make it reality? I've tried everything from university to college, graduating the second with a journalism diploma (I sucked at telling real stories), was in an all-girl improv troupe for five glorious years (if you've never tried it, I highly recommend making things up as you go along as often as possible). I've even been in a Celtic girl band (some of our stuff is on YouTube!) and was an independent film maker. My life has been one creative thing after another— all leading me here, to writing books for a living.

Now with multiple series in happy publication, I live on beautiful and magical Prince Edward Island (I know you've heard of *Anne of Green Gables*) with my very patient husband and five massive cats.

PATTI
LARSEN
PURELY PARANORMAL

I love-love-love hearing from you! You can reach me (and I promise I'll message back) at **patti@pattilarsen.com**. And if you're eager for your next dose of Patti Larsen books (usually about one release a month) come join my mailing list! All the best up and coming, giveaways, contests and, of course, my observations on the world (aren't you just dying to know what I think about everything?) all in one place: **bit.ly/pattilarsenemail**

Last—but not least!—I hope you enjoyed what you read! Your happiness is my happiness. And I'd love to hear just what you thought. A review where you found this book would mean the world to me—reviews feed writers more than you will ever know. So, loved it (or not so much), your honest review would make my day. Thank you!